T0354312

The Door

Keith Gilbert

THE DOOR

iUniverse books may be ordered through booksellers or by contacting:

iUniverse
1663 Liberty Drive
Bloomington, IN 47403
www.iuniverse.com
1-800-Authors (1-800-288-4677)

ISBN: 978-1-5320-4886-9 (sc)
ISBN: 978-1-5320-4885-2 (e)

Library of Congress Control Number: 2018905475

Print information available on the last page.

iUniverse rev. date: 05/30/2018

This novel is dedicated to my wife, Susan

without whom this book would have

been completed three years later...

or some other time in the distant future.

Chapter 1

Mason Waters studied his reflection in the bathroom mirror. *Christ*, he thought. *What happened?*

He did more than study. He examined his features. He reached into the small drawer to the right of the vanity and extracted the tweezers. Plucking small hairs from his nostrils and earlobe, he held one up to his eyes for closer examination. *It's white! What the hell!*

To discover hair in his ears and to find long coarse whiskers jutting from his nostrils was alarming. To find that the hair was no longer dark brown was simply disgusting and frankly, unacceptable. He set to work with the tweezers, pulling and plucking. His eyes watered and soon he began to sneeze uncontrollably.

"Are you okay?" his wife asked, sticking her head into the bathroom.

Mason held up a finger, trying to control the sneezing. He nodded, holding his breath.

"What are you doing?" She moved a little closer into the bathroom as he splashed his face with cold water from the faucet.

"I'm sneezing." He stood there, waiting for her next stupid question.

She did not respond, perhaps expecting him to read her mind. Her gaze drifted to the waste can in the corner of the bathroom.

Mason sniffed gingerly, testing his sinuses. The cold water seemed to be working. He glanced up at his wife, noticing her slightly raised eyebrows as she stared at the waste can. The small can held its capacity of four or five empty beer cans, and a few were on the tile next to the can. "I'll clean that up in a minute." He muttered, anticipating her disapproval.

"You really drank a lot last night."

Mason let the statement hang in the air for a moment. *Big, hairy deal! You're easier to deal with after I've had a few.* He allowed his expression to convey this thought.

He turned his attention back to his reflection. The problem left him a little confused. The man staring back at him did not line up with the man he imagined himself to be. He held an image of himself, one that lingered in his memory for a long time. Okay, he could be realistic. Through High School, he remained a lean 165 pounds. Usually tan from being outdoors, long dark hair that needed to be cut once every few months. He had a chiseled, strong jaw and never needed to shave. In fact, aside from the hair on his head, he was relatively hair free. There was the acne. Oh, yes, that was a problem. He did not miss that.

Three years in the army helped to pack on the weight. He emerged weighing 220 and most of it sat up on his shoulders, chest, and arms. Eventually, the facial hair sprouted but it only added to his charm and good looks. Mason did not consider himself vain, but my god, *this...*, *simply unacceptable!*

He decided he was most likely not the only one to blame for the lines around the edges of his eyes, the receding hairline, the gray, the extra tuft of skin under his chin, hair in places it should not be. No, not all his fault. Many long years of marriage, raising four kids, clueless bosses, unforgiving bills, he felt sure he could compile an impressive list. One thing he knew for sure. No matter who was to blame, only he, Mason Waters, could make the choices necessary to change the image staring back at him. Only he could choose to continue to sit around in the evenings, drinking beer and listening to the same drama and constant bitching. Was he entitled to some rest and relaxation after so many years of hard work? *Sure, you are.*

He gestured to the man in the mirror. *But this…, this is not what I had in mind. I'm in my fifties and sixty will be upon me sooner than I am prepared to accept.*

He placed his hands on the smooth white counter in front of the sink, leaned in close, and looked deeply into his own eyes. He studied them. They had not changed. They were bright, brown speckled with deep layers of hazel. The young man was still in there. The shell had gotten complacent. It grew older and age would soon take over completely. It would encompass the younger man, pushing him further away until he no longer existed. He always kept track his time debt, coming and going through the Door, would catch up with him one day. He wondered how old he really was. The pupils in the mirror seemed to glare back at him. *Do something! Before it's too late!*

"Are you even listening to me?" she asked again with a hint of exasperation in her tone.

He turned his head toward his wife. She was saying

something. He was sure of it; probably something important, most likely something crucial in her way of thinking. What had she been saying? That was the question.

"Yeah." He nodded without really looking at her.

In the middle of her next accusatory sentence, her voice trailed off. She stopped talking. That is when he noticed her. Mason turned toward his wife then stood motionless, looking at her. Mrs. Waters, African-American spit-fire, 5 feet - 5 inches tall, 135 pounds soaking wet, standing there with her hands on her hips.

Mason met Valerie in his Junior High drama class. At the time, he did not particularly like her. Through Junior High and High School, they seemed to land in many of the same classes. They would go out with friends as a group. On a day in early April of their senior year, they were required to give an oral report in English class. Mason found school to be rather annoying. He scored high marks in all his classes and he felt school was a waste of his time. As Valerie read aloud for the class, he hardly noticed her. He sat at his desk strumming his fingers on the edge of the desktop, humming some tune stuck in his head since morning. What was it? Boston, The Eagles, maybe it was The Doobie Brothers; China Grove. No, it was probably Detroit Rock City by Kiss. Simon Forsythe, the thug seated behind Mason nudged him.

Mason quietly looked back at Simon and gave him a, "what is it?" gesture.

Simon motioned toward the front of the class. Mason turned and looked up to see that Valerie stopped speaking. She was not finished with her oral assignment. She stood there with a folder in her hands and her eyes locked on Mason. Her hard gaze seemed to pierce him. They knew each other for years, done many things together, but she never looked at him the way she was looking at him at that moment. Mason slowly glanced around the room. Everyone was looking at him, probably because Valerie would not stop staring down at him. He shrugged his shoulders as if to say, "What? What did I do?"

"Mr. Waters." Miss Underwood, the English teacher cleared her throat softly. "If you don't mind…"

Mason looked perplexed. He was not doing anything. He sat up in his chair, flattened his palms on the desk and stopped humming. Valerie continued to glare at him. Mason waved his hand at her. "Sorry." He squeaked. "Go ahead Val."

That only seemed to make the situation worse. He watched as her face darkened and her eyes squeezed to little slits. Mason had no doubt that if they weren't in English class, Valerie would have stabbed him, cut off his Johnson and roasted him for dinner.

Miss Underwood cleared her throat again, this time it was meant for Valerie.

As she continued her report, Mason watched her with renewed interest. Of all the things they did together, all the field trips, school-sponsored activities, evenings and weekends out with friends, they never dated. Mason was not interested. Valerie seemed stuck on herself and constantly poked her nose into things she had no business. She was a perfectionist and seldom dated. The few times Mason was aware of her going out with a guy, it never lasted past the second date.

Mason asked her about one guy, Jeff, only because he was one of his friends.

Valerie looked at Mason in complete disbelief. "He is a jerk," she proclaimed and walked away as if everyone but Mason was aware that Jeff was indeed a jerk. He did not ask Valerie about any of her dates since that day.

Now, as he watched her at the front of the class, reading her report as though Mason and his childish ways did not exist, he began to notice her, really notice her. She was no longer the lanky little girl he met in Jr. High. She filled her clothing nicely. Her slender legs led up to a yellow skirt that clung to her shapely hips. She had a flat stomach and her breasts pushed heavily against her shirt. In fact, now that he was looking at her it seemed that her breasts were in a life or death struggle with the straining buttons holding them in. Valerie shifted from one foot to the other and her breasts bounced ever so slightly. Mason flinched and caught Valerie's glare once more. She did not stop speaking this time. That glance let him know she had not forgotten his rudeness.

Mason studied her face. What was happening? She seemed to transform right before his eyes. The way she kept cutting her brown eyes at him, obviously still mad, but it began to drive him crazy. She was turning him on!

52 years old, Mason Waters straightened in the bathroom, turned and gave Valerie his full attention. The two of them standing there, looking at one another. They knew each other far longer than they had not. Mason felt he had always known Valerie. He spent more time with no other person on the planet. They knew one another

so intimately that words were usually unnecessary when communicating emotions or feelings. There is a school of thought that one can never truly hate someone unless you have first loved that person. At times, Valerie and Mason Waters hated one another with a passion.

"Actually, no, I have not listened to a word you have said, Val. However, I am listening now. You have managed to invade my space and place your needs and wants above mine." He crossed his arms across his bare chest. "That's okay. I am now at your disposal. What, Valerie Waters? What is so god-damned important?"

She reached critical mass in two seconds. Her eyes narrowed and her chin trembled. She looked like she was about to blow. Instead of saying anything, she turned and walked out of the bathroom.

He followed her into the bedroom. "Oh, no, don't just walk away Val. What is it? You're upset because of a few beer cans in the trash? What difference does it make? No one else around here takes out the trash anyway. You established that as my responsibility a long time ago. Everyone around here, including you, has a license to throw crap anywhere they want and it is my responsibility to clean it up."

Valerie continued her trek out of the bedroom, away from him, down the hall and into the living room. Giving Mason her back, she tossed her right hand into the air and said, "Whatever!"

Mason's blood pressure escalated from agitation to a full boil. It was a button Valerie seemed to love to push. He hated it. The word, 'whatever', delivered the way only Val could, felt the equivalent of saying, "you are dismissed, I am through with you and your childish ways." She was treating him with pure indifference. She could have turned around, shot him the finger, told him to go straight to hell, and it would have been a lesser blow.

He stopped chasing her. What she considered a few empty beer cans in the bathroom trash was not the real issue here. This was about something else. It would have been nice to know what was really up her ass, but he was suddenly beyond the point of giving a damn. He allowed his voice to do the traveling. "You are not exactly a picture of perfect health, Val. Have you looked in the mirror? I mean, really taken a good long look. Next time you do, you might consider the cottage cheese forming on your thighs."

He held his peace and allowed a moment for that stab to sink in. Silence. Valerie was out there, in the kitchen or the living room somewhere, not saying anything, not responding. Okay, fine, she did not want to get into it with him. She hit him with her version of an atomic bomb. She knew from experience that the fallout from that one word, 'whatever' would continue to do damage whether she said anything else or not.

He turned back toward the bedroom and lowered his voice a bit, not sure if she would even hear him. "That's why you don't have any friends. Crazy black bitch." Mumbling the last three words. No sooner than the words left his mouth, he regretted it. It was a mean thing to say and he hoped she had not heard him. No such luck.

Valerie bolted into the bedroom, wired and ready to fight. "I really don't give a shit about the trash!" Spit flew from her lips as she swore. "Look at you! Look at your disgusting gut! You drink every night. It's revolting and pathetic!" Her words smoothed out and rolled eloquently off her tongue. Her lips drew in on her teeth and quivered. She looked like a woman ready to puke. "I remember when you were strong and fit. You had the ability to make me have multiple orgasms during sex. Not anymore, Mason. Your stomach sticks out. Your chest has sunk in. Your arms and shoulders are weak. I've been faking orgasms so you will just get off me."

This hit him hard. He was no longer a young man but he felt he was in pretty good shape for his age. In his current state of mind, she chose the exact subject to attack him. She flung the words at him. Each sentence landed with critical devastation. Her words had the mental effect of stabbing, turning, slicing, then tearing out. Mason looked at her, stunned, water welling up in his eyes. He opened his mouth to retort, but he'd played his ace of spades. He called her a bitch and knew that aside from repeating that adjective over and over nothing else would do much damage. Why would he do that anyway? Look at what proclaiming it once got him. Suddenly, he did not want to be here. He wanted to be anywhere else but in this room, this room full of bad memories. He certainly did not want her to see him cry. He raised his finger toward her in a feeble attempt to tell her something, anything. The words would not come. He glanced at his raised fist with one finger sticking out, pointing as if to drive home some point he just now forgot and he saw his hand trembling. It shook uncontrollably.

Valerie took a step closer to him, brushing aside his feeble hand and moving within the circle of his personal space. "You don't have any smart-ass remarks, Mason? I've been meaning to ask you something." She lowered her voice, no longer yelling at him, no longer spewing her words.

Actually, she seemed to be cooling down, becoming calm and in control of the situation. There was no doubt, she quickly gained complete control of the battle and perhaps recognized victory within her grasp. "Is it that you are getting fat or is your dick getting smaller?"

With these last few words, she managed to move within inches of Mason, getting right into his face. He steeled his mind in that instant. There was no way he was going to back up. As stinging as the words were, he would not allow her to physically move him backward with words alone. That is when he hit her. He put his balled fist into her belly driving her back and away, putting her on the floor, shutting her damn mouth. Over thirty years he'd known her and never once touched her in a violent or malicious manner. He started his Saturday looking at his reflection in the mirror. Standing there in his boxers, plucking white hair from his nostrils, now he watched his wife writhing on the bedroom floor trying to catch her breath. *Say something now, bitch.* He thought. *Let's hear something witty. Oh, yes, I suppose it is difficult to speak without air in your lungs.*

Mason knew better than to say what he was thinking. *You need to move your ass.* He went to the closet and got dressed quickly, glancing toward the closet door half expecting her to come soaring through with a baseball bat or something like it. He grabbed his keys, wallet, cell, and shades, and headed for the garage. As he walked through the living room, he saw her on the phone. She sat at the kitchen table, composed, talking to one of her so-called 'friends', one of the kids, or the 911 police operator. She looked up, saw him leaving but did not speak to him.

In the garage, Mason noticed the smaller of his two

garage doors half open. The electric garage door opener was broken on that side; an item he meant to fix a month ago. He pulled the door down manually and locked it with his key. He jumped in his truck and pressed the button to open the larger of the two doors. *Seems like nothing gets done in this house unless I do it. At least this one works.* He put the truck in drive and pulled out, heading down the street at the posted speed limit. He needed time to think through what had happened or perhaps more importantly, why it happened. He also felt sure that if Val did call the police he would be arrested. Once she reported that he slugged her they would not hesitate to cuff him and read him his rights. All the shit she said to provoke the attack would be irrelevant. Mason had no desire to wait around for that scenario to play out.

Driving down the highway gave him the opportunity to calm down. Replaying the last half hour in his mind, it all seemed surreal. He thought about the past few days, events that led up to here and now. Could he have missed something? Had there been signs that he ignored or brushed off as irrelevant? He could not pinpoint anything with meaning. His cell buzzed.

He grabbed it and read the display. "Yeah?"

"Dad. I just got off the phone with Mom."

It was Rachel, their oldest daughter. Mason recognized this tactic. Of their four children, Mason and Rachel shared the closest relationship. It had not been planned that way. He tried to be fair and share his love and attention equally with each of them. Perhaps it was circumstance. Maybe Rachel invested more of her time and interests with him. It could be that for a time Rachel needed him more than the others. Whatever the case, Val obviously phoned Rachel knowing that eventually he would speak to her and would probably speak his mind. Val would grill her later for info.

"She said you hit her. What's going on?"

"Is she okay?" Mason asked.

"Well, she's pissed. So, I guess she's okay, physically. I'm on my way to the house now. What are you doing?"

"Staying out of harm's way. I'm driving without a destination for now. Maybe I'll catch a movie. I think it's better if I put some space between myself and your mother."

"You're okay?"

There it is. Rachel had compassion for everyone but seemed to hold a special place for her father. He did not agree with her choice of lifestyle, living with a guy who did not value her for her true worth. It was her choice of course. Mason tried not to interfere with adult choices, but he was not opposed to letting his opinion be known from time to time. "I'll be fine. Don't worry about me."

"Call me if you need anything, Dad. I know how you are."

"My phone is on if you need anything."

"Okay. Love you."

"Love you too."

'I know how you are'. He played her words back in his mind. Mason knew what she meant. He hated being alone and Rachel understood that better than anyone. It was more than a simple preference. It could probably be classified as a phobia. Mason Waters had never spent more than a night or two alone in his entire adult life. Only he knew the depth of his fear, and Rachel understood his limitations. He tried to explain it to Valerie. She just didn't get it. As he drove, he thought about a particular weekend not too long ago.

He picked his wife up from the airport. She spent the weekend in Florida. Her grandmother passed. Mason was unable to attend the funeral. Work and the children kept him at home. Mason had the resources to fly them all out but honestly, attending a funeral was not on his list of preferred things to do. He made excuses and the decision was made for Valerie to go alone.

Being alone was not a subject he felt comfortable discussing. "I'm no good on my own." He would say in a joking manner. "You know I'm no good without you, Val."

She never took this seriously. Perhaps it was unfair to expect her to truly understand.

She came through the front door and the kids greeted her with joy. "We missed you!" they said, jumping on her, excited to have her home.

"I've only been gone for a few days," she proclaimed, obviously happy to be back with her children.

Once she settled in she noticed something that seemed odd. Her bed was unmade. Normally, she was the one who made the bed. Granted, coming home to see Mason had not made the bed while she'd been away was not a surprise. The odd thing, it appeared both sides of the bed was slept in.

"Mason?"

"Huh?"

She pointed at the bed with a perplexed expression. "You… slept on both sides of the bed?"

"No. I slept on my side. Oh." He realized he left the bed in disarray. "I'm sorry. That's not right. You shouldn't have to come home to that. I should have made the bed up. Here, don't worry about it. I've got it."

She watched as he made the bed and knew that she would have to re-do it later. "Who slept on my side?"

Mason stopped, straightened, and looked at her. "Rachel. I couldn't sleep. I tried, but, well you know, I can't…"

"You slept in our bed with Rachel?"

She wasn't yelling, yet. Mason realized the awkwardness of the situation. While innocent in his mind, it could have been taken the wrong way and could lead down the wrong path quickly. "It wasn't like that. I mean. I… Val, I've tried to tell you. I can't sleep by myself."

"No, you've never said that!" Her voice raised now, she teetered on the edge of fury.

Mason thought to call Rachel into the room to bear witness to his innocence, then thought better of it. He had to be smart. "Val, you know I would do nothing to harm the kids. You weren't here and I needed some company, just to get through the night. I am not trying to hide anything. Talk to her if you want. She'll tell you…"

"Why didn't you ask one of the boys?"

Mason considered this question. It never crossed his mind. At two a.m. he'd been tossing and turning, trying to go to sleep. The demons were tormenting him relentlessly. He knew the only way he would have any peace was to have another soul next to him, someone who cared about him. Rachel was the first to pop into his mind and when he asked her she came willingly enough, half asleep. He had not taken a second to think about the repercussions of that decision. He'd seen no harm. Looking into Valerie's eyes at this moment, he realized it was a terrible mistake.

He shrugged, shook his head and stammered. "I didn't

think to ask the boys. I really don't understand why you are so angry."

"Our daughter slept in the bed with you while I was gone and you don't understand why I am angry?" She screamed.

Mason remembered every detail of that day and the days that followed. They fought furiously. Val yelled accusations, not believing anything he said, him in defense mode trying unsuccessfully to match her intensity. The sad thing is that the kids heard it all, every word. They probably had no way of understanding what was really going on and to this day he had not slept in the same room with any of his children without Valerie in their presence. Mason wished he could bring his wife into his mind for just an instant. Give her a glimpse of the horror he endured. Allow her to peek into the dark behind thousands of doors. She would take one step into a black void so deep it can swallow the universe and she would fall forever.

For Mason, it was worse than that. He knew better than to drift aimlessly past the thoughts that guided him through daily life, curiously seeking to find the owners of the voices relentlessly calling his name. He learned how to ignore them, to lock them out and focus his thoughts on the boring details of the day until he drifted off to sleep from exhaustion. With the knowledge and comfort of a human spirit next to him at night, he usually slept well. For some odd reason the demons left him alone as long as he was in the presence of others even when he was unconscious. They never appeared during the day. He had no doubt they still existed but during daylight hours, he had no worries.

He had not always been so wise. As a young boy, he was tormented mercilessly. It hadn't happened right away. In fact, he traveled through the Door for years before the monsters became aware of him. He thought it was simple coincidence, he'd somehow drawn attention to himself. Maybe it was his increased visits. Perhaps it was the manner of activity. Once he realized that he could bring physical objects back through the Door with him, into his own universe, he'd been doing it more and more. He sometimes wondered what his life would have been like if he never figured out how to get through the Door. As much as he wished to live a normal life, he realized he could not undo what was done. Passing over to the other side, in one way or another inadvertently drew their attention. He realized, repeated journeys through the Door agitated any evil that lurked there. The creatures had limitations. But they appeared eager to discover avenues into this world. This was the reason he seldom summoned the Door as an adult. He felt certain that the demons on the other side would someday invade his world and inflict serious pain or even death on himself and his family.

They came into his room in the night, first in his dreams. Later he would wake, aware of them, there in the dark. They lurked in the darkest corners of his room. He sat up in bed and looked straight at them but was unable to see them standing there, the cover of night hiding their features. He knew they were there. He could feel that they were there. He closed his eyes hard, wanting to wake from the nightmare, opened them and they were at his side! Gigantic, black figures with no discernable shape. Mason closed his eyes again. *Go away, you're not real! None of this is real!* They would not go away.

"Mason." The room vibrated, the black creatures speaking as one. They stank and their voices were deep and sounded as though they spoke from the depths of a sewer. Liquid waste gurgled in their throats as they spoke. "Mason. We are going to kill you!"

Mason shoved back violently into the wall at the head of his bed and screamed. Every ounce of energy in his small body forced its way up and out of his mouth. The light to the room came on and his mother entered. "Mason, what's wrong? Why are you screaming?"

He looked up at her, thankful for the light, thankful for a friendly person in the room. Over her shoulder, against the far wall stood an impossibly tall, thin man. He was so tall he was forced to bend slightly so his head wouldn't hit the ceiling. He wore a dirty grey suit. He smiled at Mason, displaying rotten, brown and yellow teeth. Mason looked feverishly at his mother then back to the wall. The man was no longer there. Mason held up his arms toward his mother and vomited.

Chapter 2

He stopped at an ATM and withdrew five hundred dollars. Driving gave him time to come up with his next few moves. Going back to the house was not an option, for now. Fortunately, it was Saturday. He had a few days before concerning himself with work. Mason ran his own small delivery business for over a decade. It wasn't that he needed to run a company or that he needed to work at all. Since the age of seventeen, long before meeting Valerie, he'd found a source of wealth that would never leave him in need of money. The delivery company was perfect. His few customers kept him busy, out of the house, and provided a great cover for what he could tell no one. The time differential that accompanied his personal business never interfered with his delivery business or the time he spent with his family. The decision to find a cheap motel near the downtown area came easy. The fact that it sat next door to an upscale men's club was a simple coincidence. That is what he told himself.

Rooms could be rented daily and weekly. If you could spring for the weekly rate it worked out to your advantage. He took the room for a week. The room came equipped with the basic toiletries including toothbrush and paste. It was simple; a double bed split the room down the middle.

It was neatly covered with standard sheets and a blanket that looked like it might have been fashionable in the late seventies. There was a small refrigerator in the corner of the room just under an open area for hanging your coat and some shirts. He checked the fridge. It was warm, only because it had not been turned on. He set it at the coldest setting. The compressor rattled on and leveled out to a slight, steady hum. The television was not exactly large in his estimation. It sat on top of a worn out set of dresser drawers. Mason smiled. He had not seen a television set like this one in a long time. Everyone upgraded to flat screen, wall mounted, entertainment centers. He picked up the remote control; a small device he located on the nightstand. He clicked the T.V. on and set it to a local news station. It would have to do. He was not interested in going out to hunt down another room. He had no plans to camp out in a room anyhow. So, the basic stuff was fine with him. The room also came with a small table bordered by two wooden chairs. The bathroom was clean. He checked the shower and it spat out adequate water pressure. He let the shower run for a few minutes in order to be sure the water was hot. Satisfied, Mason turned back to exit the room. He set the a/c on high, pocketed the card key, and headed out the door. It was early and he would need a few things to get him through the week.

He spent the rest of the day learning the lay of the land. After paying for the room he did not speak to another person the rest of the day. He did plenty of browsing and some shopping. If a cashier greeted him or offered some pleasantry he simply nodded and smiled. The sun set by the time he returned to his room. He propped the door open and unloaded the contents of his truck; pack of underwear, socks, t-shirts, new pair of blue jeans, a magazine, chips, peanuts, a quart of orange juice, plenty of beer, and a bottle of gin. The liquids were neatly stocked into the small refrigerator. Sleep was going to be difficult to come by. So, he planned to drink the beer until his eyes got heavy. If the night got bad, he would turn to the bottle of gin, and the orange juice.

He was a little surprised at his actions. He had no idea what it would be like on his own. If someone told him at the beginning of this day what he would be doing by the end, he would not have believed it. His cell buzzed once since leaving the house. Should he be curious about not hearing from Valerie? Strangely, he was not. He sat on the edge of the bed and looked at his phone. No missed calls, no text messages. He shrugged, placed the cell on the nightstand next to the bed and picked up the television remote. Flipping through the stations he found the same thing on that was playing at his house on a Saturday evening, with one exception. The motel had adult pay channels.

He settled on the national news station. That should be boring enough. The beer was great. After the sixth can, the room began to softly sway. He sat on the bed, fully dressed, leaning back against a few pillows supported by the headboard. Three more were sufficient to knock him out. His chin dropped to his chest and drool eased out of the corner of his mouth. He breathed deeply with the lights on and the television replaying the same news stories over and over. He did not dream. His mind rested on a blank canvas in a land of nothingness. In the distance, as if carried by the wind, a whisper.

The distance seemed great like one world away from

another. There again, he could hear the voice; a rumble from far away. In the dimly lit motel room, setting on the bed, the sheets in disarray, Mason's unconscious mind turned his head slightly as if to be in a better position to hear something approach. His brow wrinkled, trying to make out the word being uttered.

The canvas was white. No, that's not right. It was made of light. The eye in his mind squinted almost in pain from the bright light that surrounded him. There it was again, the voice, getting closer. Mason focused. He could do more than hear the voice, he could see it. It appeared as a speck, a black pinpoint engulfed in the brightness. As the point grew so also did the sound that it produced. It muttered one word as it approached. In the dream, Mason closed his eyes and diverted all his energy to his ears. He needed to hear the word.

Behind his eyelids he noticed the light begin to dim, the approaching form casting a shadow. "Son! Son!" The word intensified and began to vibrate the air around him. The approaching blot in the distance repeated the same word again and again. Mason began to panic. He felt a sudden alarming urge to wake up. He tried but could not escape. *God-damn it! Wake up! It's getting too close!* His body convulsed as a man might, being bound in a straitjacket. *Got to get out!*

Unconsciously, Mason tensed the muscles in his arms and balled his hands into tight fists. As the sound of the voice grew in his mind he began to grind his teeth, bearing down hard with his jaw. He twitched and sweat beaded on his forehead. Deep within he sensed this to be a demon from his youth. One of the hideous creatures that lived on the other side of the Door. This one had some sort of hold on him. It came at him from an angle, something he never experienced. He was aware that he was asleep, and he could not open his eyes.

The light dimmed and darkness overtook every corner. The voice became silent, but Mason could feel the presence of an incredible evil. He could smell it, taste it. He was wrong about the word. The beast was not saying, 'son'.

Mason clenched his fists and flexed every muscle he could. His body stiffened and he willed his eyes open. The first thing he registered was the television. White noise crackled from the set mounted on the dresser. He opened his mouth and drew in a deep breath, but this was about all he could do. He had no control over his arms and legs. He sat at the head of the bed, frozen in place. Out of the corner of his eye, movement. Gleaming spikes eased down over his left shoulder. What appeared to be impossibly long steel fingers attached to a giant hand the color of the deepest part of the ocean moved down over his shoulder, across his chest and up to his neck.

Mason cried out in terror. He was conscious with no ability to move. The thing followed him out of his dream. He could move his eyes but he dared not look upon the face of this creature. When it spoke, the voice blasted him from above. Not 'son', "Mason."

Hot, dank breath blew his hair across his head. "I've traveled a long way, Mason!" The creature growled. "You're coming with me!"

The hand wrapped itself around Mason's neck. It had to be attached to a giant. The metal spiked fingers clanked together at his spine. It closed and lifted him straight up, the top of his head inches from the ceiling of the motel room. The beast was inches away. It's hot breath blasting the side of Mason's head. It was like being in the face of a mad bull. "Where is your mother to save you now, little boy?"

Mason's heart exploded with fear as he summoned the Door.

A silent sliver of light pierced the room from ceiling to floor. The dazzling brightness filled the room like the rising sun. The metal claws on his neck fell away immediately. "Get away from me!" Mason screamed as he fell to the bed, rolled right and hit the floor, hard. When his head slammed into the carpet he felt like he might pass out. He fought to keep his eyes open and looked up in time to see the Door wink out. He lay there gasping for air, his lungs heaving in his chest. Slowly, his heart rate diminished and he began to gain sensation in his extremities. A few minutes passed and he discovered limited control over his arms and legs. He grabbed the bed and pulled his sluggish, sweaty body off the floor. On his knees clutching to the bedspread, he scanned the room. He was alone. Had he imagined this encounter? Was it only a bad dream? A dream that caused him to rise up in the air and fall to the floor? Perhaps he drank too much. He concentrated, pulled himself up and sat back down on the edge of the bed. No. He summoned the Door. That was real.

He stood and made his way across to the bathroom. He turned on the cold water at the sink and stuck his head under the faucet. It felt good and he began to gather his senses. Mason took his time, letting the water calm his nerves. Acclimated, he looked at his reflection. Water streamed from his hair and dripped from his eyelashes. He examined his neck. The marks were easy to see. Four red lines crossed his throat from one side to the other. They were certainly real. He toweled off and slowly made his way back into the room. The television still crackled with white noise. He grabbed the remote and turned it off. That is when he saw it. The chair.

The small table against the wall came with two chairs. Standard in many motel rooms. However, Mason had not used the table. Well, he placed some of his newly purchased items on it and they were there, undisturbed. He had not sat in either of the chairs. Now, one of the chairs was pulled out and placed at the side of the bed. It was positioned in a way that suggested someone came to visit him, used the chair to sit next to him in bed as one would in the case of visiting a sick relative. Someone or something sat there, watching him as he slept. It couldn't have been the giant that held him by the throat. There were more than one. He was sure of it. He put the chair back in its place and stood there thinking. No way he was going back to sleep.

He picked up his cell to check the time. A little after two a.m. The clubs would still be open. He checked for his card key and cash. Still in his pocket. He looked around the room unsure if he would ever be able to sleep here, turned, grabbed the door and headed out into the night.

He opted to walk and entered XTC Cabaret 5 minutes later. Twenty dollars got him through the front door. The place was dark, smoky, and not too crowded. The music thumped and several women danced around chrome poles on three lighted stages. The stages and the main bar were lined with what appeared to be white Christmas lights. The further removed one was from the stages the darker it was.

He found a table back against the wall, away from any of the stages, away from most of the action.

A young woman dressed in a black lace outfit approached and asked him what he was drinking. Mason wasn't sure if this club offered alcohol and he didn't care. He had enough for one night. He placed a five spot on the table and asked for a Pepsi. The girl scooped up the money and quickly returned with a dark liquid fizzing over ice. She did not drop any change. Mason took a sip and decided it would pass but wasn't sure if it was Pepsi, Coke, or even an RC. He thought movie theater soda was expensive, cheap compared to this place. The soda was cold and felt good going down. He took a long drink and gently rubbed his neck. His eyes adjusted and he scanned the club. The place was fully nude. Some girls moved slowly on stage while others worked the floor, soliciting a lap dance where they could find a willing customer. The club favored rap and current rock music. Finding a spot in the back had its desired effect at first. He wasn't looking to spend his money. He just didn't want to stay in his room or sleep.

In time, a dancer approached; a skinny white girl with small breasts still setting up firm. "Hey sweet thing. How 'bout it?" she asked, leaning over, giving him plenty to see.

Mason remained silent, waiting for her to get closer. He pulled out a ten. "You see the lady over there?" He made a motion in the direction of several dancers on stage. "The one with the sparkling red pumps."

Small breasts stopped, considered him and his ten-dollar bill. She glanced over her shoulder, back the way she came. "Ebony?" She looked back at Mason. He nodded. She looked at the ten and frowned.

Mason pulled out another ten. "Could you ask her to come over here?"

Small breasts nodded slightly, took his money and dramatically folded the cash so it would fit into the side of her heels. She straightened, turned slowly, making sure her small flat behind was directly in Mason's face and sauntered away.

Mason did not see if or when the girl delivered his message. Approximately fifteen minutes passed and he figured he spent his twenty bucks on nothing. Maybe he'd insulted her. He finished his soda, placed it on the table and looked up. The young beauty he inquired about approached his table. She wore sequenced red pumps and a smile.

"If you want a dance, something special, we need to go up to the next level. That's VIP. Only place I give private service baby. It's only twenty to get a pass." She stopped close to him, placed her palms on the edge of the table allowing her full breasts to sway close to Mason's face.

Mason was pleased. Her face was pretty. He hadn't been able to see from across the room. Now that she was close, in his personal space, he could see her clearly. Her light brown skin was smooth and clear of any blemishes, markings or tattoos. She looked to be an inch or two over five feet, petite body with plenty of curves. She wore a little make-up, but not too much. "How much for conversation?"

Ebony smiled and looked at him for a few ticks. "I'm not sitting here," she said softly. "These chairs are disgusting. Come on." She reached out slowly, took his hand and led him toward the stairs leading up to the VIP section. At the bottom of the stairs they stopped and she held out her free hand, palm up. Mason took the meaning of her gesture and handed her a crisp twenty. Without a word, she turned and led him up.

She stopped at the top of the stairs, still holding his hand, and spoke matter-of-factly to a large black fellow standing at his post. "Rob. Send down for some food. Whatever Leon has cooked up in the kitchen. Chicken strips, fries, and something to wash it down." She pointed across the floor. "My usual table."

The big man looked at her without moving. He glanced at Mason, then brought his stare back to the girl.

Ebony, still holding Mason's hand, turned her nude body fully facing Rob. She discretely handed the twenty to him then placed her free hand on her hip, cocked her head slightly and raised one eyebrow.

Mason found this wordless communication amusing. The guy raised his arms slightly, palms up as if to say, *what do you want from me girl?* The girl moved her hand from her hip, waved it in the air and pulled Mason away from the guy toward the table she previously indicated. They guy's shoulders slumped and he trotted down the stairs.

The table she led him to did not have chairs. It was flanked with a black lounge style love seat stuck against a back wall. Once they were seated Mason realized that he could no longer see the dance floor below, which meant that they could not be seen. In fact, only one other table could be seen from this vantage point and it was empty.

Ebony moved in close to Mason on the couch, crossed her legs like a lady giving him full view of her breasts. They set perched, dark brown nipples pointing up at him, inches away. She smiled brightly. "What's your name honey?"

Mason met her full eyes. "Mike."

"Okay, Mike. When Rob gets back he's going to expect to be paid for his efforts. The twenty got us through the gate. That's all."

"Seems to me you've taken some liberties."

She cocked her head, looking up at him. "I'm pretty good at reading people, Mike. I saw you when you came in. I watched to see what table you would pick. You didn't sit up by the stage like most guys do. You didn't make a line for the VIP section. That says a lot. The girl that came to your table, Candy, you know how many men come in here that aren't interested in her, Mike?"

Mason shrugged. "I don't know. She's not my type."

"Exactly. But Mike, Candy is most guys 'type'. She gives off that young and dumb vibe. Dudes like that. They pay good for it. Have you seen her since she spoke to you?"

"No."

"That's because one of her regulars scooped her up and took her home. Or they got a room, you know."

Mason nodded. "Oh."

Rob returned with a tray full of hot food and several drinks. He set it down gently, unloaded the items onto the table and stood quietly in an obedient manner.

"What is it you want, Mike?" she asked.

Mason sighed. There is was. The million-dollar question. He was on auto-pilot, in flight mode since leaving his room. It was time to give some real thought to his situation and come up with a working plan. He had to sleep sometime and the trick he pulled, summoning the Door, might not be good enough next time. He looked up at Rob then out at nothing in particular. His mind wandered, and he was sure he could feel the steel talons on his neck. A moment passed and he turned his attention back to the beautiful creature seated at his side, her bare hip snuggled up to him. He thought about the way she took his hand and led him to this place. It felt nice. He wondered what it might feel like walking next to her fully clothed, in daylight, perhaps at the mall or going to a movie. He removed what was left of the cash in his pocket, somewhere close to two hundred he figured. Without counting it he handed it to her.

Ebony accepted the money, gently pulled three bills out and handed it to Rob. Without even looking at it, the man pocketed the cash and walked quietly away. She took the remaining cash, bent down, and placed the money into her pumps. "You haven't answered my question."

"Well, for starters, that was all the cash I walked in here with. Just FYI." He paused, took a gulp of the cold, sweet liquid Rob had placed on the table, and turned his attention back to her. "I wanted someone to talk to."

"You could have found that down on the corner. There's a 24-hour Quickie Mart and there are homeless under the bridge."

"Okay sure, but you are very easy on the eyes. So, there's that."

She shifted back. "Easy on the eyes. Is that all?" She turned and grabbed at the fried finger food.

Mason smiled. He thought maybe, just perhaps, he might make it through this night without further incident.

"Mike, I haven't had a thing to eat all night. Thanks. My feet are so sore. If I can end my shift right here without having to shake my ass it will be alright with me."

Mike took another drink and asked, "So, is this your desired profession?"

That set her up for some good one-sided conversation. She ate as she explained how she started as a cocktail waitress at some club across town. Of course, she only did it for the money. She was taking on-line courses and her goal was to be a nurse. Any occupation that fell under the heading of psychology was of interest as well. She'd taken child psychology courses and was fascinated with the effects of diseases like schizophrenia and bipolar disorder. She gave him exactly what he wanted, idle conversation, nothing serious. She moved as she spoke, using her hands to emphasize a point which caused her breasts to sway and bounce ever so slightly. Mason felt this was a particularly nice touch.

Mason was unsure how long they sat there. Eventually, Ebony informed him that the club would close soon and she needed to wrap it up, get dressed and get some sleep. The glamour of their conversation wore off but during their time together a thought occurred to him. He was working out the details for the past 15 minutes, listening to her tell him about the assholes that frequented the club.

"How did you know I wasn't just another asshole?" He interrupted her.

She took a long moment before answering. "I told you I'm good at reading people. You didn't want a dance. You wanted a very personal touch in your experience tonight. I figured you were willing to pay anything for that. Besides, I wanted to get off my feet. If I was wrong about you, I would have simply gone back to dancing and Rob would have escorted you out the door. No harm. It's obvious you like me." She turned and pressed herself into his body, brought her hand up, and traced a finger gently across his lower lip. "Right?"

He looked down at her and almost kissed her. It would have been easy. Her lips were inches away. He remembered where they were at, that she was on the clock so to speak. "Are you opposed to talking to me outside this venue?"

She didn't move an inch. "Sure. But I have to get some sleep. I've been here for like ten hours. You give me a number and I'll call you. That's how it has to go down."

Mason knew she didn't understand exactly what he had in mind. He wasn't looking for sex, though he had no doubt she would not be disappointing. He imagined a scenario where Ebony could help him get through the next week. After that well, he wasn't currently thinking that far ahead.

He jotted his number on a napkin, thanked her and made a move to go, sliding away from her across the seat. She moved with him, in the same direction. He stopped and turned his attention back to her, the naked black girl nuzzled next to him. Her worm body on his was very nice.

She moved her arm around him. "You don't say much, Mike." Her voice, almost a whisper. "I really like that. You don't smoke. I like that too. Maybe you don't think I'll call you, but I will." She stopped talking and just looked at him, trying to make up her mind about something. She craned her neck and kissed him, opening her mouth slightly to run her tongue across his lips. She pulled back, holding his gaze for an instant, then she got up and walked slowly away, not looking back but allowing him plenty of time to watch her round naked tush say, "See ya!"

After a few moments Mason rose from his seat and headed for the stairs. Rob was stationed in the same spot.

He held out his hand and for an instant. Mason thought he was going to ask for more money. Mason hadn't been lying when he told Ebony he was tapped out. Rob looked him over then said, "We get a bunch of roughnecks and perverts in here. Long as you got your cash straight, you're welcome up here anytime."

Mason smiled in return. "Thank you." He walked down the stairs and out the front door. The sun wasn't up yet but there was a Denny's not too far from here. That was his next stop.

Chapter

Mason Waters had not always been able to summon the Door. Perhaps it would be more accurate to suggest that he had not always known he possessed the ability. The Door had always been with him. From his earliest memories, it was there. Mason's Door resembled a slender break in the fabric of space. It appeared as a sliver of brilliant light, approximately six inches wide, vertical, with no discernable top or bottom. If it appeared in-doors it came through the ceiling and passed through the floor. If he summoned it outside, one end met the ground and the other stretched up into the atmosphere further than Mason could see. He referred to the opening as a 'door' because it served as a conduit between this world and a multitude of others. He considered it a passage among realities.

As a young boy, he realized that he was the only one who could see the Door when it appeared and he assumed that he was the only one who could pass from here to there, wherever 'there' happened to be. He gave up trying to explain it to his parents. He learned early on that people have a very hard time believing in something they cannot perceive when it is also something they cannot comprehend.

As an infant and toddler, the Door appeared randomly.

He saw it outside their first-floor apartment in the front courtyard, or over by the swimming pool. Sometimes he saw it inside in the living room or in his parent's bedroom. It was around so frequently that it was commonplace. Curiosity caused him to crawl or walk toward the light emitted by the Door. He could reach out to touch it but did not figure out how to pass through it until he was 7-years old. The Door was bright and vibrated slightly. Other than those two stimuli, no other characteristics. It was not hot or cold to the touch. In fact, touching it was impossible. His hand simply passed through it as one's hand passes through a beam of light coming in through the window on a sunny day.

One particular afternoon, after being dismissed from second-grade classes young Mason walked briskly toward the bus parking lot. He located his bus, number 47, came around the back and there it was. Just across the parking lot, it towered from the ground up through the clouds. Mason had a few minutes before he needed to be in his seat on the bus, so he walked across the lot. He'd been considering a new idea. When he approached the light, he lifted his right hand to give it a try. He always waved his hand over or through the light. He even put his palm up to the light and pushed only to have his hand pass through to the other side. This time he inserted the fingers of his right hand and attempted to grab as one would when pushing a curtain aside to see through the window.

The light gave way to his effort and widened. Startled, Mason yanked his hand back and the Door resumed its previous shape. Mason's eyes widened. "Cool!" he said, reaching out to recreate the move. He placed his left hand on the other side and pulled the curtain of light wide open.

As long as he kept his hands in place the opening in the Door stretched about five feet across. Another idea struck him. He lifted his right foot and stepped through the Door. He expected to still be in the bus parking lot, one step forward. When he looked up he found that he was no longer on school property. Based on what he saw he felt certain that he was no longer in the small town where he lived with his parents. He whirled in fear, looking back to where he'd come. His fear was that the Door was gone and he was stuck here, in what appeared to be a field of some kind of crop. The Door remained fixed, right where it should be. Mason turned back to study this new place. A strong warm wind blew through his hair. As far as he could see there were rows upon rows of dark green lettuce growing from the ground. To his right, very far away he could make out an area of tall trees. It was quiet here. The only sound was of the wind. He wondered what would happen if he walked away from the Door, out into the field. Instead, he moved back, reached into the light as he did before and instantly he was back in the bus parking lot at school. He didn't have to part the Door or step through this time and after returning to his world of familiarity the Door winked out. He did not see the Door again that year. He felt sure that he would never see it again. As the months passed he began to think it hadn't been real at all. Surely, he imagined it.

***

Ms. Frazier was an elderly woman with strict rules. She was also Mason's third-grade teacher. The best part of his day was recess followed by lunch. Nothing else about third-grade inspired him. On a very uneventful day, he sat at his desk, drawing with a pencil on one of his textbook covers. Ms. Frazier assigned some reading and she seemed to be occupied with some reading of her own. The classroom was quiet. Mason sighed and looked up toward the clock on the wall to see how much longer he must endure this boring stuff when he saw the tall sliver of blazing light. It fractured the space between Ms. Frazier's desk and the classroom exit. Mason sat up, looking around to see if anyone else noticed. *What was going on? How could no one else see this spectacle?* He wondered. He almost got up from his seat then remembered the punishment for disturbing the class. He sat back, gazed at the Door of light and whispered, "Come here."

He did not perceive the movement of the Door. It was there, as sure as anything, next to Ms. Frazier's desk, then it appeared at his side, less than a foot away. Mason glanced around the room again, certain that his classmates were witnessing what he could clearly see. *Just another boring day in class, except for this magnificent beam of light!* Now he understood another aspect of his own private Door to anywhere. He possessed the ability to move it, from here to there or from there to here. What he discovered the next day was the ability to summon the Door, whenever he desired. When the school bus dropped him off he ran to his apartment. He arrived home about an hour before his mother came in from work each day. He tossed his school backpack on the bed in his room and eagerly summoned the Door for his first great adventure. He planned to walk out into that field and see what he could see.

Mason concentrated and called the Door to his room. He stood before the bright light, reached out and passed through like he did in the school bus parking lot a year earlier. This time the Door did not deposit him in a field of strange vegetables. He found himself in a dark room. His eyes adjusted and he realized he was standing at the back of a movie theater.

He could make out rows of seats and a few people waiting patiently for the movie to start. Quietly, Mason found a seat, sat down and waited. After a few moments, the screen came to life with an advertisement he had never seen. There were a few previews of future attractions and the movie began. Mason remembered going to a drive-in movie theater with his parents. This was not much different, inside instead of watching the screen from the front seat of their car. He sat there for some time. No one approached him. No one seemed to notice him. The Door winked out but he felt confident he could summon the Door as he had before. He knew what was back there, where he'd come from. That was major boring. The movie he watched was animated and quite good. It was about a young space traveler who encountered many obstacles as he attempted to make his way across the galaxy toward his home planet. Mason watched the movie to the end. When the lights came up he realized he needed to pee, bad. He rose from his seat, summoned the Door and found himself in his bedroom.

He darted out and down the short hall to the restroom. "Mom." He called out. Surely, she was home by now. He relieved himself and listened for his mother to respond. He searched the small apartment then checked the time. *That's odd*, he thought. Sometimes she stopped at the store on the way home but he was never alone for more than two hours. He searched the apartment and ended up in the kitchen. He was alone. The bus dropped him off hours earlier. According to the clock over the stove, school let out like thirty minutes ago. What was going on?

He made note of the time, walked back to his bedroom and called the Door. This time the Door deposited him in a large city. A sign in front of him displayed a large map. The sign read, 'Bronx Zoo' and, 'You are here'. "What!" he exclaimed. "The freaking zoo!" He didn't need a ticket. He was already inside the zoo. He looked around at the people moving this way and that enjoying a bright, sunny day. He spent a few hours examining the exhibits. The reptiles were amazing and the gorillas awesome. His stomach grumbled and realized he hadn't brought food or money with him. He knew he could be in his own kitchen, raiding the refrigerator or pantry in a second. But, the Door was probably not going to bring him back to this zoo. So far it dropped him in a different place every time. He traveled to unknown places on this side, but always back to his world on the other side.

He was hungry and curious to see the results of his little experiment. He brought the Door down and stepped back to the exact same spot where he entered, in his bedroom between his bed and the closet. He ventured back into the kitchen, to the stove. 15 seconds; the amount of time it took him to walk from the kitchen to his room and back. He marveled at the thought of it. When he was on an adventure on the other side of his Door of light, time in the real world, his world, remained fixed. Time was passing for him. His hunger was a testament to that. He grabbed a bar of chocolate from the pantry along with a bag of chips and headed for his room.

His trips to other realities occurred daily. Mason loved it. Each time he passed through the Door he found himself in a new environment. Sometimes he would find himself in the country but mostly he ended up in a city. One day he passed through to a massive ship. It was a cruise ship far out on some ocean. He spent hours exploring the ship and eating until he was about to bust. When he grew tired he summoned the Door and passed back through to his room. He flopped onto his bed and closed his eyes. The day was far from over but Mason fell asleep and did not wake until he felt his mother shaking him.

"Mason. It's time for dinner. What's up with you? You were asleep when I got home and you've been asleep for several hours."

Mason sat up, still groggy. "Sorry, Mom. Did you say dinner? I'm not very hungry."

She placed the palm of her hand on his forehead. "Are you feeling okay?"

"Yes. I'm just tired. I think I'll shower and get ready for bed." He smiled at her. "Got a long day tomorrow." He got out of bed, grabbed some clean pajamas and headed for the bathroom. As he showered a thought occurred to him. He'd eaten a feast at the cruise ship's buffet. That food was still in his body. He brought it from one reality to his own. He never thought of bringing anything back with him. He made a note of this and decided to test this out. What else could he bring back with him? He stood there in the shower, letting the hot water soak his body.

Another thought came to him. Time difference. Of course. Why hadn't he thought of it before? Time remained fixed here in the real world while he was away. Even though he was usually only gone for a few hours each day, it had to be adding up. He was getting older while everyone else remained frozen till he returned. They weren't actually frozen. That's just how he thought of it. So, if he was gone, on average, two hours a day; he was living a twenty-six-hour day, while his classmates were only putting in twenty-four hours. Now his brain was calculating. *Two times seven is fourteen. Fourteen times four is fifty-six. Fifty-six times twelve is uh...* He reached out and turned off the water. He needed a pencil and paper. Hadn't he learned that there are a few months with extra weeks?

He toweled off. Slipped on his pajamas and headed back to his room. He pulled the super-hero calendar from his wall to count the weeks in a year, got out his tablet, then pulled out his calculator. *Fourteen times fifty-two is 728.* "Wow! Seven hundred twenty-eight hours!" He whispered. *Divided by twenty-four. Thirty! That's a whole month!* He thought about this for a while. There were times when he was away for much more than two hours. Like today on the ship. Maybe an extra month each year wasn't much, but the thought was a little scary. He had to cut back. In a few years, he felt it likely that he could be a year older than all the kids in his class. If he was careless it could really get out of hand. He decided to limit his trips to two or three days a week and not to stay gone too long. But he was absolutely going tomorrow. He didn't care where he ended up, he wanted to bring something back to his room and see if anything weird might happen.

The next afternoon he grabbed one of his matchbox cars, a blue Corvette, stuffed it in his pocket and called the Door. On the other side, he stepped into a barn full of pigs and goats. Not the most ideal spot, but it would do. Remembering what he calculated the day before he had no plans on staying long. The barn stunk and he didn't see anything interesting. He stepped outside, into the night. This was rare but he'd experienced it a few times. It was also cold. He spotted a small feeding bucket and picked it up. As good as anything else, he figured. He walked across to a wire fence held in place with wooden posts. He dug into his pocket, pulled out the race car and placed it neatly on the top of one of the posts, summoned the Door and stepped back into his room.

He wasn't sure what to expect. The bucket was still in his hand. He glanced around his room and his eyes locked on something small stuck in the wall. "Oh, man," he said aloud. He crossed the room. Jutting out of the wall was the back end of his matchbox car. He grabbed it and cautiously pulled it out for inspection. Amazement in his eyes. He passed through the Door without incident, but loose objects that didn't belong in one reality or another were thrown back into their proper environment, post haste. He set the pail on the floor and summoned the Door. Just like that, it was gone. He did not witness where the pail went but he was sure it was thrown back to its proper reality; where it smacked against the side of a barn no doubt scaring a few pigs and goats.

Chapter 4

The waitress brought him an empty cup, placed a napkin on the table and put the cup on the napkin. She poured hot coffee into the cup and sat the coffee dispenser on the table as well. She pulled out a small tablet and pencil. "What can I get for you this morning?"

Mason looked up at her. She was a middle-aged Spanish woman. She stood, poised, regarding him with what appeared to be indifference. If it were the end of her shift or the beginning, Mason couldn't tell. "I'll have the Lumberjack special; eggs over easy, bacon crispy, with a side of grits. Also, could I have some water?"

"Certainly, love." She took the menu, smiled, and headed back to place the order.

The food came hot and Mason was hungry. The food at the club was okay, Ebony put most of it away. He was also tired but sleep was not currently on his mind. The episode in his motel room was at the forefront of his thoughts. Summoning the Door to save himself was something he'd never done. He'd acted on instinct. Items from alternate realities were pulled through the Door. He never imagined it could pull in something as large as a man, an animal, or monster. He actually called the Door in an attempt to escape his attacker. He was relieved it worked the way it did. He wondered if that monster would ever haunt or attack him again.

His thoughts drifted back to when he was a boy, recalling the first time the Door returned an item; the matchbox car. He still had that car, packed away in a box somewhere. He remembered bringing a small pail through to his bedroom. The next time he summoned the Door the pail disappeared. If an item from another reality were in close proximity to the opening it would automatically be returned to its proper place. The item had to be close though. As long as he was holding the item, it remained in his possession.

He was a teenager in Junior High when he got the idea of bringing money through the Door. He journeyed from his bedroom to another reality; trying several places until he passed through into a small town. He walked until he located a convenient store. He entered, moved slowly down the first aisle and grabbed a bag of chips and a soda from the cooler. The place was empty, which was perfect. He called for the Door as he approached the cashier, a young woman in her twenties. He placed the items on the counter and waited. The lady rang up the items and the register drawer popped open. Quickly, Mason reached across the counter and grabbed a fistful of bills, turned and passed through the sliver of light.

It happened in an instant. He stood there in his room, heart racing, and looked down at the wad of cash in his right hand. It wasn't much. He laughed as he counted it, "Sixteen dollars! Mason, you've made it to the big time!"

***

Mason finished the eggs and poured himself another cup of coffee. That was the first of many where he came back to the comfort of his own room with cash. He'd gotten creative and sometimes spent many hours in one location in order to make a big haul. Once he had the money or anything else in his hands, he didn't have to worry about running or getting caught. His magical Door was right there and he was gone instantly.

Every once in a while, the money was no good. Some realities were almost exactly like his own home-world. Some were oddly different. The cash he retrieved might turn out to be the wrong color. Other times it displayed the wrong presidents or words. It was exasperating to get home with a bag full of money only to find it said something like National Reserve Note or The United States of England above the image of what appeared to be a native American Indian. Sometimes the cash was the wrong size. Mostly though, the money was perfect. He wasn't sure if the serial numbers would check out but as long as it was close enough to fool the casual business person, it was good enough for Mason.

He'd worked on accumulating as much money as he could. Not yet an adult, he didn't want to draw attention to himself with a bank account opened by his mother. It wasn't long before keeping it all in his room was not an option. For one thing, he could no longer summon the Door in his room. The money compiled from a previous mission would disappear. To avoid this, he summoned the Door after school before he got on the bus. He carried a backpack, filled it with as much as he could collect, and brought it home. Another problem was his mother. He could not afford to have her discover a stash of money in his room. He needed a place to put it so he rented a small storage unit. He stored his cash and any other items he found interesting in the storage. At a point, counting the money seemed useless. The storage unit soon filled. There was more than he would ever be able to spend.

As a matter of caution, Mason spent almost nothing. That would draw unwanted attention. He could always escape through his Door from other realities, back to his room or from wherever his point of entry was, but that trick would not work in reverse. In his own world, he could call the Door and get away from whatever danger there might be. He had to come back sometime. The Door would ultimately put him right back in danger at the exact place and time. He guessed he could live a lifetime in another reality, come back to his home world an old man. But what was the fun in that?

Over time he worked out the kinks. The only variables appeared to be in the locations the Door sent him. He had no control over that, but it didn't seem to be all that bad. That is until he recognized the inhabitants of one world in particular. Or perhaps he could say that he was recognized. It was all great fun until that day. The evil that haunted him in his dreams appeared on the street in one of the realities. The fun stopped. Certainly, the Door served to offer a variety of adventures for young Mason Waters. That stopped after the ninth grade. A trip he made as a teenager on a warm summer day was a trip that changed everything. The Door went from being an awesome path into unimaginable worlds of adventure and opportunities to the source of nightmares where demons pursued him. Monsters that wanted him dead or worse, driven to insanity, actively searched him out. They were not bound to one reality. He began to see them in different worlds. They weren't always present, but he had no way of knowing when they would appear. He had a foreboding that they were somehow tracking him. To what end, he did not know, but he was convinced they meant him harm.

As he sipped the coffee he wondered if he tipped them off or if it was only coincidence. No matter. Going through the Door became increasingly dangerous. When he slipped through the Door to find several monsters waiting for him he realized it was no longer something he wanted to do. They seemed as surprised to see him as he was to see them and he was able to escape. A mistake he did not wish to repeat.

Mason had not anticipated this particular course. Granted, when he left his home the day before he couldn't have known what was in store for him. Certainly, he hadn't expected to be attacked in the middle of the night by a creature that did not exist. Well, it didn't exist here in this reality. Aside from the fact that his personal life was not working out, he had a new problem. As pissed off as Valerie might be, the problem that presented itself now was greater. He could not stay awake forever. If and when he slept, he was confident that a beast with a deadlier bite than his wife would be waiting to greet him. He decided. Sitting there at a Denny's for breakfast. He would need money, a weapon, some help, and hopefully some luck.

He walked to a nearby gas station, slash taco stand, slash drug and alcohol store. Among his purchases were a handful of pill packets, the contents of which would help him remain awake. Back in his room he settled in, turned on the television, and waited. He wasn't sure when she would call or if she would. He roughly formed the outline of several plans. Plan 'A' involved the help of a certain young lady whom he had given his number a few hours prior. He preferred to solicit the aid of someone not related to him; someone with whom he had no emotional ties. Plan 'B' was a bit riskier; one he considered scraping as soon it came to mind. Going it alone was almost out of the question. He was no match for the creatures hunting him and he feared being trapped in another reality or perhaps being captured and taken somewhere he had no desire to be.

Hours passed and it seemed that no amount of caffeine or other such chemicals was going to keep his eyes open. The afternoon slipped away. As did Mason Waters. He slept, pretty much in the same position he was in the night before. He was startled awake by the sound of his cell phone. He glanced at the bright screen. His daughter's name and number appeared.

"Hello?" He held the phone out in front of his face to see the time.

"Dad? What are you doing? Are you okay?"

Mason rubbed his eyes. "It's past midnight. Is something wrong?"

"I wanted to check on you. Where are you?"

"I'm fine. Why are you calling so late? Man, I really passed out."

There followed a short silent pause. "Have you tried to talk to Mom? You should go come back to the house. The two of you should talk this out. She asked me not to call you or to tell you anything about her, but I'm concerned."

"Well, I have no assurance she won't call the police. I don't feel like spending time on a jail floor. It's not your place though Rachel. To be concerned I mean. I've got some things I need to work out right now. It has nothing to do with your mother."

"Like what?"

"I can't say right now. But, I'm okay." He got out of his seated position on the bed and walked to the sink. He splashed cold water on his face. "As soon as I can, I'll make some time. You and I can catch a movie or something."

Normally that suggestion would be met with a positive comment. "That would be cool, Dad." But that isn't what she said next. Silence filled the connection.

"You still there?"

"I went over there yesterday. Conrad didn't want me to stay the night so I left. She called me this morning. She told me about someone or something breaking into the house. It attacked her."

This set off an alarm inside of Mason. "Is she okay? Did she call the police?"

"She is a bit shaken. She fell in the tub and put a knot on the back of her head. And no, she did not call the police. Mckayla and I went over there this afternoon. She wouldn't let us take her to the emergency room. McKayla and I spent the day with her. I insisted she come stay with me and Conrad. So, we're here at my apartment, at least for tonight. I told her she can stay as long as she wants. Dad, I swore I wouldn't tell you this."

"I'll be discrete Rachel. You said, 'someone or something'. What does that mean?"

"Mom said it wasn't human. I know how that sounds.

It's crazy. Anyway, I wish you two would talk. When things are better, she will open up to you and tell you about it. Please, tell me you will make an effort."

"Okay, of course. I will send your Mom a text. There's no need for you to stress about it. Tell her you spoke to me briefly, I'm fine and that I will contact her."

As he spoke to her his phone chirped and lit up with an unknown number. "Rachel, I've got another call. Get some sleep. I'll call you back tomorrow."

"Okay. Love you."

"Love you too." He swiped his finger across the screen and accepted the incoming call. "Hello?"

"Hey white boy. What's up?"

Mason smiled. "You."

"My shift is over at two. You got a car?"

"A truck. Yes. You want a ride?"

Mason could hear the dance music in the club playing hard in the background. Ebony's voice came through clearly, smooth with a slight southern accent. "That depends. Are you a stalker, a weirdo, a psycho, or a pervert?"

"Oh, man! I was doing good until you mentioned pervert."

She laughed. "Meet me at the door on the side of the building at 2:15. Be prompt. Rob will escort me out and see that I get into your truck. See you then."

Mason glanced at the display on his phone again. He had plenty of time. The club was close enough to walk, but he figured they didn't allow the girls to leave without a ride. He swiped the screen to get to the 'favorites' in his contact list and tapped the icon labeled - Valerie. He wasn't the greatest at texting but muddled his way through a short message. *"If you are wondering, I'm fine. I hope you are as well. We should talk soon."* That would have to do for now. The phone call with Rachel concerned him. The thought of 'something' getting into his house and attacking Valerie was scary. Dealing with monsters that seemed to be bent on hurting him was one thing. He was terrified of what might happen if one of these creatures came after his wife and children. He tapped, "send" turned his attention to the mirror over the sink and jumped at what he saw in the reflection.

Mason turned in horror, backing against the wall, pushing his body away from the bright bar of light standing silently at the foot of his bed. The sliver of light stood between him and the exit. This was not possible. He had not called the Door. Even though the Door appeared at random when he was a child, this ceased to be the case once he learned to summon it with his own thoughts.

He stood there waiting for what was coming next. He tried to concentrate and close the Door, but it wasn't working. He felt sure a monster would come charging out. The beasts figured out how to travel from one reality to the next and they were coming for him. Nothing happened. He eased away from the wall and slowly inched toward the Door of light. Something was different. He moved closer and stopped a few feet from the Door. There was a slight pink color mixed in with the white, and the vibration was wrong. Mason realized why the Door appeared without his command and why he could not close it. It wasn't his Door. He immediately summoned his Door. It appeared as ordered at his side.

"What the fuck?" he whispered in amazement. "Two

Doors." He turned his attention back to the bright pink beam of light. He sensed movement within the new Door and he stepped back keeping his own Door at bay in case he needed a quick get-away.

The foreign Door opened and he was no longer alone. A woman stood before him. A sense of peace and tranquility passed over Mason. He could not explain this sensation. All apprehension and anxiety melted away. He felt calm in the presence of this small woman, as if he were floating. He even glanced down quickly, but his feet were still planted on the carpet.

"Greetings Mason Waters. My name is Aiden. Do not be alarmed. I am here as a friend."

Mason felt weightless, like being in a vacuum. The only thing he could hear was the sound of her voice. She was a human. However, she clearly did not belong in this reality. She looked to be not much taller than four feet and couldn't have weighed more than one hundred pounds. Her hair was a mixture of blonde and white that flowed gracefully passed her small shoulders. Her eyes were light brown and she had a pleasant smile. Yes, Mason thought, her entire being was pleasant. Very pleasant. She wore a dress that clung loosely to her body. Mason could see through the dress and she wore nothing else. Her tan skin appeared wet but the dress was dry. The effect was intoxicating.

Without actually touching him, she guided him to one of the chairs. He could not take his eyes off her. She was outwardly beautiful and inwardly magnetic.

"Mason, you can release your Door. You are not in danger."

"You can see my Door?"

"No. I am able to sense its presence. It feels like there is electricity in the air."

The Door winked out and he noticed that her pinkish Door was gone as well. "I'm sorry." He stammered. "I've never... You, you can summon a Door? You are from another reality?"

The woman answered him with a radiant smile. "I am so glad you are not afraid. We feared that you might run. Indeed, if you passed through your Door it would have been impossible for me to track you further."

"We? You said, we."

"You are very special Mason."

Mason struggled to concentrate. She was captivating and though he was seated, she remained standing very close to him. "What did you say your name is?"

"We are able to view other realities Mason, but traveling is very rare. It is political and very costly. This is an extreme exception and I am so happy to be the one chosen to come here to your world. I am here to formally greet you and to be your guide."

Mason closed his eyes. It was the only way he felt he could get control of whatever sort of spell she cast on him. This action almost worked. He realized that she smelled magnificent. A wave of floral sweetness flooded his nostrils. Even when she did not speak she broadcast a soothing sound like a breeze through the trees or a waterfall cascading over a cliff.

"Mason? Are you okay?" She gently touched his face causing a warm sensation to pass throughout his body.

His senses calmed. He opened his eyes but kept his vision on the floor. The sensation of her was still there, but it was dialed down. Mason felt he was in the presence of an angel with the appearance of a woman. A gorgeous woman, but a woman never-the-less. He swallowed and looked up at her. Even though he could clearly see her body through the sheer clothing he was not aroused. It was not a sexual thing he sensed. She was, in his estimation the closest thing to beauty he could imagine.

"Yes." He smiled. "I'm okay." You… want to guide me?"

"Mason. I am not allowed to stay here for long. I would like for you to travel with me, to my world. You are free to summon your Door and return to your world at any time. While you are with me you are in no danger. Will you accept my invitation Mason Waters?"

Mason had no reason to trust this woman. He couldn't even recall her name. Every fiber of his body wanted to be in her presence for the rest of time. The thought of declining her invitation made his stomach hurt. He was in love, true love, several times in his life. Nothing he ever felt compared to the way he felt being in the presence of this woman.

She touched his arm, pushing up his sleeve then produced a small metallic disc about the size of a dime. She placed the disc on his bare forearm and Mason watched as it painlessly melted into his skin. "Take a few deeps breaths."

He did so and looked her in the eyes. "Your name is… Aiden."

She smiled. "Yes."

Slowly he stood. He felt strong and wide awake. "What did you do to me?"

"It is a small enhancement designed for you. It has several purposes which I will explain. Mason, please concentrate. Will you travel with me?"

Mason nodded.

"Summon your Door."

As Mason's Door appeared the pinkish Door appeared beside it. "Enter through your Door. The device I put in your arm will pull you to my world."

Chapter 5

Mason passed through his Door without a word and came out on the other side. Aiden was right beside him. They were standing in the middle of what looked like an impossibly large laboratory. Men wearing skin tight black spandex surrounded them. They scanned Aiden's body from head to toe, then did the same to Mason.

Aiden reached out and took Mason's hand. "Do not be afraid. I will not leave your side."

Mason considered this. Fear was not his first or even second feeling. In fact, he felt a bit empowered. There was not one person in the lab taller than five feet. He towered over everyone. There were at least twenty, perhaps thirty people working on one thing or another. Everyone seemed focused on the two of them. They expressed concern for Aiden and curiosity about him.

A man wearing the same get-up with the addition of a long cape entered the lab. He approached Mason and extended his hand. "Mason. Very glad you have come. My name is Dr. Rasmus."

Mason took the man's hand in his own. He was a bit taller than the others but still much shorter than Mason.

"I'm sure you have many questions. Oh, is it proper to

address you in this manner?" He seemed to be speaking to himself. "Yes, yes, of course. Or Mr. Waters. Which do you prefer?"

Mason smiled, almost laughed. "I don't know how you know my name but Mason is good, Dr. Rasmus."

Aiden spoke up. She seemed excited. "The spike worked! I doubted you, but it worked!"

Dr. Rasmus turned. "Follow me. Everyone, back to work. I want all pertinent data within the hour. The Governor is going to want my report soon. That jump cost far too much not to have positive and very detailed results."

Mason was fascinated by what was happening. He was passing through his Door for decades, using it as his own personal adventure guide and cash cow. He traveled undetected mostly, interacting with people in different worlds only when he chose. He tried never to draw attention to himself and was successful with the exception of the monsters. Somehow, those creatures were aware of what he was doing and they didn't like it. This was the first time anyone demonstrated an ability to open a Door. Not even the monsters could open a Door. But he was beginning to think, even these wonderful people could not summon a Door on their own. Mason thought they relied on all the mechanical devices and computers in this lab to move from one reality to another.

The three of them left the lab, passed through a few corridors and entered a large office.

"Please, be seated," Dr. Rasmus said.

Mason and Aiden sat and Mason noted that she had not let go of his hand. In fact, she pulled her chair up against his and placed her head on his shoulder. He looked over at her small body, her breasts standing up firm against the thin fabric of her dress. If a strange passer-by were to notice them they would appear to be newly-weds. Mason felt safe with her and as a protector at the same time. He was drawn to her like no other.

The Doctor continued to stand. "Mason. We have been watching you for some time. We would have never introduced ourselves to your reality except for what has recently occurred with Adramelech."

Mason reluctantly turned his attention to Dr. Rasmus. "What's that? What is Adramelech?"

"That is the demon you banished."

"What? I didn't..."

Aiden interjected, "Dr. Rasmus. Let us begin again. That is not the appropriate starting point." She said this, all the while gazing at Mason.

"Quite right. Please, Mason. You have questions, no doubt."

"Okay. How is it, you are able to bring me here? Every time I use the Door, I am sent to a place of the Door's choosing. Or so it seems. I never know where I am going to go. To my knowledge, I have never entered the same reality twice. I figure there must be millions of realities. Yet you were able to choose to come to mine and to bring me to yours. That, to me, is very interesting. And why are you wearing a cape?"

"Mmmmm, yes. Our world is not so different from yours Mason. We have day and night. We sleep, eat, need water, etc... However, we have pursued several alternative paths. Physical enhancement is a major endeavor here. For one thing, we do not get sick. Disease is a thing of the past. We live much longer than your people and even at the end of our life-span there are several options available. One is to have our consciousness transposed to an artificial intelligence construct."

"That's certainly interesting Dr. Rasmus, but you did not answer my question."

Aiden squeezed his hand slightly. "The spike in your arm is designed to return to this world from any other reality. We were not sure it would work. As long as it is a part of you, you should be able to come here by choice."

He turned to her. "You are not sure. Are you."

"Not until you summon your Door, return to your reality, and come here again. That is why we came here through separate Doors. We knew the Door designed for me would return me here. What we were unsure of was the ability of the spike to bring you here. It still has to be tested for bringing you here at will."

"So, once I return to my world, there is a chance I will not be able to return here."

She nodded.

"A slim chance." Assured Dr. Rasmus.

"The spike affects you in other ways." She continued. "It enhances you physically. You should have more energy and should not feel the need to sleep so often." She looked down for the first time. "Forgive me Mason. I did not ask or receive your permission to introduce the spike to you. I had limited time in your world and did not feel that I would have an opportunity to explain it to you."

Mason, reached out to her. He touched her chin and lifted her face. "How could you offend me? You are the most beautiful and gentle person I have ever met."

"She has been created and designed for you," said Dr. Rasmus.

Mason turned to the man. "What?"

"When we first encountered you, we felt that there might come a time when we would need an ambassador. Aiden is a biologically designed female. I realize this may be a foreign concept for you, but it is common practice here. Her body is enhanced of course. Her anticipated lifespan is estimated at 1,000 of your years."

Something in what Rasmus just said seemed off. There was too much information coming his way and it was beginning to make him angry. He rose from his chair and approached Dr. Rasmus. He lowered his voice. "Why, the fuck, am I here?"

"Aiden invited you, and you accepted. You have an ability like no other in the known cosmos; of which the number of realities cannot be numbered, Mason. The population of a few, and by that, I mean less than one percent, are aware of multiple worlds. Of those, only two worlds, this one and another can 'see' into multiple realities. We are the only reality that has been able to open a Door or portal but it takes massive amounts of power which we harness from the sun. And the cost, astronomical. Mason Waters, you are able to open a portal with a thought. That, and the fact that you appear to be able to banish evil is why you are here."

Mason gave this some thought and turned back toward Aiden. "You cannot summon a Door."

She shook her head and spoke in a shameful tone. "No, sir. Dr. Rasmus and his team opened the portal. I only had a few moments to convince you to accompany me before the portal opened for my return. I had no way of knowing if you would come with me."

He turned to Dr. Rasmus again. "In essence, you drugged me, with this thing in my arm and with... her. She has been enhanced and modified as a type of drug."

"Mr. Waters..."

Mason realized he was no longer being addressed by his first name.

"Mr. Waters," Ramus seemed to falter. "You... you are free to summon your Door and go. But, I implore you to hear us out. We have not restrained you or..."

"You kidnapped me. That is not the best way to greet one another, Doctor. You want to study me, try to figure out how I do it so you can replicate it."

"We could have given you another type of drug. One that debilitates your bodily functions, sir. I could have had an army waiting for you here in the lab. Why would we go to the trouble of designing Aiden if our intentions were so diabolical?"

"Maybe your ability to reach out to my world is a new development. You probably stumbled upon me when I sent that beast through the Door." Anger built within Mason. He could feel it surging through his veins. "I'll admit, she's intoxicating but I'm not buying the story that she's been genetically coded to be my perfect mate."

"I don't know," he continued. "Maybe you're a big liar, Doctor. For all I know you are in allegiance with this Adramelech. Perhaps he has ordered you to fetch me since he couldn't catch me himself. Maybe he has threatened to wipe out your entire civilization if you don't cooperate."

He felt Aiden's small hand on his back. She reached

around him and gently turned his body back to face her. He looked down at her and the anger he felt evaporated through the pores of his flesh. She was silently crying. Her chin trembled and tears fell from her cheeks.

Aiden kept her gaze on Mason but spoke to the Doctor. "Dr. Rasmus, please, give us a few moments."

Rasmus did not protest. He moved quickly to the door without speaking and they were left alone in his office.

"Who is in charge here?" Mason asked, his voice almost a whisper. He reached out and wiped the tears from her face.

"No one. Our society does not have a hierarchy like you are accustomed. Please, sit with me."

He sat back down and she joined him, taking his hands in hers. "Please, summon your Door."

The silver beam of light appeared at Mason's side. He knew it was there without looking so he kept his eyes on her.

"You are free to go, sir."

He examined her. She was tense. Her jaw clenched and she held his hands tight. He could feel her slightly trembling. "But, you don't want me to go."

She began to cry again and handed him a small card. "Mason, you are free to go."

He accepted the card and glanced at it. It was some sort of personal or business card imprinted with her name and Mercer Laboratory; We Make Dreams A Reality. On the back of the card she had written; City – Thornton, Planet – Nikon. Mason thought for a second, stood and put the card in the back pocket of his jeans. He let go of her hands and passed through the Door. As expected he found himself in his room, right where he started. Only he was now alone and the absence of Aiden felt like a part of him was torn from his body. He reached out and grabbed the back of the chair to steady himself. He stood there, for a few moments then pulled out his cell phone. He checked the display. No time passed. Ebony would be expecting him soon. He reached up and felt his arm in the place where Aiden placed the small device. There was no evidence that the disc was there and no evidence that he met Aiden and Dr. Rasmus. But, there was one way to confirm their existence. It was the reason he stepped through the Door this last time. He knew he would eventually have to go home. The longer he remained in her presence he felt it was likely he would never leave her side. He had no explanation for the way he felt about her. It was as though he had known her his entire life; like the two of them had grown up together.

He had to see if he could pass through his Door and return to her. He had a 'plan A' and a 'plan B'. Maybe, just maybe, with Aiden's help, he would come up with 'plan 'C'. He grabbed the keys off the night-stand and headed out of the motel room, into the night.

Chapter 6

He sat in the cab of his truck next to the club, waiting for Ebony to finish her shift. He passed the time by going over his conversation with Dr. Rasmus. He told Mason that he had the ability to banish evil. Mason thought about the previous night when he summoned the Door and the beast in his room vanished. It was a complete accident. This made him laugh. If they only knew. He was a total coward and in no way a knight in armor as they must have believed. He summoned the Door for the purpose of running away, not 'banishing evil'."

There was something else Rasmus said. 'Her anticipated life-span is 1,000 of your years.' Why would he put it that way? The statement seemed to indicate some difference in the rate of time of this reality and the one Aiden is from. His train of thought was broken when the side door to the club opened. The big man stepped out first. He slowly looked left, right then moved toward Mason's truck. He opened the passenger door. "Hey," he said to Mason. Ebony appeared from behind him.

"Thanks, Rob." She hopped into the passenger seat. "I'll be fine from here." She turned to Mason and smiled a dazzling smile. "Hey, Mike. Let's roll."

Mason Waters cranked the truck and put it in drive. "Where to ma'am?"

She slid across the seat, getting closer to him, reached up and ran her fingers through his hair. She moved her hand down his chest and rested it on his left thigh.

Mason pulled out of the parking lot. "Don't stop there."

She looked up at him and gripped his crotch. "Better?"

"I've got a room up the road. Is that okay?"

"How much cash you got dear?"

"Oh. None, now that you mention it. I haven't been to an ATM today. However, I have been working on something. Are you in the mood for an adventure? Give me about an hour of your time. I will make you an offer, which will include money. If you don't like it…" He looked at her and smiled. "If it seems too dangerous, I'll give you five hundred and take you home, no harm no foul."

"Well! I like the sound of that." She squeezed his crotch gently. "You're not an ordinary guy, you know that."

He entered the freeway. "Really? How so?"

"No one gives me money for nothing, for starters."

"Oh, well, you are riding with me and keeping me company. That's something."

She removed her hand but remained close enough to him that her thigh touched his. "You know what I mean. I've had guys ask me if I was 'up for a good time', but never once has someone asked me if I was 'in the mood for an adventure'."

"By the way. My name is not Mike."

"My name's not Ebony. So, we're even. Are you married, Mike?"

Mason thought about that for a second. "Yes. I am."

"Children?"

"Getting a bit personal."

"He has kids. I'm okay with that Mike. How long are we gonna ride?"

"It's not far. About fifteen minutes. I'll make my proposal. That'll take about fifteen. If you decline, I've got thirty minutes to get you home, safe and sound."

"Mike, are you going to propose to me. If that's your bit, you are wasting your time."

He chuckled. "I'm already married. Remember? Anyway, you are not the marrying type. I can see that. You are young and I'm sure you love to have fun."

"You are smart and perceptive. A combination I like in a man."

"How did it go tonight?"

This caused her to pause. She put her head back and sighed. "I got stiffed. One son of a bitch threw up on me. Rob took care of him. A few customers tipped okay. I made three hundred dollars Mike. An average night."

The cab of the truck got quiet. Mason could feel her next to him. He wondered if she'd dozed off.

"Can I talk to you, Mike?"

"My name is Mason. I would prefer if you are going to be serious with me, that you call me that."

She sat there for a few moments more, silent, nothing but the sound of the truck tires on the pavement. Mason thought she may have been weighing her options. He hoped she would decide to go along with him. He liked her. She was vibrant and full of life. He had a plan to destroy the evil that haunted him. This woman could be a formidable warrior.

"Okay. You've got my curiosity bubbling. I sense something new. I hope it's not a let- down, something weird or corny. Let's see what you have to offer, Mason."

He exited the freeway, turned down a side street and pulled into a storage facility. He let his window down, punched in a five-digit code and drove his truck through as the gate opened.

They didn't talk. He concentrated on getting around to his storage unit, she remained silent, not knowing what was about to happen. Men took her to motel rooms. Not storage units. Part of her felt that she read him wrong. It scared her. This guy was like no other man she ever met.

Mason stopped and got out, leaving the truck running, the headlights pointing at the front of the storage unit. He walked across the front of the truck, around to her door. He opened it and held out his hand. "This is the point of no return, Ebony. I need you. And I hope to present a scenario where you need me as well. Working in a strip club is an end unto itself. This is going to sound stupid or maybe stereotypical. What I have to offer you is a new life. But, I cannot make you take that leap. If I were in your shoes, I'd be skeptical right about now. It's about 3 a.m. and we are in a dump of a storage facility. I wouldn't be so easily persuaded…"

Mason stopped talking and looked at her.

"You're freaking me out."

A thought occurred to him. He glanced at the small bag. She kept it at her side, away from him as he drove so he hadn't noticed it. "Do you have a gun?"

Keeping her eyes on him she reached down, opened

the purse just enough to let him see the light of the moon reflecting off a chrome barrel of a large pistol.

"38. Yes, it's loaded."

"Please, come with me."

They stood side by side in front of unit 256. Mason took out a key and unlocked the padlock. It snapped open. He removed the lock and reached down to pull the rolling door up. With the door fully open he stepped into the unit and reached for the light switch on the wall. He flipped the switch.

On the floor, in the middle of the unit was what appeared to be a pallet. The contents on the pallet were completely covered with a large green canvas tarp. The walls of the storage unit were lined with metal shelves and filing cabinets. The shelves were full but not with books or boxes. Each shelf held varying types of bags; duffle bags, back-packs, traveling luggage, and even some paper grocery bags. Mason approached a filing cabinet and opened the top drawer. He took out a small bundle of bills, closed the drawer and walked back to where she stood. He counted out 500 dollars, handed it to her and put the rest in his front pocket.

"As promised. This is yours no matter what."

She took the money and it vanished in the pocket of her small denim shirt. "What is all this?"

"The fruits of my labor. It has taken me several decades to accumulate so much. So, I…"

She brushed passed him and moved to the same filing drawer he pulled the money from. She opened it and gazed inside. The drawer was packed with cash. She closed the drawer and pulled out the one under it. Same result. She slid this drawer closed and turned to the pallet on the floor. She bent, grabbed the tarp by the corner and lifted it back. Absolutely nothing but stacks upon stacks of money. She dropped the tarp, straightened and squared off with him. "What the hell?"

Mason laughed. "That's your response? I thought maybe you'd have a few questions. You know perhaps…"

"I've got about fifty questions. The first of which is; Are you out of your god-damn mind!"

Mason stood quietly allowing her to gather her thoughts. He watched her pace several steps in one direction and then back the other way. It was rather funny but he decided it might not be a good time to start laughing or even letting out a snicker. No, she would eventually find her place. What he had to propose, he needed her to be committed. All in. His life might depend on her quick decision making and actions. One major issue for Mason was not knowing the full capabilities of the creatures that were stalking him.

She came to a stop and looked up at him. "You don't come across to me like the criminal type. I thought I had you pegged, but I was wrong. Where'd you get all this cash?"

"Oh, that's your question? I was thinking you might lead with why I have it stashed out here."

"I think that's clear. You can't keep it in your motel room. Your wife probably doesn't know about it or if she does you are hiding it from her. The bottom line is you are hiding it. Putting it in a bank is out of the question. So, my question is, where did you get it from?"

"Well, I stole it. But you can be sure, no one is looking for it. No one from around here. I will have to answer that question a bit later. When I tell you where I got it you will understand why I cannot tell you right now. I know it sounds odd, but you'll have to trust me."

"I think I've given you my trust. Take a look at where I've allowed you to bring me."

"With your gun."

"Up to this point you've been an okay guy. You're odd, but not one of a kind. I felt like we had some kind of connection. In fact, I like you. But, never would I have seen this coming."

You are in for a wild ride, he thought.

She took a deep breath. "Okay. I have a strong feeling I am going to regret moving forward with you, but I've got problems of my own; some of which money can solve. And you have got a shit load of money. Before you peel back the onion that is your life any further you should know that I have a life as well." She stepped right up to him, placed her hand on his chest and waited for him to look her in the eyes. "We should get to know one another, slowly."

Mason felt, strange. Rather he felt energetic. That was one way of saying it. Something about his metabolism was changing. The night seemed still and he noticed the smallest of sounds; a dog barking far in the distance, traffic from the highway, the sound of her breathing. He placed his right hand over hers and held it there on his chest. "I agree that we need to get to know one another. And we will. But, I don't do 'slow' very well."

She smiled. "I didn't think so. Well, you'll have to help me keep up." She eased her hand back to her side. "What's next?"

Mason flipped out the light in the storage bay and

secured the door. "We are headed to an ATM. We need to transfer the money."

He led her back to the truck and opened her door. She paused before hopping in. "My name is Sidney."

"Nice to meet you, Sidney."

As they exited the storage facility Mason said, "Look there in the glove box. You'll find a pen and something to write on. Whatever's in there, except the insurance which is in a plastic pocket container, is scrap. Find something to write on."

She opened the glove box and a small light made it easy to see. "Okay, got a pen and this envelope. Is this okay?"

"Yes. Jot down any notes you need to find your way back to this place on your own. We are just off the highway. This street is Beckley. The code for the gate is 47470 and the unit is 256. Here, put this in the envelope."

She looked up from writing. Mason was handing her a small key.

"This is the key to the padlock on the unit. I have another one at my house but I'm not sure where I stashed it. Probably on my dresser or it could be in a coat pocket in the closet."

"And you are giving it to me because…"

"If something should happen to me, I'm trusting you to take care of my family."

"I don't even know your family or where you live."

"As I said. My insurance papers are in the glove box. The card has my address on it. There is a spare key to this truck under the frame just outside my door. It's in a magnetic box. Run your hand under there and you'll find it. Rob seems to be an okay kind of guy. I mean if you need help with anything. Look, I don't plan on checking out anytime soon. But I am about to enter a dangerous arena and I am not sure what will happen."

"This has to do with all that money."

"No. Well, kind of, but not really. Just hang with me for a bit longer. I'm in the process of showing you, rather than just trying to tell you. I don't think you'll believe me if I simply tell you the details. So, I'm showing you as I explain. Would you have believed me if I told you about the cash? I mean without showing you?"

She looked at him but remained silent.

"Of course, you wouldn't. And the cash is a small part of what you will see tonight."

He drove the truck into the parking lot of a bank and pulled up to the drive-thru ATM. "I'll need that money I gave you."

Mason half expected her to protest, but she took out the five bills and handed them over without complaint. He took the cash, added it to his own and deposited all of it into the ATM. He deposited 50, 100 dollar bills. He'd done it before and never had an issue. The ATM would take up to 50 items. The powers that be didn't seem to care about a trivial amount of 5,000. One drawback is the machine's low limit on how much could be withdrawn in a 24- hour period. He only needed to give her back 500. He keyed in that amount and it came back in 20's which he handed over to her.

"You're laundering money through an ATM?"

"Yeah, in a way. I don't do it very often and it's a small amount. No red flags pop up and besides, I have a business. If anyone ever asked I would tell them it's all legit and none of their business."

"This doesn't add up. Why do you need to change the money out in the first place? I was okay with the large bills."

He drove out of the back lot and back to the freeway. "It has nothing to do with the denomination of the money. It is because of the money itself. I am going to have to open a Door when we get back to my room. If that money is anywhere near us when I do, it will vanish, or more accurately, go back to where it came from."

She said nothing to this, just sat back and stared out the front window.

"I'm getting ahead of myself. Look. You've got 500 bucks in your hands that you didn't have an hour ago. Be happy. You are in… We are in no danger. Everything's cool."

"Do you mind if I smoke?" She didn't wait for him to reply. She opened her window slightly, pulled a short, hand-rolled blunt out of her purse, lit it and drew in a heavy breath. She took a second hit, sighed and handed it toward Mason.

"I need a clear head."

"This will clear you right up."

"That's not what I mean. I may be in a situation where my reaction time must be optimal."

"More for me." She smiled and drew in another deep breath of the weed. "What's your wife gonna think when I walk up, ring the bell, and drop a bag of cash at the front door?"

Mason tried to picture that absurd set of circumstances. "Try not to be high if it comes to that. I'm sure you'll think of some ingenious method of how to carry that out. What I would like for you to do right now is pay close attention to everything that I am telling you and showing you tonight.

Help me to accomplish my task and you should never have to meet my wife."

"What's to stop me from robbing you, Mason? We get back to your room, you eventually fall asleep, I take your truck, head back to the storage unit and take all I can pack into the truck."

Mason glanced over at her. "Is that your plan?"

"I'm wondering how much you've thought this through. I mean, we've really just met. You hardly know me."

"I've thought of it. But I need your help. If not you, someone else. I don't want to involve my family. And, I don't have many friends. Well, it will sound sad but right now, you're my only friend. Either way Sidney, I can replace my truck and get as much money as I need whenever I need it. I never said that one storage unit is the only place I have money stashed." He smiled at her. "Yes, it would be a setback if you did something like that. I'm hoping you won't."

"Money is just a tool, like a hammer. It's designed to do a specific job. At least that's how I see it. You have to be careful with it though. I was not able to accumulate so much by being careless. I use it when I need it. So, I am advising you to do the same. I've given you the code and the key. It isn't going anywhere. Indulge me a little while longer. When you need more cash, you don't have to be sneaky. Just tell me you are headed to make a withdrawal. I won't try to stop you." Ten minutes later, Mason parked the truck in front of the door to his motel room. "This is it. Home sweet home."

The two of them got out and entered the room. Mason noted the time, just a little after 3 in the morning. Surprisingly, he did not feel tired. Just the opposite, he seemed energized.

Sidney headed straight for the rest-room.

When she came out Mason was seated at the table. She changed her outfit. Now she wore nothing but a loose-fitting white t-shirt and a pair of shorts that were hidden by the shirt. Mason wondered how she could keep so much in the small bag. That thought dissipated when he noticed she was not wearing a bra.

She moved to the side of the bed closest to him and took a seat. She patted the spot on the bed next to her. "Why you sittin' way over there?"

Mason pursed his lips, raised one eyebrow, then moved to the spot she indicated. "You're in a good mood."

"Why wouldn't I be? I just met my sugar daddy."

Mason laughed at that. "That's not what's going on Sidney. But, I can see your point. I need to show you something."

She took a finger and traced it down the middle of his chest. "Do you have to show me right this minute?"

She moved closer to him, pushing her breasts into his side. "We could have some fun for a while." She whispered in his ear, a strong odor of weed on her breath.

"What happened to, 'we really just met. You hardly know me.'?"

She gently traced her tongue over the top edge of his ear. "I have a feeling you are going to give me the adventure of a lifetime."

"Well, I guess that makes everything all right then. But it also sounds like a tall order to fill."

She put her palm on his chest and pushed him gently back on the bed. "Right now, only one thing needs to be filled." With one continuous motion, she was up, straddling his body and kissing him at the same time. With a few quick and apparently easy moves, she had his pants open.

He pulled back just enough to get her attention. "Sidney."

"Yes," she whispered.

"This isn't part of what I had in mind."

She looked at him dreamily. "Well, part of you, hmmm, a very significant part of you seems happily ready to go."

"He is deplorable. I cannot vouch for that part of me."

With his pants open she gathered him fully in her right hand. "You want me to stop Mason?"

"I want you to know that I had no intention of getting you in bed. I have a very real situation and I seriously need your help. I'd love to get with you, but I have an agenda. I really want you to stay with me and help me. Not screw me and leave. This will sound stupid because you don't have all the info, but it is a matter of life and death."

Slowly she stroked him, smiling. She remained quiet for a bit moving her hand on him, pushing her body into his. She raised up and removed her shirt, then the shorts. She took off his pants as he pulled his shirt off. Then she was back on top of him. She leaned in, kissed him, then whispered in his ear. "I reserve the right to pull myself out of your world at any time."

"Okay," he said, relaxing. *There will come a time of no return when you won't have the option of pulling out.* He thought.

"No more talk, Mason. Just fuck me and let's see where this goes."

"Okay."

They didn't speak after that. Their bodies moved on

auto-pilot for the next fifteen minutes. Mason found the event to be very primal. He hadn't performed in such a manner since he was in his twenties. She was hungry and he was fully able to satisfy her desire. Ten minutes in they were sweating, each one thrusting their bodies into the other. Mason was determined to keep up with her and he was doing a good job of it. He moved up off his back, got up to approach her from behind, Sidney on her knees, pushing back toward Mason's physical thrusts.

Soon, she was calling his name and begging him to stop. "Please, I can't take it anymore!" When he relented she smiled and attacked him, begging him to keep doing her.

When they were spent, each one covered in sweat and other bodily fluids they lay back on the bed breathing heavily. Sidney started laughing. "I did not expect that! How old are you Mason?"

He smiled and turned toward her. "According to my driver's license, 52."

"Shit. I know guys half your age that can't keep up with me." She turned on her side, purposely resting her breasts on his chest, her eyes fully alert now. "You are full of surprises."

"You ain't seen nothing, sister. We should get back to business."

She ran her hand down to his crotch. "What business are you gonna conduct with this? Oh my god! You are hard as a rock, man!"

"Well, what do you expect? Putting your tits on me. You are going to have to put some clothes on."

"Oh, I will. But not yet." She sat up and threw her leg over his torso. With one easy thrust, she guided him back inside and rode him until he could hold back no longer.

Chapter

They slept for hours, on top of the blanket, body's entangled. Morning came and Mason opened his eyes, noticed sunlight coming through the cheap curtains. He felt two distinct sensations. He had to pee and he was incredibly hungry. He glanced at the young woman still asleep, her warm body nuzzled up next to him, unaware that she was already fulfilling a big part of what he needed her for. He had not dreamt. No beast attacked him in his sleep, because, for whatever reason, they did not bother him when another person was next to him at night. He reached out and gently touched her face. She did not stir. He ran his hand down over her breasts, across her flat belly, and stopped at her pubic bone. She had an amazing body but more than that, he was glad she was in it with him. Well, so far. He hadn't scared her yet.

He got out of bed and took care of the first of his two necessities. He came out, stopped at the sink and washed his hands and face. As he toweled off he looked up at his reflection. This caught his attention and he stared at himself. He needed to shave. The 'five o'clock shadow' appeared to be about two days old. That was not the issue. The whiskers on his face should have been white. He still had salt and pepper hair on his head but the whiskers sprouting on his face had not one white strand. He rubbed his face in amazement. He started going grey around fifteen years ago. How was this possible? He felt the place on his forearm where Aiden placed the small device and wondered.

Sidney came up behind him, wrapped herself around his back, looking at his reflection. "Good morning sport. You okay?"

He turned and pulled her in close. "Yeah. I'm alright. You sleep okay?"

"I'm good dear. What's for breakfast?"

"There's a Denny's nearby. That's all I am aware of. You probably know this area better than I do."

"Come on. Let's shower." She pulled him back into the bathroom and turned on the water. "Go ahead, I have to pee first."

They showered together. Mason thought he did a good job keeping his hands to himself. She was probably up for anything, but he wanted to get to business.

They lingered. Letting the hot water run over their bodies. She looked up at him. "You haven't told me the plan, or what we are doing here. I have a shift at the club tonight. I should check in around 6:00."

"You can work your shift. But, I need you to come back here when you get off. I need you to stay with me Sidney, for a few days. I hope to be done with my business by then. I rented this room for a week."

"You like staying here?"

"No. I don't. If you are with me though, it's tolerable."

"What am I supposed to do? I mean, why do you need me?"

"Come on, let's dry off."

As they toweled off and got dressed she said, "I want to go to my place and get some things; clothes and some girl stuff."

"Okay, we can eat and then go do that. Before we walk out this door, I need to show you something."

She moved to one of the chairs and took a seat. "Okay, sir. You have my attention."

Mason pulled on a pair of jeans, buckled his belt, and slipped on a pair of brown canvas work boots. He purposely did not wear a shirt. "May I see your .38?"

Sidney gave him an inquisitive look but did not protest. She pulled the pistol from her purse and handed it to him.

Mason examined the weapon for a moment. It was mostly chrome in color with the exception of a black handle. It held six rounds and was fully loaded.

"It's light-weight and small," Sidney commented. "It fits easily in my hand-bag. I've shot it a few times and I like it."

"I thought girls carried mace or some kind of pepper spray."

"Oh, I have that as well."

Mason nodded. "Alright, pay close attention. I'll be right back."

He saw her begin to say something but he summoned the Door. He placed the pistol in his belt at the small of his back and stepped out of the room before he could hear her. He had no doubt that when he returned he would catch whatever it was she was saying.

***

Mason stepped into darkness. He stood there for a

moment, allowing his eyes to adjust. He turned slowly and saw a dim light coming from under a door to his left. Shapes in the lab began to come into focus. He was back in the land of Aiden, in the same massive laboratory minus the people and busy commotion. Well, he thought, the device in his arm seemed to be working as designed. Never, had the Door placed him in the same place twice. He was in the exact same place as before. The facility was quiet and dark. Perhaps it was night time and everyone was out for the evening. That seemed a bit odd though. A place this big didn't seem to be a place that would ever completely shut down.

He walked over to the door where he had seen the light, reached for the door handle and pushed. The door opened easily and he moved through into the corridor. As he walked toward the source of the light a thought occurred to him. With the device in his arm, he would be limited to this world and his own. Not a big issue at the moment, but Mason wondered if Dr. Rasmus and his team could make adjustments. If not, he would eventually need to have the disc removed. He wondered if they could design similar devices that could send him to specific worlds.

The door leading to the only source of light was marked with a sign, "Detection Office". Mason knocked lightly on the door and opened it. Inside he found the source of light coming from multiple monitors. Each monitor featured split camera views of different areas in the laboratory. A few were focused on a parking area. The rest displayed areas of the warehouse and lab. A few of the scenes were lit with ordinary light while most sported a green overlay. Mason guessed they were equipped with a type of night vision or infrared lenses. The man monitoring these cameras jumped out of his seat. Mason was met instantly by a slender man who stood not surprisingly, about five feet tall.

"Who are you? How did you get in here?"

Mason jerked the weapon from his belt and pointed it at the small man. "Easy does it. Sit back down."

The guy looked at Mason with an expression of fear and surprise. He backed up gingerly and took the seat he previously occupied.

Mason took up a position across the room a good ten feet away from the guard. He kept the gun trained on the guy and studied the video feeds displayed on the wall of monitors.

"What's going on here? Why is the lab shut down?"

The guard did not speak. He sat there staring at the gun in Mason's hand.

Mason lowered the gun but did not put it away. "Let's start over. I'm not here to harm you or to cause any trouble. I was here a few hours ago, with Dr. Rasmus and Aiden. But this place was buzzing with activity."

The guard seemed to calm slightly. "That, that can't be. This place has been shut down for the past three months. I know Dr. Rasmus. He is relocated to the main facility in the city. The other person you mentioned, I'm not familiar. Man, I just come in here and do my rounds. This is always a quiet post. There isn't anything here to steal. They have computers everywhere but they're too big, you know, not the personal type. All the chemicals were moved out when Dr. Rasmus left. I mainly watch the place for vandals. I guess if there were a fire or emergency they would want someone here to notify the authorities. But really, look how big this facility is and they only put one guard."

Mason gave this some thought. He was in new territory here. "Relax. What's your name?"

"Michael."

Mason remembered the card Aiden gave him. He reached into his back pocket and took it out. "Mercer Laboratory; We Make Dreams A Reality." He read aloud. "I was here let's see, like eight or nine hours ago, literally yesterday. Aiden, I don't know her last name, gave this to me."

Michael shifted uneasily. Mason considered his own appearance. Here stood a man with a gun. The man wore no shirt and was most likely the tallest person Michael ever encountered. He smiled inwardly but tried to remain focused. The place did appear deserted. How could it have gone from a bustling mini-city to a ghost town over-night? The fact is, it could not. So, other factors were involved.

"Yes, this is Mercer. But, I don't recognize the name of the person who gave you the card. I've had this post for three months. When I came they were still moving equipment and office stuff. That's when I met Dr. Rasmus. Weird guy, but I guess everything they do here is weird in a way. They augment or enhance plants, animals, and people. I understand they use all sorts of chemicals, drugs, and they have a massive electrical generator. I've never seen it operational but I've heard stories. They say the thing causes electrical blackouts around the country."

"Michael. Are you enhanced?"

"I'm not able to afford the procedures they do here."

"How old are you?"

The guard shot him a look. "192, why?"

The guard appeared to Mason to be in his early thirties, maybe even his late twenties. This reality, this planet, though similar in most ways to his own reality, measured time differently. This never occurred to Mason. In all of his travels, he experienced no change in his own aging process. What held constant; he aged at a normal pace no matter which reality he occupied, he always returned to the exact point in time when he returned to his home-world, the Door always, without exception, came to his location when he summoned it, the Door always deposited him in a new reality never to repeat the same place twice. This was different. He returned to the same world thus breaking a rule that he did not know could be broken. Perhaps other rules could be broken or even bent a little. He needed time to think this through and he wanted to talk to Aiden. Dr. Rasmus would do as well.

"Can you tell me how to get in touch with Dr. Rasmus?"

The guard turned in his chair and selected a small white card from a desk drawer. He glanced at it then handed it over to Mason. "This has his business contact info."

Mason looked at the card then pocketed it along with the one Aiden gave him. He raised the .38 and pointed it at Michael. "I need your shirt."

"Are you nuts?"

"Come on. Don't give me any shit and you'll make it home today. I can always just shoot you and take it. I'd rather not mess up the shirt with your blood. Don't stand up. Just remain in your chair and take it off."

The guard complied but he didn't like it. "Only damn uniform shirt I got. You know how expensive these are?"

Mason took the shirt careful to keep the .38 trained on

the man. The uniform came with attached insignia, a name-plate with Michael's name on it, and a shiny badge. Mason took off the name-plate and the badge and placed them on a table near where he stood. "You can keep this stuff. Best I can do for now. I'll be back maybe in a few months by my calculations. I'll bring this uniform shirt when I come. I might even send it back to you before I return. Either way, if you are still employed here, you'll get it back."

Michael sat there, his slender frame even more exposed. Mason could see ribs under his skin and his stomach sported a few abdominal muscles. He did not put the shirt on. He was done here and he'd learned long ago never to linger in a reality for too long. He summoned the Door and winked out of Michael's reality.

Sidney said, "You're not taking my…" She stood up.

Mason handed her the .38 and tried the shirt on. It was far too small. He looked at Sidney who seemed to be trying her best to figure out what had just happened. He shrugged and took the shirt off. "Here, maybe it will fit you better. My little plan did not work so well. I was going to return with a nice shirt, maybe even a tie, something that would fit at least."

"Return? You never left. But I cannot figure out how you made this shirt appear out of thin air. Nice trick."

"Sit back down."

She took her seat and examined the shirt in her hands. "Hey, there's a dollar in the pocket. But, it's not real, it's brown."

Mason picked out one of his own collared shirts, put it on and buttoned it as he took a seat on the edge of the bed opposite Sidney. "It's not a trick."

"What then? Man, you are freaking me out."

"Well, it's about to get even more freaky. My problem is figuring a way to explain this to you without you running right out the door. So, I brought you in on the money side of things. If you don't believe another thing I say, you can believe the part about the money."

"You like the shirt?" he asked.

"I, what? No, this thing stinks."

"Okay, put it on your lap. Don't touch it with your hands, but hold on to that bill."

She did as he said.

Mason called for the Door. The bright light filled the room for an instant then winked out. Sidney, who had not taken her eyes off the shirt sat dumbfounded. The bill remained in her hand. The shirt was no longer in her lap. "Wow. That is the best magic trick I've ever seen. How did you do that?"

Mason sighed, considering the idea that he could have long ago started a career as a magician. "It isn't magic. I left this reality, traveled to another world and brought that shirt back with me. While it was in your lap I opened the Door and returned the shirt. Well, it's a bit more complicated than that. For now, that explanation is as good as any."

Sidney threw up her hands. "I knew it. Jesus, I knew it. I meet a good guy, you seem to have your shit together. Oh, you're running around on your wife, but who isn't these days? You're a bit older than what I prefer, but not too old. You fuck like a Clydesdale, so the age thing is cool. And money, well you're loaded. But you are an absolute fruitcake. There's always a catch. The greater the guy, the bigger the damn catch."

"It's true Sidney. That's how I got all my money. Put that bill on the table." Mason got up and went into the bathroom. "Is it on the table? You're not touching it?"

"Yes."

Mason called the Door and came back out of the bathroom.

Sidney looked in amazement at the spot where she placed the bill.

"I sent it back. It's weird mainly because you cannot see the passage. Not only can I see the passageway, I can go through it. When I return through the Door I always return to the exact time I left. This is why it appears to you that I never left."

"Is the passageway here now?" She looked around the room.

Mason put his hand to his forehead. "No."

"Okay, do it again?"

"What?"

"Make something else disappear. Make this table disappear, or the bed."

"I can't. It doesn't work that way."

"But, you, you can disappear, right?"

"Well, sure, but you wouldn't perceive it. I could leave this room and be gone for a long time, like forty years. To you, I would simply go from being the man you see now to a very old man in an instant. But that is far too much of a sacrifice on my part to prove my point."

Sidney remained silent at this part of the exchange. She appeared to be thinking it over or perhaps trying to figure out how he performed the disappearing trick. She looked at him and smiled. "Make me disappear. Or, let me go through the passageway, whatever you call it."

"You're playing with me."

"No." She shook her head and looked at him earnestly. "But I am expecting to hear how you cannot do that and why."

"Okay, I will explain it. First, I'm going to get something to eat. You coming?"

She stood. "I'm definitely up for breakfast. But you didn't answer me."

"Okay, stubborn girl. The problem with that idea is that I can't let you go through the Door on your own. I wouldn't know where you have gone and there would be no way of bringing you back. I don't think you can go through without me anyway. I've never tried to take someone else through the Door. Hell, I've never told anyone else about it. As a kid, I thought everyone could see the damn thing just like me. It wasn't until I got older that I realized I was the only one seeing it and a bit later when I discovered that I could pass through it. I know you think I have some screws loose and that is the very reason why I am reluctant to explain it to anyone."

They headed out the door together and walked across the highway toward the Denny's.

"Then why now Mason? Why me? A total stranger."

"I have four adult children. I have considered approaching them as I have approached you. Well, not in the exact manner, you know. Don't be offended, but I cannot bring myself to place them in unnecessary danger."

She took his arm. "No offense taken. I get it. You love

your kids. If someone has to die, might as well be a stranger; someone you don't give a shit about."

"Huh, thought you said you weren't offended."

"Just yanking your chain sir. Continue."

"I have always dealt with the danger involved with passing through the Door. There are beings, nasty fellas, that really do not seem to like me. The danger of an encounter with them was minimal in the beginning. Now that danger is at my doorstep and I fear that if I don't deal with it, go on the offensive so to speak, they may be able to destroy me, my family, and perhaps many others."

"There's danger Scooby Doo?"

"You're not taking me seriously."

"Buy me some pancakes, then take me to my place. I will be better able to think seriously on a full stomach. Are you going to try taking me through the passageway?"

"I really only wanted you to stay with me for a while. There is no danger as long as you are with me. At least that is what I believe."

"Oh, no. You opened this can of worms, buddy. I have no intention of babysitting you till you are old and gray, no matter how much money you have."

"I felt I had to convince you of the impending danger in order to get you to agree to stay with me and take it seriously. Sidney, at the risk of sounding desperate, I need you to stick with me when I am asleep, I mean physically. I need you to be present with me as much as possible. Until I get this thing figured out."

"Well, you do sound desperate. I'll stay with you for a while. But I think it may be to your advantage to take an offensive stance. Don't wait for the danger to come to you.

I may not always be at your side. I give you some credit. The money is a major selling point. I like you even though I think you may be a little weird. Sounds like an elaborate scam to get some pussy."

"Really? You're not serious about that. All the money I have, you think I would have any trouble getting just about anything I want?"

"You have a point."

"Buying loyalty is another matter entirely."

"Mason." She stopped causing him to stop as well and to look down at her.

"Yes?"

"What we did last night. I don't do that with anyone. I mean, sure, I've been with some guys. But this is different. My life has been moving on a particular course, steady, in one way. I made a sharp left turn somewhere in the past 24 hours. I can feel it. Unless you break crazy on me, I'm not going anywhere."

Mason smiled. "Come on Sidney. I'm hungry as a bear."

Chapter 8

Over breakfast, he told her the story of Aiden and Dr. Rasmus. He left out certain details, the fact that Aiden was in effect nude, wearing a see-through garment. He did not tell her how magnetically attracted he was toward Aiden. He also failed to mention anything about the disc or spike that Aiden placed in his arm. He told her about the demons. He explained how they tormented him as a boy and how this one particular monster, Adramelech, attacked him two nights ago. He expressed his fear that the monsters wanted to kill him and he suspected they would kill anyone who meant something to him. The story he laid out was fantastic, even to his own ear, but she sat there eating her pancakes, bacon, eggs, and grits, listening intently, not questioning him.

They were sitting in their booth at Denny's for the better part of an hour when she said, "So, when do we go?"

"Just like that?"

"Just like that babe. I wanted to go to my apartment but this is amazing. The only thing I am interested in right now is going through your Door. I mean, everything you said is unbelievable, Mason. Really. It is totally, one hundred percent bull crap. I figure, if you can take me into this alternate reality, maybe I need to be committed. I cannot explain how you have a storage unit full of cash. That isn't enough to make me believe everything you say. If you can take me to another universe, another world, then I'm in it with you all the way. That's the whole thing, isn't it? If you can't open this 'Door' of yours, and can't show me another reality, can't prove it, then it's like I said; bull crap. Most likely an elaborate scam to get some pussy. If that is the case, I'm not complaining. You are great in the sack."

Mason tossed his fork on his plate in disgust, took a final gulp of his coffee and said, "You finished?"

She nodded.

"Then let's go."

Mason could have summoned the Door right then and there, but he wasn't sure how to get Sidney through. It would be better to return to his room. Once they returned he called for the Door. It appeared as commanded, bright and majestic, vibrating at the foot of the bed. He grabbed hold of her hand. "Grab your hand-bag and hold on to my hand." He passed through the Door and found himself alone in a dark laboratory; Mercer Laboratory.

"Well, shit! It didn't work." He stood there, hands on hips, in what appeared to be a lab that was shut down, closed for business as it was the last time he was there. He summoned the Door and returned to his motel room.

"Well, what's up?" Sidney asked. "Why did you let go of my hand? Don't tell me you can't do it. Mason, this is looking really lame. Let's just get undressed and do it. I'm horny. Then I've got some errands to run."

Mason held up a hand. "Hold on a second. I went through the Door. You let go of my hand."

She did not speak. She didn't have to. She lowered her

head slightly and gave him a look that said, 'Really, that's your defense?'

This pissed him off. "God-damn-it! Come here." He took her by the hand and jerked her hard, pulling her face to face. He reached down, wrapped both arms around her, picked her up. "Put your arms around me damn-it."

She clenched her jaw and looked at him in defiance. "Alright. You like to play rough? Come on!" Sidney wrapped her arms around his neck and squeezed. She leaned in, forced her tongue into his lips, into his mouth, kissing him fiercely.

Mason kissed back and summoned the Door again. He strengthened his hold on her. He would make the Door rip her away from him or he would get her through. They became one as she lifted her legs and locked them around his waist. He shifted placing Sidney between himself and the passageway. And stepped forward.

Sidney broke the kiss. The lights went out. She pulled back from Mason and placed her feet on the floor. Untangling her arms, she turned almost violently. She was no longer standing on the carpeted floor of the motel room, but on a hard linoleum surface. Her eyes adjusted and she found herself in a large warehouse full of what looked like computers things that were foreign to her understanding. She inched her body back toward Mason as fear crept into her mind. She hadn't believed him. Who would? What was this? She was in his motel room. An instant later she found herself in another, totally different environment.

"Mason?" Her voice faltered.

"It's okay. We are right where we are supposed to be.

Stand still for a few moments. Let your eyes adjust. See that light over there?"

"Yes."

"When you're ready, head that way. There is a security guard that I want to talk to."

"Mason?" She whispered. "Where are we?"

He thought it was funny, but he matched her low tone. "We are in a science lab. I've been here on two previous occasions. Which is another problem I need to deal with."

"I don't understand."

"It's not important. You ready?"

"Okay. You go first. Wait."

He started toward the door. "What now?"

"How do we get back home?"

He tried to see the thing from her point of view. He was traveling to different worlds for decades. The Door appeared to him as an infant. Sidney was experiencing this phenomenon for the first time.

She hit him with another question before he could reply. "What if that creature you told me about attacks us?"

He turned to face her and held her gently by the shoulders. "I don't think the Adramelech beast can attack us here. Don't ask me why. It's just a feeling. As for returning home. That's easy. Once I recall the Door we will pop right back in the motel room. There are some things I need to understand. You needed to experience this for yourself. So, I'm taking care of several things at once here. You won't miss anything back home cause when we go back no time will have passed."

"This may take some getting used to."

Well, he thought, *that's promising.* "Come on. The guard is down the corridor. At least I hope he is."

They found Michael in the Detection Office; reclining in his chair, feet propped on the console, hands folded over his uniform shirt, snoring. Mason motioned for Sidney to have a seat in a folding chair stashed against the far wall. He leaned against the console and slowly pushed Michael's feet till they fell to the floor.

The guard bounced forward and ended up on the floor, banging his knees.

"Good morning sunshine," Mason said.

"You! How'd you get in here without setting off the alarm?" Quickly he jumped to his feet.

"Take it easy Michael. No need to get excited. I'm not armed this time but my lady friend over there is packing. Now sit back down. I need to ask you some questions."

The guard glanced over at Sidney and his eyes bulged. "What, what happened to her skin?" He took a step toward Sidney.

Mason made a quick move, placing his own body between the two. "You've never seen an African American?"

He took his eyes off her and looked up at Mason. "A what? Did she get burned?"

This is getting better by the minute. Mason reached out and grabbed the chair where Michael was previously reclining. "Sit."

Slowly, Michael took his seat but he couldn't seem to take his eyes off Sidney.

"I see you got your shirt back."

"Oh, yeah. I had to go buy a new one. When I came in for my next shift I found this one. Someone, I assumed you, came in this office and placed it on the back of this chair. How you are able to come and go from this place is a complete mystery. I reported you to my supervisor. They went over the video from that night and there you are. Walking through the corridors. But there is no evidence of how you got in. So, they upgraded the alarm system. Yet you still seem to be able to get past it."

"How long ago was that? How long ago was it that you last saw me here in this office?"

He rubbed his chin, thinking. "Um, about six weeks ago."

Mason looked over at Sidney. "That was maybe three hours ago, max."

"What are you saying?" She asked.

"There are differences in every reality. Sometimes it's very subtle, sometimes it's major. Most of the inhabitants of this place are about as tall as you or shorter. Based on his reaction to seeing you, there are no black people. They have the ability to modify or enhance their bodies in ways I'm not completely sure of. And, there is a time difference. A big one. Michael here is 192 years old."

She shook her head. "That's ridiculous. He looks like he's around my age."

"Michael, you remember I asked you about two people; Aiden and Dr. Rasmus."

"Yeah, sure."

"Is there some way you can put me in touch with the Doctor? You gave me his card, but how do I get in contact with him?"

"Easy. I can call him."

"Right now?"

Michael shrugged. "Sure. If I do that will you tell me how you are bypassing the alarms?"

"Focus Michael. Get Dr. Rasmus for me and I'll consider your request."

The guard turned in his seat, leaned forward and made the call.

***

Dr. Rasmus frantically pleaded with Mason not to go anywhere. He informed the guard he would meet them at the lab within the hour. He stressed that Mason was to be treated as a guest. He told Michael to make him comfortable and under no circumstances was he to take his eyes off him. The guard protested, explaining that he had rounds to make. The Doctor said he was under new orders. The lab be damned. He was to guard Mason Waters with his life.

The three of them; Mason, Sidney, and Michael the security guard were getting to know one another in the company lounge when Dr. Rasmus arrived. Mason looked up as the Doctor entered; the man not sporting a cape today, clutching a small black case and wearing what appeared to be something a person would wear for snow skiing. It was a one-piece outfit that covered him from neck to ankle. It came complete with matching boots and a scarf. Mason set his cup of coffee on the counter and stood.

"Ah, Mr. Waters. Very good! I am so glad you have returned to us. It's been a while. And whom is this fine young lady?"

Mason greeted the Doctor with a firm handshake. "This is my friend, Sidney."

Rasmus bowed deeply but kept his eyes on Sidney. "I am

very glad to make your acquaintance. Should you choose to stay in our fine city I am sure you will find yourself to be a treated with curiosity as well as respect."

He turned his attention to Michael. "My good man. You have done a splendid job. You may return to your previous duties. I would also require that you omit this event from your shift report."

Michael rose from where he was seated. "I shouldn't report anything about the break-in, or any of this?"

"I believe you have previously reported Mr. Waters for breaking and entering, yes?

"I did. You know I did."

"When questioned what proof did you present?"

"The video feed was all I had. There were no prints or evidence of how he entered or exited."

"My good officer. What do you suppose the talk is about your particular performance on that night?"

Michael remained silent.

"Well, I can assure you it is not good. Word of your incompetence has been floating about. At present, the video system is off-line. I made sure of it before entering. It will not be operational until I have removed myself from the premises. You will find yourself in a similar situation as before. This time two people will have breached upgraded security and exited without a trace. You may not lose your job, but you will most certainly be removed from this fine post."

The two men looked at one another. Michael muttered. "I see." He turned to Mason. "Sir, perhaps I will see you at another time."

"Perhaps." Mason acknowledged.

With that, the security guard exited the room.

Dr. Rasmus moved closer to Sidney. "May I?"

Sidney stood, not knowing what to make of this odd man.

He did not make physical contact with her, but he certainly examined her. He walked slowly, making a complete circle around her as he scanned her body from head to toe. "Has your skin always reflected in this manner?"

"I've been the same color since I was born, sir. Same as my Mom, same as my Grandma."

After making a complete circle he turned his attention to Mason. "She cannot open a portal like you. We would have detected this ability. You... you, brought her through?"

"Yes. I wasn't sure how, but we managed."

"May I ask, to what end?"

"Have a seat Doctor." They all sat down. The Doctor placed his case on the table next to his seat.

Mason continued. "You recall mentioning my encounter with Adramelech?"

"Yes, of course. That encounter, as you put it, was a vital part of our decision to enter your world. It was the most important part of our supplication for government approval. We do many things at Mercer. 'Viewing' I'm afraid is a sort of pet project of mine as it does not produce funds. It is actually an expense. Opening a passageway on the other hand. Well, we are not clear on how you do what you do sir. I have only been able to recreate the event using massive amounts of energy, which I am afraid is very costly."

Sidney asked, "What is, 'viewing'?"

"Yes. Long ago we stumbled upon the existence of multiple realities. Just a few at first, then it became evident that there are billions of alternate realities or worlds that exist within, in essence, the same space. This science is difficult to explain without my tablet, or a laptop would do."

"Consider a novel." He opened his case and brought out a thick book. "This will do. Imagine that your world, Earth, is a letter in a word in a sentence on say, page 84 of our book." He opened the book to the page he indicated. "So, in the middle of page 84, I choose a sentence and a word, 'many' and the letter 'M'. So, 'M' represents your world, your reality. Now, all the letters on page 84 are similar and relatively close to your world. This world, my world, Nikon is also a letter in a word but it is located several pages away, say perhaps page 134."

"Over the years I devoted my spare time to this particular study. I developed a device that allows one to view another world, another reality." He sighed, closed the book and placed it back in the case. "However, a theory is only a theory to a politician. I needed proof. Viewing another reality was not enough to convince anyone to fund my project. At first, my application and evidence was a spectacular success. Once, however, the powers that be realized it could not be used for any practical purpose they became far less interested. My invention was similar to merely watching a movie but with much less drama and romance. Mason, your world is interesting, but there are realities on other pages of our book that are absolutely amazing. I believe you would be as fascinated as I am."

"Alright, let's not get ahead of ourselves. This creature, Adramelech is…"

"Not a creature." Rasmus interrupted. Adramelech is a fallen Angel, but not from your world. If your reality is on page '84', and Nikon is on page 134 a distance of 50 pages, Adramelech's reality is on page 384. In his own reality, he is ancient with immense power."

"I believe you. He and his minions have been haunting me since I was a young boy. Now they are hunting me. You asked why I brought Sidney along. She's backup."

Dr. Rasmus smiled but quickly stopped smiling when he realized Mason was not kidding. "Adramelech is extremely resourceful. I am able to view hundreds, perhaps thousands of realities that are relatively close to this one. He has managed to cross hundreds of thousands of realities to reach into yours. I cannot imagine how he was able to enter your world and to appear in your motel room. It is an amazing feat."

Mason thought about how this beast was using his unconscious dream state to reach out to him. "Doctor, are you able to get in contact with Aiden?"

Dr. Rasmus nodded. "Sure. She was devastated after you left and we shut the lab down. She took some time off. About a month as I recall. Anyway, she works under my supervision at my office in the city. Understand, her primary purpose was removed when you left. But I was able to create a new position for her. She is extremely smart and adaptable. May I ask why you wish to contact her?"

"Yes, but I'll get back to that. I've got a few matters that I need your expertise on."

That perked the Doctor up. It seemed he was keen on the idea that others saw him as an expert in any area of life or work.

"Let's begin with the spike she put in my arm."

"Ah!" The Doctor perked up at the mention of the device.

"That charm is the backbone of Mercer Industries. How is it working for you, sir?" He rose and approached Mason reaching for his arm. "You know we charge quite a sum for that bit of technology. Each one is custom made for the client. I worked overtime on yours. Have you experienced any headaches?" He had Mason's forearm in his hands now examining the spot where Aiden placed the spike.

Mason found this humorous. There were no wounds or other visible markings on his arm. He did not see what the Doctor could have been looking at. "Headaches? No but…"

"I failed to mention earlier, but I noticed the gray in your hair has diminished considerably. The device has several functions you see. The most important is to ground your passageway to this reality."

"Yes." Mason pulled his arm back. "About that…"

"Well, come along." The Doctor turned and headed for the exit.

Mason glanced over at Sidney, shrugged and the two of them followed the Doctor.

Chapter

Dr. Rasmus continued the one-sided conversation as they made their way through dark corridors. "The spike is originally designed for enhancements. Not knowing it's full effect on a person from your world, what with the time difference and other issues, I dialed it way down. However, you seem to be adapting nicely. I can design a spike for your friend if you like. No charge, it is an honor to be working with you, Mr. Waters."

They entered a small lab and Dr. Rasmus clapped his hands together. The room was immediately illuminated with bright light. "If you will sir." He motioned for Mason to meet him at a work-station and to place his forearm on the table.

"Dr. Rasmus." Mason complied but decided he needed to get a word in before Rasmus made any adjustments to the spike. "I do not want my Door to be attached to your reality."

Rasmus froze. "You. You don't like it here? I thought you wished to see Aiden."

"I do. But I also wish to be able to visit other realities. Being limited to Nikon and Earth is not what I had in mind."

"Mr. Waters, you are aware that Adramelech cannot attack you in this reality. Nor can any other being from his world."

"Are you so sure Doctor? Adramelech does not use a passageway or Door to get at me. He comes in my dream state."

"Dr. Rasmus?" Sidney chimed in.

The Doctor turned to her. For the moment, he seemed to be in stunned silence.

"Something you said earlier when you were explaining things with the book." She opened her mouth to continue, closed it and appeared to struggle with how to approach her question. "Doctor, how do you know what you know about the monsters that are after Mason? You said our two realities, yours and ours, were kind of close to one another. You said the world of this monster was like on page 384. Given the difficulty for you to open a passageway, it seems impossible for you to know the history of a world so far away."

Rasmus remained silent.

Mason studied the man, glanced at Sidney then back to the Doctor. "Well?" he asked.

"You said he is a fallen Angel." Sidney continued. "How do you know that?"

Rasmus lowered his head slightly and looked at the floor. "He came here." He remarked quietly. "Rather, I opened the portal that brought him here. I was a young man then. Hundreds of years ago. I hadn't perfected the technology. It's still not perfect, but back then, well, I didn't know what I was fooling with."

He looked up and Mason saw the man was crying. "What happened Doctor?"

The Doctor gathered his thoughts, took a moment, then began. "I have the ability to do more than view certain worlds. Your world, for example, has Internet. Many realities have similar technology, some are not so fortunate. I have the ability to access the Internet in your reality. Studying this medium is merely a hobby for me but it is how I came to understand the time difference between our worlds. There is a machine on your planet, in Switzerland. It is known as the Hadron Collider."

Mason nodded. "I'm vaguely familiar. I've seen news stories about it."

"This device interested me very much and I watched with interest, how it was to be used and what results or discoveries came from its use. It took approximately ten Earth years to be constructed using over 10,000 scientists and engineers. It fails in comparison to what I built. For roughly seventy-five years I constructed a machine that is as vast as a city. It had one purpose; to open a portal into another reality."

Sidney spoke softly. "It works."

"It exceeded my expectations. When I engaged it to full capacity it opened a portal to every reality, all at once. The result caused a black-out over half the planet. Of course, the machine shut down as well, but not soon enough. The angelic beings from Adramelech's world have advanced technology. They have in essence an alarm system that is triggered when an anomaly such as the one I created occurs. The portals I opened only lasted for a few seconds. In that time, a host of beings from that reality entered our own."

The Doctor walked slowly to a large metallic device that dispensed water. He took a long drink and continued. "At first we were in awe. These beings are massive, at least four times our size. They appeared bright and they have the ability to defy gravity. Their leader, Adramelech dispatched them to all the major populated areas of our world. He alone remained at the location where they came through the portal. The next few decades were horrible. They took whatever they wanted. Our women suffered the most. What they did to our women. It is unspeakable. They are not good angels. They set about taking over our planet. Hundreds of thousands of people were killed. Our military prowess was laughable against them."

"But they are here no longer," Mason said.

"I was given a specific duty by Adramelech. My machine suffered significant damage during the power-up event. I was tasked with the machine's repair. It took me years to get the damn thing functional again. Our power grid suffered a major blow and that was a big part of the delay. There wasn't much I could do without adequate power, so I had to start with that. They did not realize that my machine had not worked as I planned. They wanted me to reopen the portal so more of their kind could come through to our world. They also wanted to use my machine to visit other worlds. I assume their intent was to invade and conquer everywhere they could possibly go. I did not tell them what I believed would be the effect of powering up the machine again once repaired."

"The day I announced I was going to open the portal, Adramelech called all of the angels back to the location of the machine. That proved to be a mistake on his part.

When I powered up the portals opened again, for about five seconds. The power grid failed again. What happened here is the same thing that you experienced Mason. Adramelech and the host of angels that traveled through the portal with him were returned to their own reality, and the passage-way closed behind them, forever."

The three of them stood in silence for several minutes.

"You want to know how I know about Adramelech? He told me to my face."

Rasmus abruptly cleared his throat. "I am the Adolf Hitler of this reality. I should have been tortured and thrown into prison for my crimes. A new government was established and I was forbidden to work on anything without approval and supervision. It has taken a long time for me to be able to work on my viewer. I'm allowed to use it in my spare time without much oversight. They do not believe it to be dangerous. I constructed a much smaller machine that creates only one portal. I have very little authority to use the device. We have to get permission and the reports I must submit are long and tedious. It still uses a large amount of energy." His chin began to tremble. "If you will excuse me. I shall return shortly." He walked slowly out of the lab.

Sidney waited for him to leave the room and turned to Mason. "Wow."

"Yeah." Mason agreed. "Maybe you should just stand over there in the corner. You know, quiet like."

She shot him her middle finger. "How was I supposed to know about all that? And, what is it with time in the place? He said this took place hundreds of years ago."

"I was only gone this last time for a few hours. The guard, Michael said I was gone for about six weeks. It's one of the questions I have for the Doctor. I was getting around to it till you caused him to remember this world's version of the apocalypse."

When the Doctor returned he was his old chipper self again. Mason was not sure what the man had done, but he was happy to see him get it together. Perhaps he had some magic pills.

"Now, let's see what we can do with your spike, Mr. Waters."

Rasmus took Mason's arm and placed it on a device that displayed a purple light across his skin. Mason felt a slight tingle but no discomfort. "Please, remain still Mr. Waters. This will only take a few moments." He moved over to a computer on the wall, pulled out a keyboard, and began typing.

"Doc. Sidney and I were wondering…"

"Yes?"

"Could you explain the time difference?"

"Certainly. A day and night in your reality is approximately a year in this one. I meant to explain this to you, but it slipped my mind. Aiden should have informed you of this fact. When she asked me to step out of the room I had no idea she was going to tell you to summon your Door to leave. While you spent only a few hours in your own reality, months passed here. I was very displeased with her actions. In my opinion, it was a reckless and a very risky choice on her part. She assured me that you would return but of course had no way of guaranteeing this outcome or of assuring me how long you would be gone. You can imagine my joy when Michael called me to inform me that you were here."

The Doctor continued to tinker with the device in Mason's arm for some time. Finally, he looked up. "Done."

Mason was processing what the Doctor just explained. "So, how does the time difference affect us, Sidney and I?"

"The effect is minimal at this point. According to my studies, you should feel no different and your bodies are aging normally. I believe, if you were to remain here, for perhaps a year or so you would begin to adjust to this world's time. Right now, you are aging just as you would in your own reality. That would be a matter of study however and one that I would gladly conduct."

Mason held up a hand. "Okay, Doc. Let's file that for now. You mind telling me what you've done with this chip in my arm?"

"You seem to have adjusted well to the minor enhancements I previously employed. So, I have increased the dosage, so to speak. You will notice this adjustment shortly. Unfortunately, I have no answer for your concern about the spike grounding you to this reality, at present. Foreseeing this particular problem, I took the liberty, in your absence, to solve it."

"I'm listening."

"I believe I can create another device that will give you the ability to choose the reality you visit."

"You can do that."

Rasmus nodded. "It would be something small. In theory, you would pass through your portal to an unknown reality; as you are used to. If the world you visit is one to your liking you would need to fix the device to a solid object in that reality. You will give the device a name or number or some other sort of code and sync it to your spike. You should then have the option to return to that world by choice. You could create a type of running log."

Mason smiled. "I really like that idea Doc. You're going to make me feel indebted to you."

"My motives are not completely unselfish. I would like to work with you on some other projects. We can talk about that later. Give me a little time and I will design a spike for Sidney as well. I will program it to give her specific enhancements. I am also working on a program that I can use to call you."

"How's that?"

"I can place a program in both spikes that will give me the ability to contact you. It would act as a one-way pager. Since I cannot freely visit your world, I would be able to call you to come to me."

Mason looked at Sidney. "What do you think?"

"What sort of enhancements are you talking about Doctor?"

The Doctor's face lit up. "Well, your options are as open as your imagination. We can change the pigmentation of your face so that it is not necessary to apply cosmetics. That option comes with several designs. Depending on your feeling on a particular day you can change the color of your lips, the length of your eyelashes, the shade of your cheeks. We can eliminate wrinkles, and shape your body to your desire. Most people desire strength, energy, vitality. I will need a few weeks to create your spike, the homing device, and the programs I have mentioned. Once I've produced the spike you simply tell me what options you want. It works like a blank hard drive waiting for the user to download programs and applications."

He turned back to Mason. "You are welcome to stay here for that time period. You mentioned Aiden. I have a place you can stay and I will let her know you are here. She may wish you to stay at her home. Or, you can go back to your own reality for about an hour; return and meet me back here."

"What do you think Sidney?" Mason asked.

"I am liking the enhancement idea. Actually, I think his entire proposal is good. I have to say, Mason, I doubted you. But this, well I am blown away. As for our next move, that's your call. I would like to clean up and get a change of clothes."

Mason thought for a moment. He asked her to stay at his side at all times, but he had not impressed upon her how vital it was that he not be left alone. He considered what occurred to him over the past few days. His life was always this way. He often marveled at how events unfolded. A conversation with himself played out in his mind. *If you told me yesterday that I'd be here today…. If you would have told me last week that I would have experienced this or that… Well, I wouldn't have believed you.*

He was grateful that Dr. Rasmus reached out to him, though he was not so keen on the method. Nevertheless, if the Doctor could do what he advertised, it would change things dramatically for Mason. Over the years he visited many worlds that he wished he could return to. He may never see those places again, but there was an abundance of undiscovered realities.

He walked over to Sidney and handed her his keys. "I'll send you back to the room. Take my truck. You think you can go to your place, change your clothes and be back in the room in an hour?"

She nodded, accepting the keys. "Sure."

"I'm staying. I think I'll be okay here. Maybe I can assist the Doctor. I'll be back to get you in one hour. You ready?"

She gave him a questioning look. "I got the impression you really wanted me to hang with you for the next few days."

"It's only an hour."

"For me. It's two weeks for you. I've been paying attention."

Rasmus cleared his throat. "Mr. Waters, you are aware…"

Mason raised one hand to silence the Doctor but kept his eyes on Sidney.

"Okay, babe. This is your party." She clutched her bag and stepped up to him, so close the front of their shirts touched. She lowered her voice. "I don't think you are planning to do anything with the Doctor. I get the feeling that Aiden is a female."

Mason nodded slightly but did not speak.

Sidney put her finger in his chest. "We are going to have a conversation about that when I return. You behave, Mason."

He looked down at her and smiled as she reached out to put her arms around him. "No need to hold me on the return trip." He bent and kissed her; long and passionately. "Brace yourself," he whispered.

Sidney did not see the Door appear. She did not know what Mason surely knew. One second she was standing in a laboratory with Mason and Dr. Rasmus, the next second she was on her butt in Mason's run-down motel room. She felt as though she was slugged in the gut. The return trip to her reality was not a simple step from there to here. It was a violent blast. The reality where she did not belong pushed her back to the one where she did. At the same time, the reality of her birth yanked her. She hit the floor, rolled, and came to a stop, her back knocking against the air conditioner. Oddly enough, laughter burst from her mouth as pain thrummed in her hip. "Mason, you bastard!" she screamed. "You knew that was going to happen. Just wait till I see you again boy! You are so gonna get it."

Mason turned and froze. Dr. Rasmus stood like a statue, his gaze fixed on Mason. "What?" Mason asked.

"Have you considered sir, that I would have enhanced myself?"

"Yes. That thought has crossed my mind. Given that you are in the business of tailoring the enhancements I would guess you have targeted your brain. You are overly cerebral."

"Quite right. When I made my suggestion that you could return to your world for an hour, I meant for you and your friend to go together. You can stay here on Nikon for two weeks or two years. You and I both know when you return to your world no time will have passed."

Mason strolled back across the lab and took a seat. "What do you suppose she is doing right now Doc?"

Rasmus shrugged. "The part of the equations that I am having trouble with is why you sent her back in the first place. It accomplishes nothing."

"Really? You don't see the advantage it gives me? I'll let you work on it a while. But it makes me wonder. Every time I travel through the Door and back to my world, am

I creating a new or different reality? Are there thousands of identical versions of me out there? Do they all possess my ability to open a portal?"

The Doctor looked distressed. Mason wondered if the man was having trouble processing this information. Perhaps he was actually trying to make sense of it. "What would we see if we looked through your viewing device right now. Would we see her getting into my truck and heading to her place? If so, how could I possibly return to the exact second I left?"

Rasmus shook his head. "I already know what we would see. I've done it. We wouldn't see anything."

"Why not?"

"Every time you leave your world my viewer blanks out, as it applies to your reality. Actually, it is like watching three-dimensional static. Furthermore, I've never been able to track you when you leave. It is as though, when you pass through the portal, exiting your reality, you take reality with you. It is not reestablished until you return."

"Do you think that is possible? When I leave time stops or that reality freezes? That would suggest that I am pretty damn important. What happens to Earth if I were to die in another reality?"

"There are many things I do not fully understand concerning the phenomena you create with a mere thought. I have opened a portal to other realities. We have successfully sent people through the portal and brought them back. But it is different. For example, when I sent Aiden through to retrieve you I was able to watch her through the viewer. She did not call the portal when she was ready to go. I made the call as to when we opened it a second time for her to pass back through. She was in your room for about fifteen minutes. Four days passed here."

Rasmus stopped talking and Mason sat there, considering what the Doctor said.

After a few moments of silence, Mason said, "You are aware of my issue with being alone."

Rasmus nodded. "You are concerned about being alone here?"

"I've spent extended periods of time in alternate realities. I didn't have my wife at my side during those times. I always made sure I had someone with me when I needed to sleep. If I couldn't find someone to 'babysit' me I would just come back home."

Rasmus chuckled. "Well, Mr. Waters, I do not plan on spending tonight or any other night with you, just to be clear."

"Yeah, I don't want to spend the night with your skinny butt either Doc. Let's give Aiden a call."

"Indeed."

"You know, I'm beginning to feel the effects of your adjustments to this device in my arm. It is rather euphoric. Oh, have you figured it out?"

"Why you sent her back?" He paused, then raised one eyebrow. "You didn't want her with you when you visit with Aiden."

Mason smiled.

"Let me know if it the enhancement becomes overwhelming." He turned and headed for the door. "Follow me please."

Chapter 10

She expected him to return later that evening. She lay there in bed, in the dark. The house was quiet. The display on her cell phone told her it was half-past eleven. Almost midnight and he hadn't returned, called or sent a text. It was very much not like her husband. They were married for 28 years. Counting their friendship and dating period, Valerie and Mason were together for three decades. She thought about the few times they were apart during their marriage. No matter the situation, a dispute, a family or business trip, they were never apart for long. Even now, after this fantastic blow-up, she still expected him to return before she slept.

When she finally dozed it did not last long. She woke around two in the morning. Her abdomen hurt like she had done a sit-up work-out before going to bed. She threw the blanket aside, planted her feet on the carpet and felt her way through the darkness to the bathroom. Out of habit, her fingers found the light switch. The light flickered above the vanity. She fumbled in the medicine cabinet and retrieved a prescription bottle, half full of white pills. The label on the bottle read; hydrocodone bitartrate 5 mg and acetaminophen 325 mg. She took two.

As she turned to head back to the bedroom she caught a

glimpse of something in the vanity mirror. She stopped and snapped her head back toward the mirror. What she thought was movement came in the reflection of her dark room. Instead of moving toward the room she slowly moved closer to the mirror, searching the reflection. She moved to within inches of the mirror. *What is that?* she thought. Something glistened in the darkness, a small sliver of light that should not be there. She moved back to the set of light switches on the wall and turned on every light in the bathroom. This illuminated the bedroom enough for her to be able to stand in the doorway and scan the room. Bed, dresser, wardrobe, chest of drawers, love seat, bench, several paintings on the wall, everything in place. Something wasn't right.

"Mason? Is that you?"

Silence. She glanced over at the bed and saw her cell phone on the night-stand. She hesitated, began to step from the bathroom to the bedroom, then relaxed. A deep instinct was warning her not to cross into the room. She stood there, frozen in place, focusing all of her energy into her ears. *Was that breathing?*

Through the door, to the left, where the light was very dim, something moved. She could see only a small portion of the object and the movement created a wet sucking sound like a snake uncoiling from mud. Whatever it was stood between her and the exit from the room. There was no way to run for it. The movement, a continuous smooth motion, shifted, getting closer to where she stood. Valerie backed into the bathroom putting as much distance, about fifteen or twenty feet, between herself and the bathroom door. The lights blinked out.

Valerie froze. The bathroom had one large privacy

glass window. One could not see through it from either side but it did allow sunlight to pass through. The heavy curtains in the bedroom blocked all outside light, day or night. Mason protested but Valerie insisted on being able to stop any light from the outside to illuminate their room. As her eyes adjusted she began to make out the dim outline of the bathroom as some moonlight found its way through the privacy glass. The doorway to her room looked like a rectangular black hole. She stared at that spot and fear gripped her as she watched the being in her room fill that space. It was not a man. It was not human though it appeared to have arms and legs. It wore no clothing. She could make out the outline of a large appendage between its legs. The skin of the creature was gloss black and appeared to be moist. Valerie could make out the arms, legs, and torso. It had hands but she could not see fingers. It began to crouch, bending down to try and fit through the door. The creature moved in slow motion and it made the sound of a shallow stream of water traveling over rocks. The beast reminded Valerie of a ware-wolf, in one of the movies she saw as a teenager, without the bushy hair.

She was trembling. The creature bent low enough for its head to clear the upper portion of the door and she saw its eyes. The entire body of the beast was black, except those eyes. Light escaped two holes in the head where the eyes should be. It fixed those beams of light on her. She jerked backward and screamed. She struck the large tub with both ankles and fell backward. Her back slammed into the tub and the back of her head struck the tiled wall.

***

When she woke the sun was blasting through the privacy glass, illuminating the bathroom with light. It took a few seconds to find her orientation but she soon realized that she had fallen back into the tub. She hit her head and must have blacked out. Judging from the brightness of the light coming through the window she was unconscious for quite some time. The fall mixed with the medication really knocked her out. She touched the base of her skull where she hit the wall and found some caked blood in her hair. Slowly she pulled herself out of the tub and made it to the bathroom sink.

The vanity mirror revealed evidence that she had not imagined the intruder. Her nightgown was torn from top to bottom. It looked like someone used a razor to slice it open. She backed up to see her full reflection. With the gown destroyed she was nude with the exception of a small pair of panties that appeared to be undamaged. Four distinct lines of something black and sticky ran from just above her breast-bone to her navel. She removed the gown and placed It on the sink counter; added her panties to the pile, and stepped into the shower.

When her daughters arrived, she was dressed and sitting at the bar in the kitchen drinking a hot cup of lemon tea. The doorbell did not ring nor was there the sound of a knock. The two girls simply appeared as they entered the kitchen. They both approached tossing their purses and jackets on the dining table.

"Mom, what happened?" Rachel asked.

"I tried to tell you over the phone."

McKayla the younger of the two, Valerie's last-born

child, examined the back of her mother's head. "I'm getting a warm wash-cloth. You've still got some blood here."

"You should go to the hospital." Rachel continued. "At least get checked out. You don't have to say anything about an intruder. Just tell them you slipped in the shower."

McKayla returned with the washcloth and soaked it in hot water at the kitchen sink. "The front door wasn't locked, Mom. Was it like that last night?"

"No. I unlocked it when I realized you two were on your way." She continued to sip her tea. "Rachel, help yourself to some tea. There's plenty."

Rachel took a seat at the table but did not acknowledge the offer. "Dad still isn't home? I'm calling him." She moved to retrieve her cell from her purse.

Valerie held up a hand. "Don't. I don't think he had anything to do with what happened last night."

McKayla, gently sponging the back of her mother's head. "What happened? You spoke to Rachel I know. But go over it again."

"I woke up around two. I went to the bathroom. When I was coming back to bed I noticed someone or something was in the bedroom."

"You didn't imagine it? Like you weren't dreaming or sleepwalking?"

She flinched. "Ouch. I think that's where I bumped my head."

"Yes, there's a knot."

"Anyway, I considered the idea that I dreamed it or something like that. I could have stumbled into the tub on my own. But that doesn't explain how my nightgown got torn or the scratch marks. Also, every light in the bathroom is burned out. The lights around the vanity, the shower, those in the ceiling, twenty-seven lights don't burn out at once."

McKayla appeared confused. "A power-surge that focuses on the master bathroom?"

Rachel said, "Can I see the scratches?"

Valerie stood and lifted her blouse exposing her midsection just under her bra. She managed to wash off the black stuff but there were distinct scratch lines running up from her navel.

"Were you raped?" Rachel asked.

"No." She shook her head. "I'd know." She replaced her blouse and sat back down. "If that thing, whatever it was, tried anything like that... Well, I might not have survived that kind of assault."

McKayla walked back to the sink to rinse the cloth. "What do you mean?"

"As far as I could tell... I mean, it was dark." Valerie's eyes wandered and she seemed to be looking off into the distance at something that wasn't there. "It was so black. It wasn't wearing anything but it seemed natural. Like you wouldn't expect a dog or cat to be wearing pants and a hat. This thing wouldn't wear clothing. So, I saw it."

Rachel stared at her. "You saw what?"

"She saw its dingus," McKayla said.

"It was so big." Valerie whispered. "The entire creature was so big. It stood well above the frame of the door. It was twice the size of any man. If that creature raped me, it would have broken me in two."

Rachel stood and grabbed her purse. "Okay, let's go."

"Where?"

"You aren't staying here alone. I think some shopping is in order and you can stay with me tonight."

McKayla grabbed her things. "Me too."

***

The three of them spent the day together. Valerie's encounter the night before faded in her mind. It seemed like a distant dream and details of the home invasion became fuzzy in her mind. She was very stressed, spending the day with her daughters had the beneficial effect of taking her mind off what occurred.

Rachel lived in a two-bedroom apartment with her boyfriend, Conrad, a tall German with brownish-blonde hair and dazzling blue eyes. She explained the situation to Conrad and he seemed to be fine with having their space invaded, given the circumstances. The apartment had two levels with the master bedroom upstairs. It sported an open floor plan. The second floor overlooked the first floor. If one stood at the top of the staircase they would be able to see the living room, kitchen, and dining area. The only place out of sight was the first-floor guest room and half bath. The guest room shared a wall with the kitchen. Valerie took the room. McKayla grabbed a few blankets from the closet and made a place for herself on the couch in the living room.

They stayed up late playing Monopoly in the dining room. Conrad needed to be up early the next day so they each retired to their designated area. Rachel, ever the ambassador called her father. It was late but she wanted to check on him and start a conversation that might lead to a solution between him and her mother.

Keith Gilbert

Conrad came out of the bathroom, hearing the tail end of the conversation.

"Please, tell me you will make an effort. I'm concerned." A pause followed this, then… "Okay, I love you."

"Who was that?" Conrad asked.

"My Dad. I think the only way we get my Mom out of here is for the two of them to lay down their weapons and talk this out. It's so stupid. They have been together like, forever. I don't know what they hope to accomplish by not talking."

"Sometimes people need some time apart. I'm sure they will work it out. In the meantime, your Mom is welcome to stay here. She cleaned up the kitchen." He smiled.

Soon they were all asleep with the exception of McKayla. She sat up on the couch using her I-phone to do some research. She may have been the youngest of all her siblings, but she was by far the most analytical. She searched for meaning in most everything and the recent event with her mother a big mystery. She was supportive but now she slipped into detective mode. Taking what her mother told them about the creature that broke into her home, she did a thorough search on Google. There was an abundance of material on giant beings that have inhabited the Earth. Her search eventually brought her to text from the Book of Enoch and the sixth chapter of Genesis which speaks of the 'sons of God' having sexual relations with the daughters of men, producing giants called Nephilim. The information fascinated her and she was surprised to find that she was still awake at three in the morning.

She forced herself to stop and placed the cell on a charger. The couch wasn't very comfortable. She grabbed the blankets and joined her mother in the guest room. Careful not to wake her, McKayla slipped into the bed beside her Mom and waited for sleep to come. Eventually, she slept. A few hours later she opened her eyes. It was still dark and she was unsure how long she was asleep. It had to be getting close to the morning but, what woke her? She raised herself slightly. Mom was snoring gently on her left. A few moments passed then her mother jumped. She mumbled something incoherently and turned on her side.

"No." she moaned in her sleep.

McKayla watched her mother, unsure whether to wake her or not. She never knew her Mom to talk in her sleep.

She tossed her body to the other side and whimpered.

McKayla reached out and found that her mother was perspiring. Something was wrong.

"Mom." She shook her. "Mom. Wake up."

***

Valerie stirred slightly, groaning like she was in the chair at the dentist office. In her mind, she was trying to run. Her legs would not respond to anything more than a brisk walk and even that seemed to be slowing. She found herself in an open field bordered on all sides by a thick line of trees. The sun was high in the clear blue sky. She was walking on an old dirt and gravel road that constantly curved to her left. She looked over her shoulder and saw the man behind her. He was following her, about one hundred feet away. The man walked in an awkward manner, barely bending his knees, a kind of double limp, and still, he was gaining on her. He was tall and incredibly slender. He wore old slacks and a dirty suit jacket. Valerie turned her attention forward and tried with all her might to speed up. The road curved and turned back in the direction she just came. It was like walking on an unpaved NASCAR track. In the distance, she could see that the road passed under a structure. She felt that if she could reach the structure, she would be safe.

She was not able to get off the road. If she cut across the field she could reach the building quicker. Her body had a mind of its own. She looked back over her shoulder and the man was closer. She began to sweat. Her heart was pounding even though she was merely walking. The tall man behind her was saying something, but she could not make it out and turned her full attention to reaching the safety of the building ahead.

It was not much of a structure. The building was an old wooden barn. It was open at both ends and the road passed through. It was large enough for a truck to pass under but not big enough for something like a tractor trailer. Valerie was getting close, but the building seemed to be inching away from her, making it harder, giving the man behind her more time to catch her.

As she approached the barn-like building she was panting, her shirt wet with perspiration. She could see through to the other side and noticed something dangling from the rafters inside. It was blurry and she needed to get closer to see it. She could hear the footsteps of the man chasing her. He was on her now, ten or twenty feet behind her. She dared not look back, her heart would stop if she saw his face. She could hear what he was saying and it made no sense. The man was not speaking English or any other language she was familiar with. It was gibberish like he was speaking in reverse.

In her dream, her feet stopped when she crossed into the shadow of the building. She stood at the entrance and waited for the man to grab her. Why her feet would not move was a frustration she could not understand. She waited. When nothing happened, she turned. The man was not there. No one was there. She saw nothing but the high brown grass blowing gently in the wind, the dirt road, and trees in the distance.

She turned and moved into the building. As she inched forward she could see what was hanging. A long rope was attached to a high cross beam. At the bottom was a child, the rope bound around the feet, the child hanging upside-down. Once she realized what it was she moved toward the middle of the barn. The child was a girl, perhaps ten or eleven years old. She was unconscious and wore only a small pair of gym shorts. Her blonde hair hung down and when Valerie reached up she could just touch the girl's hair.

The inside of the barn was cold and dark. She could see the field and daylight stretching out on either end of the barn, but in this darkness, her eyes had to adjust and she looked frantically for something to stand on. Against one wall was a relic of a ladder, made from what looked like thick tree branches. She grabbed the ladder and leaned it against the cross-beam where the rope was tied.

As she put her foot on the first rung of the ladder she saw movement to her left. She turned and saw the tall man again. He had to be seven-feet tall but was so thin he may not have weighed one hundred pounds. He stood at the opening of the barn where she entered. She waited, but the man did not advance, the toes of his dusty black dress-shoes held in place by the line of shadow cast by the barn.

The girl whimpered, snapping Valerie into action. She was not sure why the man did not advance. What she did know was that she had to get this girl down. Bringing her down and getting her to safety was suddenly more important than anything else. At the top of the ladder, she laid her hands on the knot. It was tight on the beam but she felt that it could be loosened. The girl was hanging at least six feet from the ground. Valerie had no way of cushioning the fall once she loosened the rope. She prayed the fall would not injure the child. Her shirt clung to her body, soaked in sweat. She fumbled with the think rope, cutting her fingers as she pulled on the knot. Once she had the knot loose enough she grabbed the rope and held tight. She did her best to ease the girl down. It seemed she weighed much more than she should and with a few feet to go the rope came free. The girl dropped the remaining distance to the dirt floor with a thud and Valerie realized the sound caused movement against the far wall; movement in the darkness. Something else was in the barn and perhaps the reason the tall man refused to enter.

Half-way down the ladder, her foot hit a weak rung and it gave way. The ladder cracked and buckled under her weight. She found herself hanging by her hands, feet dangling free. The only way down was to let go and drop. She let go and hit the ground, hard. The movement in the dark became much more pronounced. It was not a man, not a human. Perhaps it had been sleeping. Not any longer. She could see its eyes. They appeared like the head-lights of a locomotive approaching from a cavernous tunnel. Slowly, it stood, towering over her and the girl.

The tall man stood, guarding one side of the barn. She

had to get the girl out through the other side. She scrambled and scooped up the girl. She stood and once again, she was not able to run. She turned her back to whatever was standing in the darkness and she walked toward the exit. Dread filled her chest. She knew she was within reach of the creature in the dark. Not looking back was her only defense, but it was like hiding under the blanket hoping the monster in your room won't see you.

Valerie made it to the edge of the barn, where the shadow of the structure met the light of day. She felt like she made it. For whatever reason the beast let them go. She would make it out and wake up, safe and sound. The rope around the girl's ankles became taught. Valerie stopped, inches outside the exit and turned. The rope was suspended in the air, stretching from the girl's feet straight back into the darkness; the other end of the rope obscured, floating in the air.

Valerie was faced with a choice. Let go of the girl and walk out into the warm afternoon field of grass; or fight back with all of her strength, refusing to let go of the girl, risking certain death for them both. She pulled and the creature in the darkness pulled back, toying with her. From around the corner of the building, the tall man appeared. Valerie dug in. She pulled against the monster at the other end and was surprised when she began to make positive ground. The creature did not let go, but she was winning the battle.

The tall man was on them before she could break free. He reached out and grabbed Valerie by the arm with one hand and latched onto the girl's throat with the other. Valerie was repulsed by his touch. His palm was cold as stone, his breath smelled of decay, and his presence against her body caused her stomach to lurch. She cradled the unconscious girl in one arm and with the other she held the rope, pulling with all of her strength, the rope beginning to burn her palms. Her attacker said something in his backward speech then sank his teeth into the girl's cheek. Blood sprayed into Valerie's face. She glanced back at the black exit of the barn and saw the massive fist holding the other end of the rope. The monster was incredibly big. It reached out into the light with its other arm and latched on to the rope with a meaty paw. As this happened the tall man reared back with a hunk of flesh in his ragged teeth, strands of blood trailing from the girl's cheek to his mouth.

Valerie screamed, pulling the girl with the little strength she had left. She was no match for the beast at the other end of the rope. It gave a mighty jerk and the girl came free of Valerie's sweaty grip. The girl's limp body hit the ground and the monster reeled her in. Valerie fell onto her back, exhausted. She looked back where the monster was pulling the girl back into the barn and noticed something odd. When the monster reached out of the darkness into the light of day, smoke billowed off its dark skin. She realized this beast could not come out of the barn because of some kind of adverse reaction to the light. The tall man was bearing down on her now. She knew if she did not get up, right now and run, he would catch her and no doubt drag her back to the barn for the monster to string her up along-side of the girl.

Valerie scrambled to her feet and took off. She put the barn behind her and set her feet on the road. In her mind, she was trying to run. Her legs would not respond to anything more than a brisk walk and even that seemed to be slowing. Once again, she found herself in an open field bordered on all sides by a thick line of trees. The sun was high in the sky. She was walking on an old dirt road that constantly curved to her left. She looked over her shoulder, knowing what she would see; the tall man behind her. He was following her, about one hundred feet away.

***

The apartment shook. McKayla felt like the entire building lifted a few feet and suddenly dropped. Everything in the apartment that wasn't nailed down rattled, moved, shook, cracked, or broke.

McKayla leaped from the bed, her feet struck the floor and she bolted from the room.

"What the hell?" Rachel was screaming from upstairs.

McKayla searched for a light switch but the lights popped on without her finding the switch. She glanced up the stairs and saw Rachel at the top, her hand on a switch at the head of the steps.

"Mac! What is that? Get out of there!" Rachel was staring into the kitchen, terror in her voice.

McKayla turned toward the kitchen and saw what she could only process as a monster. She'd never seen anything like it in her life, in reality, online, or in a publication. The creature stood, hunched over in the kitchen. It was entirely black. The beast had no face. It had a head with what appeared to be eyes made of light but where its mouth, nose, and chin should have been was a flat, slick, surface. Its massive body was all muscle, no clothing, and no hair. A noise emanated from the creature that reminded McKayla of a musical recording being played backward. The noise rose

135

and fell in volume and only ceased when the beast spoke. It uttered one word, "Mason."

McKayla could not figure how this giant creature got into the apartment or how it got into the kitchen. She stood there, frozen. The beast seemed to be focused on her. It moved slowly, like a panther, calculating each movement of its' legs and arms as it stalks its' prey. It carried something in its fist, a long piece of rope frayed at both ends. The creature stopped and jerked its head up toward where Rachel stood, screaming. It wasn't interested in Rachel. It locked on to Conrad who was bounding down the stairs in his underware, sporting a 12 gauge Mossberg.

Conrad stopped halfway down the staircase, pulled up the shotgun and leveled it at the creature below. McKayla watched what happened next as though it occurred in slow motion. The black creature dropped the rope and leaped in Conrad's direction, flying over McKayla's head. Conrad pulled the trigger on the rifle creating a magnificent blast of sound and shrapnel. Impossibly, he missed. The rifle bucked and Conrad shot high into the ceiling, missing the beast completely.

The beast did not miss Conrad. It reached the man in a second. In a fluid motion, it backhanded Conrad and the shotgun, sending both up, past the screaming Rachel and into the bedroom he just came from. As Conrad's limp body sailed up the staircase the creature landed on the spot Conrad previously occupied and slammed into the wall causing sheetrock and plaster to crumble.

What McKayla did not see was her mother dashing from the bedroom, across the living room, to the glass patio door on the other side of the apartment. She yanked the curtains aside and frantically turned the rod that opened the horizontal blinds. Dawn crested the building adjacent their own and sunlight filled the apartment. The creature let out a back-masking sound that pierced the morning and caused the three women to clutch at their ears. The beast exploded.

Rachel and McKayla, within striking distance, were instantly saturated in the hot black and red sludge and what could only be the creature's internal organs.

Chapter

Aiden Waters was a few months shy of her 200th birthday. The whole thing amazed Mason. The good Doctor Rasmus 'discovered' the Earth and its inhabitants a year before Aiden was born. That worked out to roughly six and a half months ago for Mason.

Mason sat next to her in what he figured was the living space in her home. There was the small couch they were seated on, a coffee table that held the hot tea she served, and a large window currently closed and covered with a heavy dark curtain. Just before the entrance to the kitchen stood a large wooden desk with an elaborate office chair. On the desk set a dual monitor computer system. Mason felt sure that she was able to do much of her work right here at home.

The Doctor arranged for transport from the laboratory, into the city. He'd placed a tiny blue rectangular wafer in Mason's palm, which of course, melted into nothingness as soon as it touched his skin.

"It is currency." The Doctor explained. "Magdon, your driver and personal assistant while you are here will take you wherever you wish to go. Explore our fine town. Get some new clothes and sample our varieties of food. Magdon is specifically enhanced for the task he is assigned."

The Doctor placed his hand on Mason's shoulder and lowered his voice. "Magdon will defend you to the death if need be."

"Will that be necessary, Doc?"

The Doctor laughed robustly. "Certainly not."

Mason doubted his confidence for some reason. "Magdon," Mason said. "Does anyone in this world have a normal name?"

This made the Doctor laugh even harder.

As it turned out, Magdon was Mason's type of guy. They got along very well. He was talkative, hospitable, and knew his way around the city. He was not as tall as Mason. In this world, no one was. Mason was sure he could handle himself. His clothing stretched in all the right places, telling Mason the guy spent much of his time at the gym. Perhaps they could enhance a person to be strong and to specialize in some form of martial arts.

The transport vehicle could fly, of course. *Can't be bothered with slow-moving wheels*, Mason thought. It had room for at least ten people. It was shaped like a mini subway car, narrow and sleek, with gadgets, lights, and switches of which Mason had no idea how to operate. There was no steering mechanism. Instead, Magdon spoke to the onboard computer and it responded accordingly. The vehicle actually held conversations with Magdon and Mason got the impression the two of them were good friends for a long time.

"You understand that I am not from your planet?" Mason asked.

Magdon nodded. "Yes, sir. Doctor Rasmus filled me in, somewhat. I don't understand the dimensional, alternate reality stuff, but I get it that you weren't born here like everyone else. Heck, anyone can see that. You're the tallest person I've ever seen."

"Yeah. I was wondering. Since it seems your people can enhance themselves in any way they wish, why doesn't anyone wish to be a bit taller?"

Magdon looked at Mason like he was a lunatic. "Why? I mean, why would anyone want that? You might as well say, I'd like to change my body to be more obese."

"No, it's not. That is not the same at all. Don't you have basketball?"

"Basketball? So, you need a ball and a basket. What kind of basket?"

"Oh. Wow. Is there any sort of sports here?"

"Sure! Why wouldn't there be? I've just never heard of that one, basketball," he said it, pausing between the two words. "Not everyone is enhanced, you know." He continued. "It's expensive and most people cannot afford it. Those of us who have enhancements are either independently wealthy or, like me, we work for the government. Well, I work for Doctor Rasmus and he works for the government. Anyway, most, I'd say 95% of all enhancements are career-related."

Mason had not realized this, but it was beginning to make sense. The enhancements were specialized for a person's line of work. There were obvious exceptions as to what the Doctor was offering Sidney. Mason figured cosmetic enhancements were petty options. The main purpose was to achieve high marks in ones preferred career and enhancements helped in attaining those lofty goals.

Magdon helped him pick out some trending clothes and the two of them shared a meal at what Magdon described as one of his favorite diners. Mason had no idea what they were eating but he found it similar to a lamb and cheese sandwich complete with brown soda and what must have been fried potatoes only they were shaped like pancakes. Magdon notified Aiden that they were in route and she sounded excited to hear the news.

"Doctor Rasmus has informed me of your arrival. I am very pleased to have you in my home Mason."

Mason smiled. Her voice was incredibly smooth. She sounded like a professional actress doing a commercial for some luxurious brand of shampoo for women. He realized that even though it had not been long for him; he saw her the day before, that over half a year passed for her. "I'm looking forward to seeing you too."

That was about an hour earlier. Magdon dropped him off and assured him that he would be nearby at all times.

Her home was very modest. She obviously lived alone. It was small; a single bedroom, bathroom, living area and a kitchen. "It meets all my basic needs," she said. "Of course, I go into the office daily. On most days, I am able to leave at lunch-time. I can come home and complete my work here."

"I notice there is no television."

"A television? That is a device for watching entertainment?"

"Aiden, you have to be kidding me. No one on this world watches T.V.?"

She laughed and it sounded like music to Mason. "My dear. I love to be entertained. I'd go crazy around here without some distractions." She motioned toward the desk and computers. "That is not only my work-station it is also my entertainment center."

Mason was mesmerized by her. Everything about her, her beauty, her personality, her intellect, and her mannerisms were intoxicating. He understood what they did, Doctor Rasmus and his team; how they genetically designed her. They did a magnificent job. Once the Doctor discovered Earth, he quickly focused in on Mason and his family. While studying the culture and history of the planet he made Mason a special project. To him, Mason was indeed a special individual. In all known realities, the Doctor had not found a being that could open a portal like Mason Waters could. Aiden informed him that the Doctor was amazed at how easy Mason opened the portal to other worlds. She recalled a remark he made, "It takes an act of Congress for us to get the funding and permission to open a portal. Then it takes a massive amount of power. This primitive fellow does it with so much ease like he is simply taking a breath of fresh air." She also recounted how angry he was about the fact that he had no way of tracking him when he disappeared from the Earth.

"I get a feeling that you don't indulge in much entertainment," Mason said. "You enjoy your work."

She smiled. "Sure, I do. It has recently taken an unexpected turn. I did not plan to be reassigned but I still enjoy what I do."

"You were reassigned because of me."

She nuzzled up next to him and placed her small hand on his chest. "One can only anticipate the choices of another; plan for several outcomes, but in the end free will is unpredictable."

The thing that Mason found bewildering was his conversation with her. She had the wisdom and intellect of

143

a learned professor yet she appeared to be no more than a teenager, still working on her high-school diploma.

"When you told me, I could leave and even urged me to do so, I had no idea of the time difference. I reasoned that I would only be gone for a few hours. I planned to take care of some things back in my world and then come straight back. Honestly, I had no idea it would be so long for you."

She reached up and kissed him on the chin. "Don't be silly. I knew the cost, even if you did not. The point is that you needed to make that choice. I did not want to confuse the matter by giving you facts that did not pertain to your reality."

Mason returned her kiss with a light peck on her lower lip. He had a few items on his mind, one question in particular. His body had other ideas. The upgrade the Doctor gave him was working. He felt different, euphoric. He resisted this urge for the time being.

"There is one question I wanted to ask you Aiden. When I arrived, you met me at the door and I did not think it an appropriate time to ask. You know, Magdon was standing right there."

She pulled back a bit, but not enough to break contact with his body. "Sure dear. I understand. Go on."

"Your name is engraved over the door outside; Aiden Waters. I find it kind of odd that anyone would put their name on the door like that, but I'm thinking it is cultural."

"You are wondering why my last name is the same as yours."

"Well, yes, I am. It's kind of stalkerish. Don't you think? Is that your legal name?"

"I was born Aiden Waters. When Dr. Rasmus found

you, he decided to create me in the event that your world and ours ever came together. It was a very wise choice on his part. I was created, and raised at Mercer. No one knows who my biological mother and father are. The system under which I was created is designed that way."

"So, Doctor Mercer is like a father to you."

She nodded. "I suppose giving me the same last name was his way of designating his creation. He has a tendency to do things like that. It's his way of keeping things in order."

"We have the ability to birth a child outside of the womb. Test tube babies, they call it. I don't think it is done very often," Mason said.

"Does it bother you?" she asked.

"Well, I guess not. Just have to get used to it."

She moved her hand to his thigh. "Mason. I am so glad you are here. Would you like anything? Are you hungry?"

"No. I'm good. Magdon and I ate before we arrived."

"You look very good; even better than when I saw you last."

Mason chuckled. "I think you can thank Doctor Rasmus for that."

"He has his ways." She rose and moved across the living room.

To Mason, it seemed that she floated. Her shear clothing clung to her body, accenting her curves. Mason could not see through her outfit as he was able to before, but the way the cloth held to the shape of her body, not much was left to the imagination. He liked the effect very much. He wondered if she traveled outside of the house looking like that and figured he was going to be staying long enough to find out. "How is it that you are not married or that you have no boyfriend, Aiden?"

She crossed to the entrance of the bedroom, stopped and turned back to him. "I'm going to clean up. My home is your home. Feel free to scavenge something from the kitchen. You can turn on the computer and poke around. There are no passwords. I'm sure you can find your way around our technology."

As she spoke she removed her clothing. The outfit came off easily. Mason admired her beauty. He had no interest in navigating his way around anything technological.

She stood there, naked, holding her clothing in one hand. "I'm not married. I have no love interest. Because I am for you, Mason Waters. I would also like not to enter my 200th year of life, as a virgin." She smiled coyly at him, turned and glided out of the living room.

Mason decided he had no interest in food, entertainment, or any other thing that did not involve lying next to this woman. He got up from his seat and followed her, undressing along the way. When he entered her room, he stopped and stared in amazement. He assumed the home was small and from what he'd seen it was, but Aiden's bedroom defied logic. It was a master bedroom that belonged in a castle from England or Spain. The walls were crafted out of what might have come from massive redwood trees. Four brilliant chandeliers hung from the ceiling each spaced at least fifty feet apart. The ceiling would be a masterpiece painting on Earth. He could not imagine how it was done. Rich, thick draperies hung lavishly in the corners of the room where Mason figured they covered incredibly large windows. The floor was wood as well covered with an intricately designed rug. The walls were lined with beautifully crafted dressers, chest of drawers, and a magnificent wardrobe. Mason was impressed. There was a stone fireplace along the wall opposite the bed. It was large enough to walk into. Mason never saw a bed so large. It was easily twice the size of a king-sized bed on Earth. It was mounted by a massive canopy of wood that looked impossibly heavy and covered with thick blankets, stacked with several dozen pillows of different shapes and sizes.

The sound of wind blowing like a heavy storm caught his attention. He turned toward the sound and saw an opening leading to another room. It must be the bathroom. Aiden went to shower. The sound was odd. Not the sound of water falling. He heard a continuous blast of air. He walked to the opening and found Aiden standing before a mirror in a bathroom equally as majestic as her bedroom.

She turned to him. "I am pleased to see you have removed your clothing. Take those off as well and join me."

Her body was glistening as though she just stepped out of a sauna. She crossed the bright room and stepped into an opening in the wall. Steam billowed out of the entrance and she stopped, looked back at him and smiled.

Mason removed the last article of clothing and followed her through the opening.

This smaller room was the source of the wind. As he entered it swirled around him. The wind was mixed with hot moisture and something that made his skin slippery. It was the equivalent of a shower but he didn't have to use a washcloth or a bar of soap. The rushing air pushed the chemicals over his body, cleaning every inch of him. He even felt a tingling sensation at the bottom of his feet and he figured the floor was somehow scrubbing his soles.

Aiden turned and met him in the center of the cleansing storm. She pulled him into her body, wrapped her arms around his neck, pulling him down. Mason reciprocated. He enveloped her small body with his arms and lifted her off her feet. She put her face into his and they kissed passionately, tasting one another.

Mason's head swirled. He ran his tongue over her lips and down her neck. Her skin was sweet. He wondered if it was an effect of the storm of wind and rain that soaked their bodies or if she was engineered to taste this way.

He lowered her and she urged him to continue in a downward motion. She was leading him to the floor. This place was amazing. The hot moist air never ceased to spin around their bodies. They were able to lay down, stretch out fully and never once did his feet or his head touch a wall. It was the largest shower he'd ever been in. He expected the floor to be hard and cold. It was neither. It felt more like they were laying on a large bed of soft leather. At no time were they overcome by the moisture. No matter their position, breathing was never a problem.

Mason experienced a sudden surge of energy. Perhaps it was a combination of things; Doctor Rasmus's enhancements, the wind and hot rain in this place, or it could be the nude and extremely vibrant young woman pressing her body into his. She sat up and beckoned him into the same position. The two of them face to face, their legs wrapped around one another. Mason was fully erect. He was for some time. Pressed into her this way he was poised at the entrance to her body. He throbbed with the constant beat of his heart and she pushed herself up onto him.

Aiden placed her arms around his neck and her lips next to his ear. "I am for you." She whispered. With that, she flexed her arms around his neck and lifted her body slightly. When she felt she was positioned just over him she hovered for an instant then lowered her body taking him deep inside her. She experienced a pleasurable spasm, tossing her head back.

Warmth spread throughout Mason's body. It started at his groin and advanced to his head and feet. He could feel her body quiver. With the first thrust, she held him tight for a moment, shaking, head back, her breasts pointing to the ceiling. He began to feel that something was wrong. She clung to him like the bark of a tree, not moving. Then she relaxed, coming back to him, and lifted herself slightly, her breasts on him now, sliding up his slippery chest. She stopped at the highest point, not losing control, and came back down gripping him, eating him up with her small body. The third time she made this move Mason exploded inside her. Aiden pulled away just enough to look into his eyes. She did not look surprised but rather had a dream-like appearance.

To his surprise, Mason remained firm and strong inside her. His heart pounded and his body thrummed with a feeling of electricity. "Are you okay?"

She smiled and kissed him again. She slid her tongue over his lips and answered him without speaking. She lifted herself again and slowly began riding him as before. They made love for some time; on the floor, their bodies as one. Mason could not remember ever being able to perform in this manner. Even when his hormones raged as a teenager. He was very satisfied with this ability. He was also very aware of the bond forming between himself and Aiden. He recalled how he felt when he first met her; how his heart hurt at the thought of not being with her. That feeling was magnified many times over. What he was experiencing with her was magical. It was something he knew he would never forget and he wondered what the future held for himself and this magnificent girl.

They spent the next two weeks together. For Mason, it was like an incredible vacation from life. He forgot about the monsters and focused all his energy on Aiden, enjoying the time they were together. He was well aware that as soon as he opened his Door and stepped through he would exit at the exact second Sidney left the lab and that no time would have passed in his own reality. A part of him wished the bliss he was experiencing now would never end.

Aiden insisted on showing him everything she could about Nikon and the city where she was raised, Thornton. Doctor Rasmus assigned her duties to another scientist and gave her as much time as she wanted to spend with Mason. Which after all, was her original mission. The day would come when Doctor Rasmus would expect a return on his investment. Aiden knew what she was, a lure and hook for an Earth-man, but she tried not to think about it that way. She was in love with Mason and wanted to be with him forever.

They spent every night in her massive bed, making love and exploring vast possibilities with one another. Mason wondered how he was possibly keeping up with her. There was something magical about this world that fascinated him. Each morning he woke, sure that he dreamed it all. He would turn and see her lying next to him. It didn't take long for him to fall. He passed the feeling off at first, sure that he was experiencing the effect of the enhancement and the butterflies of young lust. Toward the end of the second week he knew, beyond any doubt, he was in love with her. He knew she was in love with him.

Chapter

"Doctor Rasmus summoned us," she said, bringing a hot meal to the table.

Mason accepted the food and pulled out a seat for her.

"He says he has completed his work on the devices he spoke to you about and needs you to come in for final programming and implantation."

"He's early. But I'm excited to see what he's accomplished."

She reached over to him and brushed the side of his face with her palm. "You're letting this grow out?"

He had not shaved since leaving Earth. The dark whiskers across his face came in nicely. It wasn't long enough to brush but he thought it made him look ten years younger. He felt even younger than that. "You like it?"

Aiden smiled, chewing her food and sipping hot tea. "With or without it, I like you." She was ever smiling.

"This food is great. Thank you. There is something I wanted to talk to you about. How long before we head to the lab?"

"Since you made Magdon leave us alone, he's not just around the corner. Doctor Rasmus will have him here soon though. We have time. If he arrives before we are ready, he'll wait."

"Once the Doctor implants his new device, if that is what he is going to do, I am going back to Earth. I have business there and I'm not sure how long I will be gone. I've been thinking about the extreme time difference between your world and mine Aiden. If I spend a full 24 hours over there, a year passes here. That is a long time to ask you to wait for my return." He paused and looked at her. She did not speak.

"You're aren't saying anything. How do you feel about that?"

"I don't like it. I don't want you to be away from me so long."

He nodded. "I understand. Well, since we are on the subject... How do you see things going forward?"

"Don't you want to stay here with me?"

Mason gave this some thought. He had to be careful in his response. "You've seen my world through Doctor Rasmus' viewer? You've seen my life, right?"

She nodded.

"You know I have a wife. We have children. Yes, they are grown but I love them and have a relationship with them. Even though Valerie and I are not on good terms right now, she is my wife and always will be."

She put her head down. Mason watched tears drop to the table. This tore at his stomach and he was no longer hungry. He lowered his voice to a whisper. "Maybe I should go visit the Doctor on my own?

"No," she said immediately. She rose from her seat and crossed to the counter where she used some tissue to dry her eyes. "I'm coming. Please, give me a moment." She walked away, entered her room and closed the door.

Magdon arrived and entered the house without knocking or ringing a bell if there was one.

Mason looked up from the table. "Hey."

Magdon stood, looking uncomfortable. "Ummm, you ready?"

"I'm ready. We are waiting on Aiden."

He nodded and took a stance like a bouncer at the door of an upscale night-club.

Aiden emerged looking absolutely delicious. Mason could see no visible sign of distress on her face. She was smiling again, looking almost exuberant. "Alright fellas, let's go."

Mason got up and noticed that she was carrying a small bag over her shoulder. He decided not to ask and headed out the door behind Magdon.

***

"Mr. Waters!" Dr. Rasmus greeted them each with a big hug. "Aiden, my child! I am so happy to see you. How have the two of you been? Come, sit. Mason I've got some wonderful news. Please, take a seat. May I get something for you? Something to drink perhaps."

Mason liked this quirky man. He was dressed in all black. Johnny Cash would be proud. He had a black cape only it was hanging on a hook instead of on his back. He also had a habit of asking questions he had no intention of getting an answer to. He would ask you how you are doing today and keep on talking. It was rude, but Mason thought it was funny.

They settled in and the Doctor brought out a small chrome box. He opened it and began, pulling something from the box. "First, we have this little switch. I considered your request to be able to go to any reality you desired and I have solved the problem in two stages."

The device he held in his palm was about the size of a fly. It was black and sparkled a bit. "This is stage one cut-off switch. Your arm please, sir."

Mason extended his forearm. Rasmus glanced at Aiden as he took Mason's arm.

Aiden approached Mason and took his face in her hands. She bent slightly and kissed him full on the mouth. The pain was sharp and quick.

Mason jerked his arm back. "Aggh! That hurt. What the hell did you do?" He was rubbing his arm where the Doctor stuck him with a needle or something.

"That little switch does not meld with your arm like the spike. When you rub your finger over it you can feel it there, just under the skin."

Mason calmed and ran his finger over the spot the Doctor indicated. Simultaneously he glanced at Aiden with a bit of contempt. "I'll be ready next time you try that. How does it work?"

Rasmus moved to a computer on the wall and began typing instructions. Mason felt several sensations in his arm where the spike was located. After a few moments, the Doctor walked back to where Mason sat. He took Mason's finger and gently rolled it over the switch. The spike made a wobbling sensation.

"The spike has received a signal to turn off. Your enhancements are not being interrupted. Only the homing portion of the spike is disabled. I am sure you are used to these enhancements by now and that you have enjoyed the results."

Mason grinned. "Stay on topic, Doc."

"Indeed. Turning the spike's homing program off allows you to pass to other realities as you once did. So, turn it off when you do not intend to come here. On, when you wish to return to Nikon." The Doctor repeated the same motion with Mason's finger in reverse. "I have also programmed your spike to signal you when I call." He made a motion with his hand as if he were waving an annoying flea away.

Mason felt the spike vibrate inside his arm. "That feels weird."

"But you can feel the difference in the two signals?"

"Yes. The vibration for calling me is much faster than the 'on/off' sensation."

"Good." The doctor was visibly excited. He moved quickly to the little chrome box and produced a small bag with a drawstring on top. He opened the bag and poured out a handful of miniature six pointed jacks. "I call these stickers. Take these with you, back to your reality. Put them in a safe place so they don't get pulled back to this reality. When you travel to other realities, you take one of these stickers and fix it to a solid object that cannot be pulled through the portal. It is voice activated. Give the reality a name. Speak the name over the sticker before you leave. When you return home, write it down or do something so you can remember that reality. Give it some specific description that means something to you. When you wish to return to that particular reality you will need to touch the switch, turning off the homing ability for Nikon, and

157

speak the name you designated to the sticker of your choice. I realize it's a great deal of information…"

Mason held up his hand. "I got it Doc. I am blown away by what you've done. I've been using the Door in a halfhazard manner for decades. In two weeks, you have given me an ability to bring order and meaning to my plight. With these devices and upgrades, I may be able to find a way to defeat Adramelech and his ability to harm others. But, I see no need for the switch. Why can't I simply attach a sticker somewhere here in the lab? Switching the spike on and off seems redundant."

The Doctor stood, not answering him. He seemed to be waiting for Mason to figure it out on his own.

Mason looked at him. "You don't know if the stickers work."

"Theoretically, the devices should respond as designed. This is a rare case where I cannot test it in my lab. You have to test it in the field. If there is a problem, I want you to have a backup plan for returning here. I may have to make some adjustments; work out any problems that may arise. Once you have returned to your reality and have flipped the switch on your spike, open the portal and travel to a few alternate realities. Place the stickers, program them and see if you can return to the reality of your choice."

"Okay, Doc. You promised something for Sidney."

"Yes. I have her spike. It is ready to go. I need to make specific adjustments. I would need her input."

Aiden asked, "Who's Sidney?"

"Mason's friend," Rasmus said. "He didn't mention her?"

Thanks a lot, Doc! Mason thought.

Aiden looked at Mason with an expression of

bewilderment. "No, sir. He most certainly has not mentioned Sidney."

"With everything going on, it slipped my mind. It isn't important anyway."

Aiden stood. "Mason, could I speak to you, privately?"

Mason exchanged a look with the Doctor and followed Aiden out of the room, down the corridor, and into an office. He figured it might have served as her office space when she worked here.

Once he entered and shut the door, she turned and closed the distance between them. She stopped within inches, as close as she could be without actually touching him. She looked up at him with obvious pain in her eyes. "Mason. I love you. I'm sorry if that is a problem, but I love you very much. I am aware that you are married to Valerie. I know you have children that you are close to." Her chin began to tremble. "But I am in love with you and I am afraid of what comes next."

Mason gently put his arms around her and pulled her in. He held her for a few moments then responded in a low tone, "I fell in love with you a week ago. I am sorry for not saying it. You deserve better. As for what comes next, I don't have the answers Aiden. If you believe that I love you, and you believe that I would never intentionally hurt you, then we can make it through whatever comes next."

She was trembling. Mason felt like a one hundred percent asshole. Aiden did nothing but be the perfect friend and lover. She opened her home and her heart to him. What had he done? It made him question his relationship with Valerie. Had he treated her in a similar manner? Had he taken her for granted?

"How can you say that you love me and you have a relationship with your wife and with Sidney?"

"I don't know how to answer that question. Sidney and Valerie exist. They are in my life. I cannot deny that. I love you Aiden. You are not obligated to accept my love or to reciprocate. But with all my heart, I love you."

She reached up and pulled him to her. They kissed passionately. There was a long leather davenport against the wall. Aiden took him by the hand and led him to the sofa. They shed their clothes frantically. Mason sat down and Aiden straddled him, guiding him inside her. She pushed her breasts into his face and began working herself up and down on him.

Mason quickly lost any ability or desire to resist her. He knew what was coming and he let it happen, joined in and made deliberate reactions to her every move. He lost track of time, finding that nothing else mattered but this young girl and the climax he was quickly reaching. They moved from the sofa to the floor, hungry for one another. Every time he had sex with her was a new adventure. He could not say that one session was better than another as they were all wonderful.

They got up from the floor and pushed an abundance of paper and office items off the desk. She would not allow him to take over, pushing him back across the desk. She climbed on top of him, straddling him with her feet planted on the desk on either side of his waist. She placed her palms on his chest for balance, lowered herself, moaned and started a slow bounce. She held still when he arched his back, thrusting violently upward and held him in place. He slowly lowered himself and she followed him. His body shook beneath her.

She waited for him to calm then began her up and down motion once again.

***

As they dressed he said, "I see you brought a bag with you."

"Yes. I planned on asking the Doctor if there was any way I could travel back to your reality with you. I am quite certain he will refuse this request, but I came prepared."

Mason realized that she didn't know he brought Sidney through the Door with him. The Doctor described her as a friend and revealed nothing more. "I thought it took time, permission and a lot of money to open a portal."

She looked at him. "Or, you could just take me with you."

Mason froze, his shirt half unbuttoned. "You know something I don't?"

"We could try. I don't know how it works. But maybe if we hold hands I can go through with you."

"You can't even see the Door."

She shrugged. "I can sense when you open it. I don't know Mason. I don't have it figured out. I just want to be with you. Is there something wrong with that?"

When they returned to the laboratory they found Doctor Rasmus busy at some sort of computation. He turned and smiled. "Aiden. Could you wait for me in my office?"

She looked at the Doctor then turned to Mason. She reached up and kissed him softly. "I love you." She turned and left the two men alone.

Rasmus continued working on the computer as he spoke. "My apologies Mr. Waters. When it comes to science, chemistry, mathematics, physics, biology, well you understand, I'm at the top of my game. As for matters of the heart. I'm not so good. I had not anticipated you and Aiden becoming so deeply attached, so quickly. Not that I mind, in fact, I am elated. I should not, however, have mentioned your friend Sidney. That is my mistake and I am sorry."

"It's okay Doc. For now, I need you to refrain from mentioning anything else about Sidney and about how I brought her through the Door. Aiden wants to go back to Earth with me."

This made Rasmus stop what he was doing and look over at Mason. "What have you decided?"

"The plan does not include her tagging along. I need to move without having to worry about her for now. The problem I am facing is the time difference."

Rasmus nodded his head and rubbed his chin. "Yes. I see. With her permission, I can put her in stasis."

"What is that?"

"We have some stasis chambers here at the lab. They are relatively low maintenance. I can program it for as long as needed. The client, or in this case, Aiden, would be unconscious while you are away. The chamber sustains her."

"You think she will allow you to do it?"

"I can tell her you have requested it and that you strongly suggest that she takes this option while you are away."

"You can't simply order her to do it?"

"I could. But I won't. How long will you be gone?"

Mason shrugged. "I'm not planning to be gone for long."

Rasmus picked up the small pouch of stickers and handed them to Mason. "I suggest you go now. Better that way, wouldn't you agree?"

Mason nodded, summoned the Door and winked out of the reality known as Nikon.

Doctor Rasmus marveled once more at the man's ability. He wanted more than anything to unlock that mystery. He considered the relationship forming between Mason and Aiden. Things were back on track and he was glad to see them so close. When he engineered Aiden Waters, he spent considerable time enhancing her female reproductive system. She was waiting for him in his office and he had a little test he wished to perform on her.

Chapter

She hit the floor, rolled, and came to a stop, her back knocking against the air conditioner. Laughter burst from her mouth as pain thrummed in her hip. "Mason, you bastard!" she screamed. "You knew that was going to happen. Just wait till I see you again boy! You are so gonna get it." She looked up and saw Mason standing there, laughing.

He reached out to help her up. "Are you okay?"

She took his hand and pulled herself up. "That felt like falling down an elevator shaft. Not cool, Mason!"

"How was I supposed to know that would happen?"

"Then why did you tell me to brace myself? I can see it in your face, you knew." She stopped fussing and took a good look at him. He was wearing different clothes, his beard was growing out, and he lost weight. "Hold on. What's going on here? You... You followed me straight through, but how could you have a beard? And... How long were you away?"

"I stayed for a few weeks."

"I just got here. You said it would be an hour."

"Do you really want me to explain it?"

"No. Not really. My ass hurts."

He held out his hand, palm up. "You want me to drive?"

"Hell, no. Get in the truck. I'm driving."

On the way to her apartment, he filled her in on what Doctor Rasmus designed. "I'm going to visit four or five realities and plant these stickers. You up for the challenge?"

"I've got to work."

"Really? After everything you just experienced, you want to go back to a life of dancing for money? You've traveled to another world. Something no one else on planet Earth has ever done. Well, except me. I have given you the key to a storage room full of cash. You want to shake your ass? Well, you can shake it for me anytime you get the itch. Besides, as long as you are with me, no time passes here. You are going to have to get that through your head."

She remained quiet as she drove, thinking. "You've got a point. Okay, I'll call in and tell them I'm on my period and won't be in for a few days."

"Unbelievable. You really don't get it, do you?"

"I noticed you have said nothing about your girl-friend, Aiden."

Mason chewed his lip. "Well, I didn't think there was much to tell. I just met her a few days ago."

"You just met me a few days ago. You just spent a couple of weeks with her."

"I never said I spent the whole time I was away with Aiden."

"Don't try that crap on me, Mason. I'm not a fool. I don't appreciate you treating me like one."

"Hold on. You just told me you needed to work. Your job requires you to take off your clothes in front of men who want nothing more than to shag you. I'm supposed to be okay with that, but I can't have a female friend? Christ, I'm married. Have you forgotten that?"

"I'm not concerned with your wife. She was in the picture before I came along. Law of the jungle and all that." She looked over at Mason. "Is your wife black?"

"What does that have to do with anything?"

"Yeah, that's what I thought. She's black."

Mason laughed. "Sidney, are you jealous?"

"You think I go around fucking every guy I meet? You're damn right I'm jealous."

"Wow. I did not see that coming."

"We're here." She pulled the truck into a parking spot close to a large apartment building.

Mason nodded his head slightly. "I'm impressed."

"I make pretty good money at the club and it helps that I share the place with two girls that work with me. Are you okay hanging here while I shower and change?"

"Why can't I come inside?"

"Are you that out of touch? I don't want you coming into my apartment that is no doubt littered with dirty panties. One of my girl-friends has a guy she's seeing. They're probably both in there. You, coming in only complicates things."

"You afraid they will say something about you dating an older guy?"

"Are we dating Mason?"

He shrugged. "Well... see, I like a woman who loves her freedom, a woman who can hold her own. If you fit that description baby..."

"You are funny."

"I also like a woman who is quiet, a woman that carries herself like Miss Universe."

She started laughing. "Stop that bullshit. As for you

167

being an older guy, man, you are looking younger every day. Your wife isn't going to recognize you." She leaned closer to him, sniffing. "You smell funny. What is that?"

He pulled back. "You know what I want you to do? I want you to float on baby. Go do what you have to do. I'll wait."

She looked at him for a moment, took the keys from the ignition and jumped out of the truck. "You don't just look younger, you're glowing. I'm not finished with the topic of Aiden. Also, I see how you changed the subject."

When she walked through the door to her apartment Mason opened the glove box, pulled the pouch holding the stickers from his pocket and placed it inside, keeping one of the stickers in his fist. He got out of the truck and walked till he was a few hundred yards away. He touched the switch on his arm like the Doctor showed him, summoned the Door, and stepped through.

***

On the other side of the portal a blast of cold air, mixed with heavy snow hit his face. Mason threw up his arm to shield his face. The wind howled and blew him hard enough he almost fell back. He changed his footing, placing one foot several feet ahead of the other and lowered his arms enough so he could see what sort of world he entered. He stood at the edge of a forest at his back facing a large open area of white land. The entire place was being punished by an amazing blizzard. He exited the Door in some unusual places, but nothing close to this. He wasn't dressed properly. He knew he would not be able to last long without freezing to death. There didn't seem to be any place to stash the sticker and he saw no reason to stay when he heard a magnificent crashing sound behind him. The noise came from the forest and sounded like trees were being torn from the ground.

Mason turned his back to the storm and faced the line of large trees. At least the snow and ice was no longer punching him in the face. He stumbled forward into the trees hoping for some protection from the storm. He would later look back on this encounter and wonder why he hadn't simply opened the Door and returned to Sidney's apartment complex. Something about what Dr. Rasmus did in fine-tuning his body, Mason felt invincible, like when he was a teenager. Several yards deep into the woods he spotted a rabbit hunkered down next to a tree trunk. It was shaking violently but not moving from the spot it occupied. Mason assumed it was shaking because of the cold wind coursing through the trees but he realized the rabbit was not alone. From behind the tree trunk, a large grey wolf emerged, its teeth bared and glistening. A low growl emerged from his gut and Mason realized the rabbit was shaking with fear.

"Hey!" Mason shouted. "Over here!"

The wind caught his words and carried them away. The wolf did not seem to notice Mason. It inched toward its prey. The trees to Mason's left popped and came crashing down. Mason turned toward the sound as did the wolf. Through the trees that were, unfortunately, standing in his way a giant man entered the scene. Mason wished he was dressed like this guy. His body was covered with the hide of a bear. He wore heavy fur boots and a thick leather hat. Mason figured him to be 12 feet in height and probably weighed around 500 pounds. He was grinning like a boy playing hide and seek.

The giant glanced at Mason then turned to the wolf. Mason followed his gaze and saw the wolf was no longer interested in the rabbit. The creature stared at the giant and backed away. The giant took a step toward the wolf and it sprang back, turned and started to run. Too late. Mason watched in amazement as the giant pulled a double-bladed ax from where it hung on his hip, leaned back and flung it toward the wolf. The weapon flipped through the cold wind like a bullet. The steel blade struck the wolf, driving the animal into the nearest tree and stuck into the wood, pinning the wolf in place.

"Ha! Ha, Ha!" The giant bound across Mason's line of sight reached out to the rabbit and gently scooped it up into his arms.

For an instant Mason forgot the cold wind and snow pelting his back. He was in awe of what he witnessed. The giant of a man transformed from a vicious hunter to a child. The rabbit was completely safe and warm in this behemoth's arms. The giant turned and moved slowly toward Mason, extending the rabbit to him, beckoning Mason to take the small brown ball of fur. Mason did the only thing he could do; he accepted the rabbit which was now wrapped in a thick blanket of some other long dead animal. The big man turned and trudged to where the wolf quivered, dripping blood, stuck to the tree. He reached down, grabbed the handle of the axe and yanked back, releasing the dead wolf. The giant kicked the wolf and watched it sail through the storm landing a few yards away.

He cleaned the blade of the ax on an old piece of cloth, sheathed the weapon and turned back to Mason. "You must be cold. You have no coat." The giant's voice boomed and made its way to Mason through the howling wind. "Come with me. I have a shelter with my family just over the hill. I can carry you if you need."

Mason turned and walked beside the giant. He was speechless. The top of his head came up only to the man's waist. He was thankful that the man took a position between him and the storm, blocking most of the snow and wind with his massive body. They moved slowly and quietly through the forest. Mason took note of the trees that the giant destroyed and realized the incredible strength the man must possess. In spite of all that he experienced he refrained from summoning the Door. He moved with purpose, sheltering the now still rabbit. He was getting a second wind like a long-distance runner might.

As they crested the hill Mason looked down on an open valley covered in a blanket of white snow. There must have been one hundred homes and structures in the valley, each one with grey smoke billowing from massive chimneys. Judging from the size of each building they were a race of giants and this man that ended the life of a wolf with one blow of his ax; a man who now sheltered Mason and a small rabbit, he was perhaps not the largest of his race.

They walked a bit faster down the hill and stopped at the front entrance of a large house. The home was simple as homes go. It was built most likely with wood cut from the forest they just exited. Even though it was a simple home, it was without a doubt the largest house Mason ever saw. It towered above him and reminded him of pictures of castles in Spain and England. All of the homes were about the same size and now that he was closer he could see that they each had multiple chimneys pouring hot smoke into the cold sky.

The giant, who had not spoken to Mason along their trek to the village pushed the big doors open and they moved inside knocking snow off their clothes and bodies as they entered. The giant reached and took the rabbit. "I'll be back in a moment. There is a fire in the next room. Go, warm yourself."

The floors were crafted with cobbled stone. The walls were made of think wood that stretched incredibly high. The fireplace in the adjoining room was very large. The heat it produced was welcoming. Mason knelt before the fire and warmed his body, considering the situation he now found himself in. He had the sticker in his shirt pocket and he wondered if there was anything about this reality that might work to his advantage. Was there anything about this cold world that would make him want to return? He was willing to allow the scene to play out a bit more. After all, he was losing no time in this quest.

The giant entered the room carrying a pot of something hot, two big mugs, and two spoons. "You will accept my apology, sir. I was tracking that wolf and had no idea you were in the forest." He motioned for Mason to join him at a gigantic wood table. Mason felt like a little boy at the table. He would have to stand to eat anything but the big man brought a large wooden block and placed it in the chair so Mason could sit and comfortably serve himself from what appeared to be a steaming pot of stew.

"Before we continue…" He bowed deeply. "I am Sid. Pleased to make your acquaintance sir."

Sid. Could that be just a coincidence? Sid, Sidney. What were the odds? Mason was unsure if he should bow, besides he just climbed into his chair. So, he bowed his head. "My name is Mason Waters. I too am pleased to meet you."

The big man took his seat and served them both a large helping of the stew. "Hope you like that. I've been reheating it for the past three days. Now, I have to ask the most obvious question. How is it Mason that you are so small? Are you stricken with a disease? Perhaps a witch cast a spell? I've never seen a grown man so little. You surprised me for a second, but seemed harmless, especially when I noticed you were about to freeze your butt off out there."

Mason sampled the stew, then dug in with the large wooden spoon. "This is delicious."

Sid grunted and shoved a large spoonful into his mouth.

"I'm not sick. And I don't know any witches. On my world, I'm relatively tall."

"Don't go saying such things around here, man. That kind of talk will get you hanged. Just tell folks you were bewitched and you'll be fine. Me, I have an open mind about such things. You, showing up in the woods like you did... That's a real trick. I'm a good hunter. I would have known about a man in the forest. Where is your coat?"

Mason threw caution to the wind and said, "Well, I had no idea what I was walking into. So, I was not prepared for the cold weather."

"Ha! Cold? This ain't cold. Wait till the winter."

As they ate and conversed an older, taller woman entered the room. "Sid. You will have to make a trip to the apothecary. Sarina is getting worse." She looked at Mason, opened her mouth then closed it. "As soon as you can, Sid."

"Okay, Mom. Give me time to gear up. I'll be back by tomorrow afternoon."

The giant woman turned and exited the room.

"There is a sickness that plagues our village and the villages across the land. It has ravaged the old and the young. Do you have similar struggles in your village?"

Mason considered the question. "Who is Sarina to you, Sid?"

"She is my sister. I had a little brother but he died last year of the sickness."

"May I see her? Your sister?"

"Sure."

Sid gulped down two more spoons of the stew than led Mason through the mansion to a room where his sister was bedridden.

Mason studied the giant girl. She was covered from neck to toe with thick blankets yet she was sweating and her breathing was labored. Each breath came with a deep rasping sound. "What are you giving her for treatment?"

Sid brought a bowl half full of a white powder. "The healer gave us this and said we should mix it with water or juice and give it to her periodically. She has not responded positively to the medicine. I saw this same thing last year with my brother."

Mason put his finger in the powder, sniffed it and touched it to his tongue. It was bitter and reminded him of aspirin. "That's not going to do the trick. She's got a fever. Her body is fighting the infection but it's not enough. She needs an antibiotic."

Sid looked at him for a long moment. "Do you have this thing? Antibiotic?"

"No, but I can get it. I can get it faster than tomorrow afternoon."

"The Gods have sent you Mason. I understand it now. Over eighty percent of our village has this sickness. We believe it comes through the water. We boil all our drinking water but we also think the sickness is passed from one to another through bodily contact. How can you retrieve the medicine you speak of? May I help you in some manner?"

Mason shook his head. "She will die soon if her body temperature does not come down. Stay with her and I will return to this room." He pulled the sticker out of his pocket and walked over to the wall. He said, "Ice world" over the sticker and pressed it into the wall. He turned back to Sid and said, "I will return shortly."

Mason took a moment to scan the enormous room where he stood. He wanted to remember it well and sketched many details of the room in his mind. Satisfied, he touched the switch on his arm activating the Nikon grounding device in the spike. He summoned the Door. For an instant, he saw the parking lot of Sidney's apartment. In the next second, he was standing in the Mercer Lab. Finding the lights on and many people bustling around the lab was a pleasant surprise. Several of the lab techs saw him and gave him a look of shock.

Mason looked down at them and said, "I need Doctor Rasmus, right away."

In a matter of about an hour, Dr. Rasmus was able to gather several medications for Mason. He gave him a large quantity of the equivalent of penicillin and morphine along with a large backpack to keep the items fixed to his body. He also equipped him with several hundred sterile syringes and gave him a quick tutorial on how to administer the antibiotic. Mason thanked the Doctor and prayed there was not a massive time difference between Nikon and Ice World. He was also unsure if the sticker would work. He said, "Doc. if it works, you will have a hand in saving countless lives in another reality. What do you think of that?"

The Doctor gave him a big smile. "Go. Please come back and tell me what happens."

Mason summoned the Door and stepped back onto the parking lot where his truck was parked outside Sidney's apartment door. He switched off the homing device in the spike and thought of the Ice World. He pictured it in his mind, the room of the giant woman Sarina. Then he called his Door to many worlds and stepped through.

Sid gasped when he saw Mason appear in the room in the same spot he disappeared. Approximately two minutes passed from when he vanished. He stood. "Mason Waters, what kind of magic is this?"

Mason looked up at the massive man. "Do you want to help your sister live?"

Sid the giant relented. "Yes," he said in a humble manner.

"Then step aside and let me do what I can do."

Mason accepted the offer to stay in a guest room and was relieved to find that he did not dream. But it was risky. He should have brought Sidney with him. He was not prepared to take such risks on a continual basis.

The next day Sarina was setting up in bed, consuming a light broth. Her mother offered Mason anything they could give him, wealth, food, clothing. They were very grateful for saving their daughter.

"What you have done is a miracle." Sid was saying. "No medication or incantation has had such a positive effect as the medication you administered. We took the supplies you brought and are administering the medicine to those who are very sick in the village. Already, there are positive results. Some say you are a magician. But I do not believe that, Mason. I believe you are a man of compassion, as am I. I believe you have access to a type of technology that is advanced to our own and that you are willing to share what you know with us for our better good. You are a man of mercy."

"I've been called many things, Sid. That is the first time I've been called a man of mercy. I was not in much danger in the forest. However, you couldn't have known that. Your quick instinct to help me showed me what kind of man you are; what kind of people you must be. I believe friends can be found in the most unusual places and the most unlikely of circumstances."

"I see your logic, Mason." Sid nodded. "However, you must consider my perspective. You have potions and devices that are unknown to us. You disappeared and reappeared before my eyes. How do you explain such things if you are not a sorcerer? It is believed that a person who practices such magic cannot be trusted."

"I have not caused you harm. Quite the opposite. Besides Sid, you are far stronger than I am."

"There is a saying that the devil appears in the light. A deceiver would not present his true nature. He would study his prey and wait for the right moment to strike."

"Hmmm. And yet your sister and others in your village are recovering their health and their strength. I have to say, that isn't much of an attack plan on my part. Okay, you deserve some semblance of an explanation. I would not normally remain in your world or any other world so long as to be questioned. I have an adversary that wishes to harm me and perhaps my family as well. So, I am reconsidering my methods."

"You said, other worlds."

"Sid. I have a unique ability. I am able to travel beyond this world. This would explain why you found me out there in the middle of a blizzard without proper clothing or protection. There are places beyond this one, that exist with other people, other societies, places with abilities and medicines you have yet to discover. You do not have to accept what I am telling you as the truth. However, you have seen that I have the ability to vanish. If you or anyone else were to try to harm me, to hang me, I would simply vanish. That is why I was in no real danger in the forest and why I am in no danger now."

Sid nodded and considered the situation. "I do not believe it is an accident or random set of circumstances that you and I met. I must give you my trust, Mason. You are a little man, but you carry an extraordinary talent. You mentioned an adversary that wishes to harm you and your family. Perhaps there is something I can do to help. I know many men in this village and others that would jump at the opportunity to repay the kindness you have shown us. This must be a cunning creature to be able to cause you fear."

"He has the ability to track me, especially at night. He is much bigger and stronger than I and he knows much magic." Mason was surprised to see that Sid was grinning.

"Are you able to retrieve more of the antibiotic?"

Mason nodded.

"You are welcome to remain with us as long as you like. I can post men to guard you. We will do our best to protect you and if this fool should decide to attack you in my home he will most assuredly perish."

Mason shook his head. "You won't see him coming. He can appear in this house just as I appeared in the woods and in your sister's room. Right now, I do not think he knows where I am. If I keep moving I can most likely keep him off my trail." Mason got up from his seat. "Let's go check on your sister and continue our conversation."

Sarina was clothed but still in bed. She sat upright, her back against the post, reading a book. She smiled as they entered.

"Sarina, how are you feeling?"

"I am well. Thank you, Sid. Thank, you Mason. We are in your debt, sir. I wanted to go out to the shop…"

Sid held up his meaty palms. "Oh, no you don't. Give yourself time to get your strength back. I am sure you are feeling better. You look great. But let us not be hasty."

Mason walked over to where he pressed the sticker into the wall and began jiggling it, trying to get it out.

"What is this device Mason?"

"Well," Mason struggled with the small piece of metal. "Not so long ago, I was not able to control where I traveled. I could always return to my homeworld, but when I opened the Door to another world it had a mind of its own. This little device has changed that."

He popped the sticker out of the wood. "There. I wanted to return to this room because your sister needed that medicine quick. What I would like to do is take this to a special location. Can you think of a good place where I can place this permanently? The location needs to be close to this village. Consider what we said in the other room. If

I were on the run and needed your help, I would need to get to you fast."

Sid's forehead wrinkled in thought. It was Sarina who offered a suggestion. "What about the village square? It isn't far. The winds are not so strong there."

Sid shrugged. "She has a good idea. Let's go. I can show you where it is. I will get you some wraps that will keep you warm."

They moved slowly down the village streets. The town seemed deserted with the exception of the smoke billowing from the chimneys it was a winter wonderland to the extreme.

"How long will the weather be like this?" Mason yelled.

"Storms like this go on for days, sometimes a week. We will get a few weeks of warmth then another storm will blow through. During the winter, it snows for months and the clouds always cover the sky."

"That sucks."

Sid gave him an odd look. "You mentioned a family. Has this creature you speak of ever attacked your family?"

"I'm afraid he might. He would know how to find them. I'm sure of that. If he ever did attack them I am sure he would kill them quickly. They do not possess the ability to escape like I do."

They reached their destination and Mason liked it at once. It was more the shape of a rectangle, a massive open space surrounded by shops and restaurants. Trees grew sporadically. Under their huge branches were gazebos and play areas for children. Mason could imagine marriages and family reunions being held in the square.

"Everyone knows where this place is located. There is a

similar square in every village. During the warm months, it is heavily populated with families shopping or simply coming out to socialize. There is a saying among the men, 'it is a good place to die.'"

"That's what the men say?"

Sid shrugged. "Sure, but I don't think anyone has ever died here. It's an old saying. I'm not sure how it started."

Mason crossed the square and approached two shops that were built so close to one another there was no way Sid or anyone his size could fit between them. "There is only about four feet between these buildings. It doesn't seem wise to build them so close."

"The snow builds up between the buildings. It's easier to clean out small places. We use a horse, a long rope, and a blade."

"You have horses?"

"Sure. Do you have horses on your world?"

"Yes. Do you ride your horses?"

"Personally, I'm not much into that," Sid said. "I can ride and many of our men travel from village to village on horseback."

Mason could only imagine how large a horse would have to be to carry someone as big a Sid. "Here." Mason handed Sid the sticker. "Reach in there and put it up high."

"Okay. Why are we putting it in this little gap?"

"You want to explain to anyone who sees me appear or disappear?"

"Oh," Sid grunted. "I see your point."

"I'm not staying Sid. There is a man I need to see. I will return with more medicine."

"You know the way back to my home?"

"I was paying attention. Just over that way, about ten minutes. But, I don't think it matters."

Sid gave him that odd look again.

"When I 'disappeared' from your sister's room, I was gone for a few hours."

Sid shook his head. "No. You reappeared very quickly. I wondered how you retrieved the medicine so fast. I just figured you had that handy little backpack waiting for you from wherever you went."

"I was gone for several hours. It took me a while to gather those supplies. I had to go visit a Doctor friend of mine. When I reappeared here, only a few moments passed. I'm going to disappear again, Sid. When I reappear here, it is most likely only a few moments will have passed."

Mason paused and took a long look at his surroundings. He made mental notes about the details of the square and the alley he was standing in, just as he'd done when he was in Sarina's room. He looked back up at the big man. "If you will do me a favor and remain in this spot for a few moments. I'll be right back. Then we can discuss something I think you will really like."

"What's that?"

"A battle-plan."

Sid straightened and gave Mason that big grin as he watched the little man wink out of view.

Chapter 14

Rachel stopped screaming. She appeared to be in shock after being covered in hot blood and entrails. Her body shook, she fell back against the wall, then crumpled to the floor.

"What the hell is this shit!" McKayla shook her arms in an attempt to rid herself of the sticky goo that fell down on her. It was in her hair. She tried pulling it out but it was no use. She would have to shower. She heard her mother on the phone.

"We need an officer fast! And an ambulance!" Valerie located her cell and was currently on the line with a 911 dispatcher. She spoke quickly, almost in a panic, but seemed to be holding it down, all things considered.

McKayla waited for her mother to end the call. They were in a highly populated area of the city and she knew it would not take EMT long to arrive. She feared Conrad may be dead. She was unsure if this stuff on her body was toxic. "How did you know?"

"What?" Valerie looked at her youngest daughter seeing for the first time how much she was covered in monster goo.

"The blinds. The sunlight. How did you know that would work?"

"I...I dreamed it." Valerie stammered. "I dreamed the

whole thing. That thing…" She pointed to the top of the stairs where it landed. "That thing was in my dream. I woke up and it was real. Somehow I sensed it wouldn't be able to withstand the sunlight."

McKayla moved to the bottom of the stairs. "Rachel? Rachel? Are you okay?" She did not wait for an answer. She climbed the steps and knelt next to her sister. Rachel's eyes were open and she was muttering something.

McKayla heard sirens in the distance. She stood and moved to the bedroom door. The shotgun was lodged in the opposite wall just above the headboard. She did not see Conrad but heard him moaning. She saw him pulling himself up on the other side of the bed. He lost his grip on the blanket and slid back to the floor, groaning.

She moved around to the other side of the bed. "The ambulance is on the way, Conrad. Stay still."

His voice came tiny and weak. "I'm busted up inside. It's hard to breathe."

She grabbed a pillow from the bed and placed it under his neck supporting his head. "Try not to move."

She breathed a sigh of relief. She felt sure they would all be okay. The wail of the sirens was just outside. Explaining what happened was going to be challenging. She walked back to the head of the stairs. Her mother stood at the front door, holding it open. "What are we going to tell them, Mom?"

"You want to tell them it was a bear?" Valerie asked.

McKayla crossed her arms. The blood was beginning to dry. "Okay. How did it blow up?"

"I'll think of something. If they try to question you or Rachel just clam up and act the part of a victim, too emotionally upset to talk about it." Valerie turned back to the door. "In here officer. We need medical attention upstairs."

The police and EMT entered at the same time. Three medical personnel climbed the stairs. Two police officers remained on the first floor to question Valerie.

McKayla coaxed Rachel to her feet and put her in the upstairs shower; closing the bathroom door as the EMTs entered the room. Rachel calmed considerably and the warm water seemed to do the trick. "Don't use all the hot water. I need to get this crap off too."

Rachel opened the curtain. "Come on," she said in a low tone. "I don't think I'm ever coming out of here."

They showered in silence. McKayla spoke up quietly. "You got your wits about you, Rachel?"

Rachel nodded. "I'm okay now. I guess I need to get out of here so I can follow Conrad to the hospital."

"Rachel. That thing. Did you hear it? What it said?"

She nodded. "How do you suppose it knows Dad's name?"

McKayla looked up at her. "I wasn't sure I heard it right. But you heard the same thing."

"It made a terrible noise. I will never forget that sound, Kay. It said Dad's name. I know that for sure."

Conrad was in bad shape. He suffered from multiple broken ribs, a punctured lung, a broken collarbone, a broken arm, a dislocated shoulder, and a concussion. The prognosis was good. In time, he would recover and would most likely experience no long-term effects. The medical examiner was impressed at how healthy the young man was and said if he were an older man, say in his fifties, he would not have been so fortunate.

Valerie Waters proved to be very improvisational. The following is the tale she spun. Before going to bed she placed several pots of stew on the stove to simmer over-night. Sometime early in the morning, an intruder broke into the apartment. She heard the stairs creaking and felt something was not right. She got out of bed, failed to turn on the lights, tripped over her dangling nightdress and startled the intruder. Quickly looking for something to defend herself and her daughters she grabbed one of the pots of stew and flung it at the man. In the dark, with all the commotion things got pretty crazy. The stew ended up on the stairs, the walls, and her two daughters. As for Conrad's injuries; he came out of his room brandishing a shotgun. Not really knowing how to handle the rifle, in the dark, with women screaming, he shot a hole in the ceiling. As a result of mishandling the weapon, he suffered an injury to his arm and shoulder. In the confusion, he ran back into his room. Why? She wasn't sure officer. But he surely tripped, hurling the gun into the wall and falling down causing further injury to himself.

Given the fact that Conrad was whisked away to the hospital, the police did not question the man nor were they aware of the extensive nature of his injuries. As for the girls; they saw no reason to harass them. The older of the two was hysterical and wanted nothing more than to get to the hospital to be with her boyfriend. The officers were glad the younger of the two seemed to have her act together and were willing to allow the younger to drive the older. Valerie impressed upon them that the intruder may be close by, perhaps in another unit. He would be the guy with food stained clothing.

Valerie was grateful they did not press her on much of her story. They did look skeptical when they inspected the 'food' stains on the walls, the stairs, and the floor. The woman was obviously a very bad cook or the stew was far from done. In fact, it was down-right raw. It was a bizarre scene. The guy with the shotgun could have killed someone. No sign of forced entry. Had they gone to bed without locking the door? The officers excused themselves and began canvassing the apartment complex with the help of a few additional cruisers. They would no doubt be talking about this particular call for many days to come.

Finally, alone, Valerie touched the number one favorite tab on her cell and waited for Mason to pick up the call.

The call came through on one of Mason's many trips from this reality to another. He saw Valerie's name and number light up the screen but he was far too busy to handle a family matter at the time. He touched the screen and traced his finger down on the screen, thus giving him six options of a preprogrammed text response. He chose, 'I'll call you later.' And pocketed the phone.

Valerie looked at the text. "At least I know he's alive." She muttered. She hadn't shared the entire dream with the girls. In light of the circumstances, she dared not. The creature that invaded Conrad's apartment was possibly one of many. It was similar to the monster that found its way into her room at home but it was smaller. She thought the dream would have continued to repeat itself if she hadn't awakened. It was Rachel's scream that woke her up.

She recalled a conversation with Mason before they were

married. It was long ago but some of what he told her came back to her now. He described the night terrors he suffered as a young boy. He said they came at night when he was alone in his room. He mentioned his fear of being alone after they were married, but she did not take it seriously. She also recalled how upset she was when she came home from a trip to find that he asked Rachel to stay with him through the night. Was he trying to tell her these creatures were haunting him? If a creature as terrible as the one that assaulted her in her bathroom visited young Mason Waters as a boy she could see how it would have traumatized him.

She glanced at the text on her phone. 'I'll call you later.' "What are you doing Mason?" She said aloud. How was he getting through the nights alone? She typed out a text of her own. 'Mason. We need to talk. I know you are worried I will call the police, but I promise you, I won't. Something very serious has happened involving me, Kayla, and Rachel. Please, call me as soon as you get this.' She pressed 'send'.

She pressed the number three favorite tab and waited. She paced the first floor of the apartment and noticed something on the kitchen floor.

Clinton, her oldest child answered on the second ring. "Hello. Mom, what's up?"

"Are you busy?" She bent down and picked up a three-foot piece of tattered, thick rope.

"No. What I'm doing, it can wait."

"I'm at Conrad's and Rachel's apartment. McKayla and I spent the night. There was a break-in and Conrad got hurt. He is on his way to Methodist Hospital over on Seminary. Rachel and McKayla are on their way there also."

"A break-in? You mean like a burglary? Is anyone hurt? I mean, besides Conrad. How bad is he?"

"Hold on, hold on. Do you know where Steven is? He never picks my calls."

"He may be at the recreation center. If he is, his phone is in a locker."

"Can you break away from what you are doing?"

"Sure. You want me to pick him up?"

Valerie nodded. "Yes. I'm headed to the hospital now, myself. We need to come together, all of us. Find your brother and meet us at the hospital. We will be in the ER waiting room most likely. I'll fill you in when you get there." She ended the call and examined the piece of rope in her hand. She noticed her own palms. They were sore and red with what appeared to be rope burn.

Mason sat at a stainless-steel table in a chrome chair. The place reminded him of a germ-free examination room. Most of the furniture of similar color and texture, cold steel. On the table were two backpacks full of medicine and syringes. Doctor Rasmus had one of his assistants gather the supplies and the young man brought it in and placed it on the table in front of Mason.

"I can get as much of that as you need Mr. Waters." The Doctor stood, looking a Mason with fascination in his eyes.

Mason figured his appearance was fairly odd. He popped back into this reality bundled up in animal skin coats, looking like he'd spent the week in the Earth's Arctic. "Thank you, Doctor. Two packs are probably all I can carry through the portal. If I don't have a firm grip on what I'm taking through... Well you know it's just going to stay glued to this reality."

"Indeed. I am very pleased with your report on the stickers I created for you."

Mason pulled off the heavy clothing, stacking them in a pile on the table. "Well, the first one worked, as advertised."

"I suspect if you copy the process on every world you visit... Those that you wish to return to, the result will be the same."

Something about the stickers seemed off to Mason. He made a mental note to come back to this topic at a later time. "You remember a conversation concerning the stoppage of time?"

Rasmus nodded. "You suggested that when you open the portal and travel to an alternate reality, that time freezes on Earth until you return."

"Yes. Yes. I dropped Sidney at her apartment and decided to take a trip. What could it hurt? She wouldn't notice my absence."

Rasmus nodded remaining silent, considering Mason was aware this was not new information and he was forming a foundation for the purpose of demonstrating some new point, theory or fact.

"I travel to what I have dubbed, 'Ice World' where Sid and his people live. I leave, come back here to Nikon, spend several hours here with you, then go back to Ice World. When I returned, only a few moments passed; maybe two minutes at the most. I spent that day, the night, and half the following day on that world. Which brings us to where I am right now, in this shiny room with my favorite doctor."

Rasmus placed one hand on his chin, the other on his

elbow supporting the one on his chin, a classic thinker's pose.

"It stands to reason that when I return to Ice World, only two minutes will have passed from when I left. I asked Sid to stand-by saying, 'I'll be right back.' I feel certain that I can stay here with you as long as I want. When I return to Earth, no time will have elapsed. When I return to Ice World, two minutes." He held up two fingers.

Rasmus looked at him. "Your point is?"

"Doc, let's say I put these stickers on one hundred worlds. In essence, I would have incredible control and power. All I have to do is make a mental note concerning the time element of each reality. Are you following me here?"

"You are becoming aware of what Adramelech and the inhabitants of his world already know. They desire to use you Mason for purposes I can only imagine."

"What about you Doctor? What is it you desire?"

Aiden entered the room.

The Doctor was about to respond. Seeing Aiden, he felt it prudent to remain silent.

Mason watched her approach and saw fire in her eyes. This was not a happy woman. He braced himself for what was to come.

She stopped well within his personal space, clinched her jaw and her small fists. She closed her eyes, dropped her head, blew out a long breath of air, then fixed her eyes on him again. "Don't ever do that again. You can open your portal and leave whenever you want, but do not ever leave me without saying goodbye. Even if it means breaking my heart, Mason. You tell me goodbye." This last sentence was hardly audible as she broke into tears.

Mason reached out and brought her into his arms. He held her for some time gently telling her how sorry he was. He looked up. Rasmus was gone. They were in the middle of an important conversation and he wanted to ask him some questions about the stickers. He also wished to have the switch removed and for the Doctor to place a sticker in the lab somewhere. He didn't like the switch device. It felt funny under the skin of his forearm.

"What are all these blankets and coverings for?" She pulled back, no longer crying, trying to put a smile on her face.

"I've had a small adventure." He motioned toward the back-packs on the table. "I need to get this medication to the world I came from where heavy coverings are essential."

She wiped her face with some tissue. "When I came back and you were gone. I insisted on using the viewer. But your world was static. The Doctor told me you left and he had no idea where you were. He assured me you would return, but the last time you were gone for months. I was so upset."

"Well, I'm here. I wish the time difference wasn't so massive. It would be better if you were on Earth."

Aiden looked at him in shock. "You talked to Doctor Rasmus about sending me there?"

"No. I am merely making an observation. If you were on Earth, I could leave and you would never know I was gone."

"Well, there has to be a very important reason to open a portal for us. I'm afraid a request from a woman who wants to be with the man she loves is not going to move any mountains."

"The Doctor told me you have the option of sleeping."

"Being put in stasis?"

Mason nodded. "Yes."

"I don't want to do that. Please don't make that demand of me. Please."

Mason sighed. "Can we get Doctor Rasmus back in here?"

The door opened and Doctor Rasmus reentered the room.

"Are you listening, outside the door?"

Rasmus smiled. "No. I prefer to call it monitoring. You caught my attention when you mentioned my name."

Mason decided to let it go. It was the Doctor's lab. "I'm considering taking her back with me, to Earth. I would like your input on the matter."

"Physically, she should be fine. Biologically, she would continue to age at the same rate as she does now. I am not sure how long it would take, but in time, perhaps a few years her metabolic rate would begin to sync with that of your reality. I must warn you, she will outlive you, your children, and your grandchildren. On a side note, be very careful opening the portal if she is near. She will be pulled back to Nikon instantly."

The doctor cleared his throat and seemed to be a bit uncomfortable. "Aiden, you haven't told him?"

She did not speak, only shook her head slowly.

Mason looked at her, then back to the Doctor. "What is it?"

"If you insist on taking her to Earth, and I know she wants to be with you no matter what. I suggest you leave Nikon and remain on Earth for approximately 20 to 24 hours. This will give her adequate time to give birth while under my care."

Mason turned his head sharply toward Aiden. "You're pregnant?" Mason's head began to spin. He felt light and sat down.

Aiden looked up at him. "I was going to tell you."

"It seems awful fast. Are you absolutely sure?"

"I am. The Doctor tested me and confirmed it. In case a nasty thought is coming to your mind, I have been with only you."

What was he going to say to Valerie, to his family? 'Hi everyone, this is your new brother. I had an affair with his mom. She's from another planet.' Yeah, that wasn't going to cut it. "I need some time to process everything. What the Doctor proposes; you, staying here to have the baby, how do you feel about that?"

She looked into his eyes. "I can do it if you will promise to come see me; I mean before the baby comes. You have to help me with a name."

Mason could not believe he was having this conversation. He felt he was having an out of body experience; he was a bystander, watching his life play out on a big screen. "Doctor. In all the worlds you have viewed, all the different societies, have you ever come across one that practices time travel?"

"No, sir. I have not. But I am hopeful."

Aiden tensed. "You want to go back in time and change something?"

Mason shook his head slowly. "Forget it. I feel like what little control I had, just came way undone. Please, don't take offense. Give me some time to absorb this. It's kind of big, you know."

***

After saying goodbye properly, Aiden left the two men to attend to their business. She agreed to remain on Nikon under Doctor Rasmus' care for the duration of the pregnancy. Mason agreed to return at least every other month and promised to call her if he was in town conducting business with the Doctor. The plan was to bring her and the child to Earth and it was Mason's responsibility to make sure they had an adequate place to live when they got there. Suddenly, Mason had a hell of a lot to do in a very short amount of time. He had to get the medicine back to Sid, devise the battle plan to combat Adramelech and his cohorts, call Valerie back to find out what was going on with her and the kids. Maybe he could convince Sidney to help him find a furnished apartment in Dallas for Aiden and the baby.

"Mr. Waters?"

Mason looked up.

"I called you several times. Are you okay?"

"I'm sorry, Doc. I was just thinking."

He nodded. "I would like to tell you that I admire you, sir."

Mason chuckled. "Don't start stroking me Doc. It ain't over yet."

"Excuse me?"

Mason waved his hand passively. "Forget it. We need to attach a sticker here in the lab so I can have this switch removed."

"I have one right here." He produced what resembled

a small metallic edged jack. "I've taken the liberty of magnetizing this one." He snapped it in place on a large cabinet, perhaps it was a stainless-steel refrigerator. "No danger of it being yanked out of place as this is its home reality. So, that should do nicely."

Mason spent a little over an hour at the lab. He memorized the place. He walked over to the jack and whispered, "Nikon" over the device.

Surprised, he noticed Doctor Rasmus chuckling, like there was some inside joke. "What?"

Rasmus waved both hands in the air. "Oh, nothing. I'll share it later. Here, let me see your arm." The Doctor produced a slender instrument about the size of a toothbrush, passed it over Mason's arm making a very tiny incision.

It felt like someone scratched him. Mason watched in amazement as the Doctor retrieved the small switch without causing him to shed a drop of blood.

"There you go. You should be free to pass between three realities now. Add as many as you like. You know I will always welcome any information you want to share. Any insight or discoveries will always be of value to my research. Should you have any requests; an adjustment on your enhancement spike, or any challenges you are facing, please do not fail to communicate with me, Mason. We are partners, you and me. It appears we shall soon be family."

Mason bundled up in the thick heavy animal skins, picked up the two backpacks, and secured them across his back. He looked at the Doctor. "Don't you think that happened a bit fast?"

"Not really. It's quite common here. Additionally, I have equipment here in the lab that is very accurate."

"Normally, on Earth, a woman might notice something like that after a month or so. She misses her cycle, becomes concerned, it's like four to six weeks along, you know."

"You are forgetting that I engineered Aiden from the womb. I expected this outcome, in precisely this way."

"That sounds suspicious, Doc."

"How so? I at no point encouraged the two of you…"

"You designed her specifically with me in mind. You gave her characteristics you know I find very attractive, perhaps even irresistible."

"However, I would point out you still have free will."

"Doctor Rasmus. You are formidable. I am going to be very careful with you from this point forward. At the very least, you held the deck and arranged the cards in your favor."

"Are you not practicing the same methods, Mason? You are using the tools at your disposal to form a plan of action against Adramelech. You are arranging the cards to favor you, as you put it."

"That is a matter of life and death. It's not the same."

"Are you so sure?"

Mason considered his words. "We were having a very serious conversation before Aiden came in earlier. Have you forgotten or simply choosing not to revisit the subject?"

"We will have many similar conversations, and many dissimilar, in times to come. No, I have not forgotten, and I would welcome the revisiting of that topic. I find you equally formidable and engaging."

Mason grunted. "Remember what I said about that time travel thing. I'll see you in a few months. If you need me before then, just buzz me."

"Be safe Mason Waters. I look forward to our next meeting."

Mason secured the back-packs, fixed his gaze on the Doctor, smiled, summoned the Door and stepped into the parking lot of Sidney's apartment complex. He glanced over at his truck, still setting there, the engine no doubt hot as only about a minute passed in this reality. The amount of time it took him to walk over to this spot and open the Door.

He concentrated on the village square on Ice World and called the Door again. Frigid wind and snow hit him on the side of his face. He looked toward the spot where Sid should be standing. Sid was not there.

Chapter

"Mason!"

Mason heard him calling from across the square. The large man ran toward him, knocking the snow into the air like an industrial snow blower. He stopped a few feet away, a large grin on his face. He reached out and took the backpacks off Mason's shoulders. "That is scary, Mason. I do not want to witness your coming and going. It will give me bad dreams, no doubt."

"Ha! You, big scaredy-cat. Let's get back to the house where it's warm. You got any of that delicious stew?"

"Sure. Um, I know what a cat is, but I'm not familiar with 'scaredy-cat'. What is that?"

"You're not cold? Come on. Let's get to the fire."

They began the return trip to Sid's home, pushing through the snow drifts. A task much easier for Sid. He walked ahead of Mason, clearing the way, a cruise ship cutting through the ocean. Mason kept up, walking close enough to Sid's back to take advantage of the shelter his large body created.

"I moved that little device."

"What?" Mason yelled back. The wind took Sid's words

but Mason thought he said something about moving. "I didn't hear that."

Sid turned his head to the side continuing to move forward. "You were right. You were only gone for a few minutes. I thought of a better place for that little metal pin. I moved it while you were gone."

"Sid! Stop!"

Sid stopped and turned.

"That's why you were running across the square. Where did you put it?"

"I remember that there is much traffic around that alley during the warm months. It's next to a popular restaurant. I felt it was risky."

Mason moved close enough so he did not need to scream. "Sid, where did you put it?"

"Oh, it's just across the square in a more secluded place. A spot close to a garbage disposal, so no one ventures over there."

Mason's mind went into overdrive. He reentered the Ice World in the exact spot he expected. He told Sid to fix the sticker in the alley, took a mental picture of that spot just as when he was in Sarina's room. "Come on. Keep moving."

"Did I cause a problem?"

"Keep moving, Sid. No, you didn't cause a problem."

Once they were seated in front of the massive fireplace, eating something delicious and hot Sid's mother baked, they continued the conversation.

"The sticker, that's what I call it, is designed with a purpose. It is a new technology for me. My first time using the device was when we were in your sister's room. I placed it there and returned to the exact spot. You saw me do it."

Sid was nodding and chewing. He stopped nodding and started shaking his head slowly, still chewing. He looked at Mason with a measure of pain in his expression.

"When you jump straight up, you land in the same spot." Mason tried to explain. "The 'little device,' you moved works in a similar fashion. When I disappear, it makes me reappear in the same spot."

"You did."

The big man was right. He returned to Ice World in the exact same spot he left. Doctor Rasmus hadn't said he would return in close proximity to the stickers. He assumed this. Something in the back of his mind troubled him. Something wasn't right about the stickers. He meant to talk to Rasmus about it. The Doctor instructed him to speak the name of the world or any other sort of code over the sticker and create some sort of database so he would be able to remember all the realities where he left a sticker. That part seemed odd. How scientific was that? Was the sticker able to record his voice? More importantly, how was the sticker communicating with the Door? Furthermore, if the physical location of the sticker was of no consequence, then what governed his reentry location? That was the question he needed to be answered. Sid moved the sticker across the square. What if he took it to another village? What if he sent the thing to the other side of the world? He couldn't have done that in two minutes. Mason was beginning to think the Doctor gave him the equivalent of a placebo.

He finished his food and turned to Sid. "I need to check something out."

"Okay. You need some help?"

He handed the empty plate to Sid, getting up and

shaking his head. "I'm going to step out for a few minutes. If it makes you uneasy, close your eyes. If I do not return here in this room in two minutes, come looking for me in the village square."

Without a word, Sid put his big paw over his eyes.

Mason summoned the Door. It lit up the house, a silent bolt of lightning, frozen in place, from the floor it stretched up high through the ceiling. Mason regarded the Door for a second and considered what he was about to do. The Doctor was playing a little game. If he was right, he was about to do something he never attempted. Worst case scenario, he would end up in the parking lot of Sidney's apartment building. He closed his eyes and pictured Mercer Laboratory on planet Nikon. He blocked out the sounds of the wind howling outside, the warmth of the blazing fire, the smell of food simmering in the kitchen. He imagined himself in the bright and sterile environment created by Doctor Rasmus and his team. He could see the chrome chairs and tables, the workstations, the walls lined with large computers. His physical eyes remained shut, but the eyes in his head guided him and he stepped forward.

As his right foot came down on a solid surface he felt a numbing sensation throughout his body. He brought his left foot forward to meet his right and he stood still. He opened his eyes and found himself in what appeared to be a vast room of light. There was no floor, no ceiling, no walls, no outside world for perspective. The numbness abated as he turned slowly. He was inside the Door; not through, not out, but in the middle of here and there. There was no way to discern north from south, up from down. He was in the middle of nothing or perhaps it was the middle of everything.

He felt calm like a child feels in its mother's arms. He stopped turning and looked down at his feet. He was standing on a solid surface, but he could not see a floor. He bent at the knees and reached out. His hand passed the point where a floor should be. He was floating in the center of all this light yet he could take steps.

Which way to go? He thought. *There is no, way.* Mason closed his eyes again, focusing on the pulsing light that engulfed his body. He breathed in and out and considered the air. *How can there be air?*

Okay, let's move. He took a step forward, then two. The pulsing stopped with a popping sensation, a loud clap. The bright light surrounding him winked out with the clap and he was standing in the laboratory looking at a surprised Doctor Rasmus, seated at a workstation. Mason smiled. He moved from one reality to another without passing through his own homeworld.

Doctor Rasmus stood. "You have not been gone long, Mr. Waters. Did you forget something?"

"No. You and I are going to come to an understanding. Right now." Mason shrugged off the heavy skins and tossed them on the table.

"You seem agitated."

"Sit."

The Doctor took his seat and waited.

"There was something off about the stickers. Aiden clouded my thinking and I didn't see it at first. Do the damn things actually do anything, Doctor?"

"I will admit. I wondered how long it would take you to figure it out."

"Doctor, you do not know the level of my anger. I'm not here to chit-chat. Answer my question."

Doctor Rasmus regarded him and shrugged. "No. Well, they do stick to things nicely. However, they have no working parts. They are a means to an end. I believe you have untapped power Mason. I believe you have the ability to move freely from one reality to another. In time, you may also discover that you can bend and break many other laws of physics. You pass through a portal to alternate realities not knowing where the portal is taking you. You have never revisited one reality because you did not believe it was possible. I could have tried to convince you it was possible to go where you wanted, but I felt it may be better if you discovered it yourself. I simply applied a gentle push."

Mason recalled how the Door appeared to him when he was very young. He had no control where it appeared or when it appeared. He remembered setting in Ms. Frazier's third-grade class. The time he first moved the Door verbally, how he was able to call the Door at will from that point on with just a thought. He considered the first time he discovered his ability to step through the Door to another world, to slip back into his own reality. Other discoveries followed; items strongly gravitated toward their own reality, time differed from one world to another, and recently that he could bring another person through with him. It followed logically there were things about the Door he had yet to discover and it made him wonder just how powerful this ability might become.

"Creating a portal to another world is old science for me.

My problem is it takes a great deal of power, which costs a great deal of currency. Opening a portal to the desired destination, a specific place, into your reality, on your planet, in your small motel room, is a mere mathematical equation. I thought if I can do it, why can't Mason do it? I suspected my answer was; he can, he just doesn't know he can."

"Once again, I do not appreciate your methods. I will agree, you are smarter than I am. It does not give you the right to play games, Doc. How foolish would it have looked; me jumping from world to world placing those little pieces of worthless metal in each one, believing it was my only way to return?"

"I would have told you. I am actually pleased you figured it out so quickly. I do not know how you are communicating with the portal. Your Door to other worlds is obeying a mental command. It was not much of a leap to theorize that you should be able to control your destination in the same manner."

Mason decided not to mention the fact his discovery was an accident. Had Sid not moved the sticker he would not have realized so quickly. "Was the switch you put in my arm necessary? Because that actually hurt."

"Oh, yes. The switch was connected to the spike and it worked perfectly. It was insurance if you will. We are discovering new things together, Mason. I wanted to take some precautions and the switch was one of those precautions. Fortunately, we no longer need it."

"Doctor. I can take my toys and go home. And never come back."

Rasmus gave him a puzzled look. "Toys?"

"A figure of speech. I appreciate your position,

considering what Adramelech is and the threat he poses to you and to me. But, I am not a test subject. I have to trust you, Doctor. If you continue experimenting on me, I won't know when something is authentic or when it is some kind of maze you designed so you can study which path the mouse chooses and why."

Rasmus nodded and appeared to be in thought.

"If you have a theory; something you want to study or test, just talk to me. You have to have a little faith. Everything is not going to be a 'sure thing'. There are some things in life that are simply 'no win' situations. You take the good with the bad."

"That is very difficult for me to accept, Mason."

"You better work on it. You cannot control me. If I find out you are operating in this manner again, I'm gone Doc. I'll scoop Aiden up and you will have to be content watching us through your viewer because we won't be back."

The Doctor fell silent.

"Tell me now if you have any other little experiments in the works."

"I have another theory. Your mentioning time travel really got me thinking."

"Go on."

"You are able to move from reality to reality by concentrating. You are picturing the place you wish to travel and somehow your doorway is plugged into this thought. I am wondering what would happen if you used that same process on a past event."

"Not just picturing a place, but a place that corresponds to an event I witnessed from the past."

"Yes. We all have vivid memories of traumatic and of

wonderful past events. Say, a birthday party, or the death of a loved one. Those memories are strong. If you were able to move through the portal and revisit a past event, it would open up many possibilities."

"See how easy that is? Two guys talking, working on the same goals. What a concept."

"I apologize. I see I was wrong to lie to you about the stickers."

"Okay. Accepted. Let's put time travel on the shelf for now. I've read some books on that topic and watched some movies. People that start toying with time travel ultimately create a real mess of things. If in the days to come we try it and it works as you say, I can always travel back to this very moment and tell myself to go ahead and give it a go. What do you say?"

He frowned. "The fact that your future self has not appeared this very moment is a bad sign."

"Says you, Doc. Maybe my future self decided not to visit us here at this time for some good reason that we are yet unaware."

He raised his brow. "Indeed."

"You thrive on this stuff, don't you?"

Rasmus flashed a big grin.

"I figured as much. But, it's starting to make my head spin. I wasn't planning on coming back here so soon. I was on Ice World talking to Sid and I need to get back. I've got an idea of how he may be able to help us with Adramelech. I need to be with him to implement the plan. I can't tell him what to do and leave, cause I'll just show up two minutes later. I have to tell you Doc., it took me a while to get used to the fact that when I return to my world, no time has passed. It was freaky at first, but I got used to it. Now that I can revisit other worlds that issue has cropped up again. This time it's worse."

"Each world operates differently as it applies to the passage of time."

"Well, I don't know if everyone is different. When I was busy collecting a fortune I often found currency was different on other worlds. However, many of them have a currency that appears to be an exact copy of what we have on Earth. I have a feeling that I will experience the same effect as it applies to how each world experiences the passage of time. I am hoping the good places will be similar to Earth in this regard."

Mason called for the Door and it parted the laboratory on command. He grabbed his animal skin coats and turned to go. "Pray this time you do not see me for a few months, Doc."

"Until then Mason. Good luck."

Mason pictured the large living area on Ice World. In his mind, he pictured Sid, still perched before a roaring fire with his hand no doubt, still covering his eyes.

Sid still covered his eyes. He heard Mason's feet on the floor. "Is everything okay, Mason Waters?"

"Yes."

Sid dropped his hand and looked at his friend.

"I want to assemble as many warriors, hunters, and able-bodied men as you can find. Is there a place, a town hall or convention center, anything that will accommodate a large group like that?"

"Sure. The church is the largest building in the village. It is on the north side of the village square. It will do. You need to draft letters stating your intentions and needs. I would send a few runners and riders to neighboring villages. They can carry the medication with them and deliver the letters to the leaders of the villages."

"How long do you think all that would take?"

Sid thought about it. "A few days to reach all the nearby villages. Several days for the men you request to make the journey here; five maybe six days."

Mason paused then nodded. "Okay. I'm about to disappear again. When I return I will have a guest with me."

"A guest?"

"She is a friend of mine. She can stay in the room you have prepared for me. Make sure your Mom is aware. She is even smaller than I am, so you won't notice her much. I have to remain here with you while we assemble our small army. I need her to keep me and your home safe."

Sid stood and roared with laughter. "You are describing a mouse to me. How can a mouse keep us safe?"

Mason looked up at the giant. "I'll explain it to you later. Oh, she will need warm clothing, like these skins you gave to me. Stop laughing. I'll be back in a few minutes so shag your big ass."

In the parking lot of Sidney's apartment, Mason walked casually back to his truck. He removed the heavy coats and tossed them in the back, opened the passenger door, and sat down. He'd been gone for quite a while; visited two worlds, found out he was going to be a father again, played a part in saving the lives of hundreds perhaps thousands of giant humanoids on a frozen planet, and he was currently hatching a plan to take on a world of demonic angels who were determined to kill him, his family, and perhaps taking over control of the Earth. He sighed and peered out the front window wondering how long Sidney was going to take. He sat back and closed his eyes. His cell phone chirped.

"Hello? Clint?"

"Dad? What's up? We've been trying to reach you."

"I got a text from your Mother but haven't had the time to call her back. What's going on?"

Clint was their oldest child. He was in his early thirties, unmarried, the father of three children. Mason allowed space to come between himself and his son though Clint enjoyed a great relationship with his Mother. It wasn't that they were at odds; nothing like that. They simply had a difference of opinion when it came to the definition of family. When they were together, Thanksgiving or Christmas for example, they got along just fine. There was a mutual respect between them, but Mason wished for a closer relationship with the young man. Clint was always too busy and how could he complain? Mason had a non-existent relationship with his own parents.

"I just picked up Steve. We are on our way to Methodist Hospital. On Seminary."

"Yes, I know where it is. Why are you going to the hospital?"

"We are meeting Mom there. McKayla and Rachel are there also. Mom said someone broke into Conrad's apartment and he was injured."

"Injured? How?"

"She didn't say but there was a sense of urgency in her voice. She told me to pick up Steve and meet them there. You should call Mom. Maybe you should think about coming as well."

"I'll call her, son. Be safe and I'll talk to you soon."

Mason ended the call and pressed the tab to call Valerie's cell. She picked up on the first ring. "Mason. Thank god."

Mason looked up and saw Sidney coming back to the truck. She wore painted on jeans, tennis shoes, and a grey t-shirt that said, 'Sassy, Classy, and a bit Smart Assy'. She opened the driver side door, tossed her bag on the seat and climbed in. She stared at Mason but remained silent while he spoke on the phone.

Mason returned her stare. "Calm down. Start from the beginning."

Sidney could hear a woman's voice. The woman spoke quickly and obviously wanted Mason to get himself to the hospital as quickly as he could. What was he doing anyway? Why wasn't he picking her calls? Why hadn't he come home?"

The questions were coming faster than Mason could respond. "Valerie. Calm down. I just spoke to Clint. I'm on my way. I've got a call I need to take. Yes, yes, I will call you back in a few minutes. Get your thoughts together. I want to hear the whole thing from the beginning."

He ended the call and sighed, looking at his lap.

"What did I miss!" Sidney said, shutting the truck door.

Chapter 16

She drove him toward the hospital as he attempted to bring her up to speed. On the way, they stopped and picked up two bags of cash from the storage facility.

"You won't be gone for long." He was saying.

"You just said it would take maybe a week."

"No. I said five or six days. Honestly, I cannot be sure. It could take longer. But that is irrelevant Sidney. When we step through the Door time stops here."

"You can stop time?!"

Mason shook his head. It wasn't as easy talking to Sidney as it was to Aiden. He needed to be very specific with her. "No. I said it wrong. No matter where we go, or how long we are gone, we always return to the same point in time in this reality as when we left."

She nodded. "Right. You can stop time."

Mason threw up his hands. "Okay, if it helps you to see it that way, fine. My point is we can be gone for a few days, but we are not really going to be gone at all... Kind'a."

"I'd like to revisit the subject of your relationship with Aiden."

"Oh, right," Mason said, as if he were remembering

something urgent. "The cash we picked up. I need you to help me rent an apartment, a nice one, a furnished one."

"Why? Have you tired of the motel room already?"

"It isn't for me."

Sidney drove in silence for a moment then turned to him. "You want me to find an apartment for her?"

He nodded. "Is that going to be a problem?"

"You want me, to find an apartment for another woman; a woman who is not your wife, who you just spent two weeks with? Then you want me to travel with you to another planet to spend a week with you? Have I got it about right, Mason? In the meantime, we are rushing to the hospital so I can drop you off at a meeting with your wife and kids."

Mason returned her gaze. "Well, when you put it that way, it sounds a bit sleazy."

She turned her attention back to the road. "It doesn't sound sleazy, man. You are a real piece of work. What's up with the beard? Are you going to just let it keep growing like that?"

Mason pulled down the visor and peered at his reflection. She was right. He could run a small comb through it. "Huh. What do you think? I think it looks pretty good."

"You would."

He looked closer pulling down his lower eyelid. The color of his eyes changed from brown to hazel. "What has the doctor done?" he whispered.

"I told you. You've changed. You don't look like you did when I met you the other night."

Mason flipped the visor shut and dialed Valerie on his cell. She answered on the third ring, calm in her tone. She told him about the creature that attacked her in their bedroom; how it scratched her, how she fell into the tub and hit her head. Because of the attack, she went to Rachel's place. She was afraid of staying at home alone. She told him about the animal that attacked Conrad, Rachel, and McKayla. "I've never seen anything like it Mason; not even in a movie. The creature that hit Conrad could not have come from Earth. That's not all. It said your name."

Mason listened with increasing dread. Each detail of her story matched something he experienced from his youth. The creatures she described were not Adramelech, but he had no doubt they were buddies.

"How does it know your name, Mason?"

Mason sighed. This was exactly what he feared would happen. He managed to evade the evil beings that wanted him dead so they were turning their attention to those that were closest to him. If they couldn't get to him, they would surely get his family. He said quietly, "I'll be there soon Valerie. I'll try to explain everything when I get there."

"It isn't over, is it?"

"No. For you, it's just the beginning. I was afraid something like this might happen. The reason I have not come home is that I have been trying to deal with this on my own. I hoped it would not come to you or to the kids."

"We're in the ER waiting room."

Mason ended the call and sat in silence. The only sound was of the truck tires clicking along as they ate up the miles on the highway.

"That didn't sound good." Gone was the edge in her voice. She actually sounded sympathetic.

"The creature that attacked me the night I met you. It sent... Well, I don't know what to call it. Valerie has been attacked twice by monsters from the same realm as the one that wants me. In this recent attack, my daughter's boyfriend got hurt, bad."

Sidney reached out and placed her hand on his thigh. "We're going to get through this. I don't really understand everything that's going on. I'm playing catch-up here, but I'm doing my best. If finding an apartment helps in some way, I'll do it. God knows you've got enough dough in those bags. You could buy a house if you wanted. Anyway, just tell me what to do."

Mason remained quiet for a while. He turned his gaze to the hillside out the passenger side window. He pursed his lips, running through options in his mind. Eventually, he turned to her. "We've got less than 24 hours to take care of business here, then we are traveling together to the Ice World. I prefer not to push our luck though. Drop me off at the emergency room entrance when we reach Methodist. Take the truck and the afternoon. I don't care how much you spend, Sidney. Get a house, an apartment, a condo, whatever. If it is not furnished, go online and get what you would want if it were your place. I mean, it has to be ready; food, electricity, water service. Get a television, a big one, and call the cable company to come out and hook up the internet. Also, get everything an infant would need; bassinet, mattress, blankets. Treat it as though a friend of yours is having a baby shower. Pick up the stuff she would need for the first few months."

"I can't get all that done in one day."

"Get your friends to help. Make it worth their efforts, financially I mean. Call Rob and the girls you live with. It has to be done today; within the next ten hours. What you are not able to get done in that time, set appointments. Get the ball rolling."

"Mason, you haven't told me why I'm doing this. Why does it have to be done so soon?"

Mason rubbed his forehead. "Please. It has to be done this way. Trust me. Yes, it's for Aiden. I'd prefer not to discuss all the 'whys' associated with it. It has nothing to do with our current problem. Do you understand the danger we are in?"

"No."

"Well, that is good for you. Doctor Rasmus explained to both of us what happened when he opened the portal that allowed Adramelech and his 'angels' into Nikon. That is what is going to happen to Earth, only worse. We have to stop it before it does. My family has been attacked, but that is the tip of the iceberg. All of humanity is in danger and that includes your pretty little tail."

She smiled. "You think it's pretty?"

***

Mason walked into the ER waiting room and was greeted immediately by Rachel. She met him halfway across the floor.

They hugged and she stepped back, looking at him. "Dad? What's happened? You... You look amazing."

Valerie approached and Mason put an arm around her. She reached up and rubbed his face gently. "What is this? A beard? Have you colored your hair?"

"Dad?" McKayla approached. "You've lost weight."

Mason ushered them back toward the section of chairs they previously occupied. Clint and Steven did not get up.

Clint extended his hand offering a shake. Steven put his right fist out, waiting for his father to do the same."

They all sat. Mason taking the chair next to Valerie. "How is Conrad?" he asked scooting up to the edge of the seat.

Rachel said, "He's in surgery. He suffered broken bones and internal injuries. We're waiting for the surgeon to come out and give us an update."

"Mason. What is going on?" Valerie asked. You've been MIA since Saturday. You return looking like a different man. And these creatures. I'm scared, Mason. I've been attacked in our home and now, another attack in Rachel's apartment. The monster that hit Conrad said your name. We each heard it clearly, me, Rachel and McKayla."

Mason raised his hands up a little. "Let's keep our voices down. Give me a few moments and I'll do my best to explain."

They fell silent, each one giving him their full attention.

"What I am about to tell you is going to sound, well, unbelievable. Hear me out though. Everything I say is completely real."

"Given what I have seen with my own eyes…" Valerie said, then her voice trailed off. "Does this have anything to do with the night terrors you told me about? You said it happened when you were a kid."

Mason nodded. "Yes. That's part of it."

"What was that thing that attacked us?" McKayla asked.

Mason could see they were not just going to let him lay it out. "It was a demon. It came from another reality. A world that is ruled, I think, by a demonic angel known as Adramelech."

Clint sat up and chuckled. "Okay. You've already lost me. How did something like that get in Rachel's apartment?"

Mason turned to Valerie. "You told me you hit your head and passed out during the first attack. Was that creature the same as the one this morning?"

She shook her head. "The one that came into our room was bigger. It moved slowly, like a snake. The one that came into Rachel's apartment was agile and compact. But they were both incredibly strong."

"So, it attacked Conrad, then ran away?"

"Oh, I didn't tell you."

McKayla interjected, "Mom, bolts out of the bedroom like a cheetah. She runs over to the sliding glass doors that lead to the deck and opens the blinds. Sunlight comes shining through and the thing explodes. There was nothing left but guts, goo, and blood everywhere."

"You guys need to let him talk," Steven spoke up for the first time. "He said he was going to explain and we aren't letting him."

They fell silent again and Mason took a deep breath. "I was not aware of any reaction they may have to sunlight. That is something I need to think about. It may be helpful." He made a mental note to ask Valerie what caused her to think that course of action would work.

"What you have witnessed, you girls anyway, is the product of events that have taken place in my life since I was a toddler." Mason gave them snapshot versions of events that took place from when he was a baby to when he was in the third grade. He told them about the portal and how he came to discover what he could do. He watched their facial expressions as he spoke and felt certain that Valerie and the girls were not simply dismissing him as nuts. The boys were another story. Steven looked skeptical, Clint was clearly incredulous. He began to consider that he might have to summon the Door and take them through one at a time to prove himself.

Revealing this talent was not something he ever considered. First, until Sidney, he never attempted it with a person or even a pet. Second, it served no practical purpose, and third, he thought it to be an unwarranted risk. He caught the attention of a malevolent force by traveling through the Door. He never wanted those same forces to see his children and focus their attention on the ones he loved. He did not mention the stash of money in the storage unit.

"I left the house on Saturday. I got a small room in Dallas. I was planning on spending the weekend, you know, wait till things cooled down. That night, one of the creatures attacked me in the room. I thought I was dead. It had me by the throat. There was no way I could have defended myself. Out of complete panic, I opened the Door, thinking somehow, I might be able to escape. Doing that had another, unexpected effect. The creature attacking me was sucked through the opening and it immediately shut behind him. I fell to the floor gasping for breath, thankful for my life."

Steven laughed. "You almost bought the farm in a motel room in Dallas? Man, that would have sucked."

"Thanks for the sentiment."

"Why didn't you call me?" Valerie asked. "Why didn't you just come home?"

"And tell you what? You don't believe me when I tell you I cannot be alone, especially at night. If I told you, any of you, what I am telling you now, you wouldn't believe me. Even now, Clint isn't buying any of this."

Clint smiled. Somehow, he seemed to find it all a bit humorous. "No disrespect. You can easily make me a believer, Dad."

Mason nodded. "I can summon the Door, whenever I want. But you can't see it. None of you can. If I pass through it and return, you won't see that either."

"Wow. That is convenient."

"I'm not going to knowingly put you in danger, son. I would rather you don't believe me. I'd rather you think I'm loony toons and know that you are safe."

"How can you say we are safe?" Valerie asked.

"Well, obviously, things have changed. These creatures can track me. I don't know how, but I know they can find me. I've been moving around for the past few days. I think they figured out I have a wife and family and have refocused on you guys in order to get to me."

Valerie placed her hand on his arm. "I was wrong not to believe you, Mason. I see that now. These monsters, they come in your dreams?"

Mason regarded her, a bit stunned. "I tried to tell you. What's changed? Why would you suddenly believe me?"

She opened her hands, palms up, exposing minor rope burns. "I was struggling against that thing in a very bad and vivid dream. I was injured in the dream and I am injured in the same way, look. I have marks on my body form the attack the other night. I cannot dismiss these things. I do not understand what is happening, but something is very wrong. If you believe we are in danger, I believe you."

She turned her attention to Clint. "You don't believe

your father. Go in there and tell Conrad you think it's all a coincidence."

Clint responded, then Rachel made some comments. McKayla chimed in and Steven actually joined the conversation. Mason tuned it all out. The whole thing was beginning to spin out of control and instead of being fearful, he was getting angry. He looked up at the clock on the wall. He'd been in this reality for over an hour. Mason wanted to talk to Doctor Rasmus. There had to be a way he could take the fight to Adramelech. When he was attacked his reaction was to run; to get away and keep running. His family was attacked. He clenched his fists and tensed his jaw.

Valerie placed a gentle hand on his arm. "Mason?"

He looked at her.

"The boys and I are going home. Rachel is staying. McKayla is going to get her something to eat. We've decided it is best to stay together until this situation is resolved. You seem to be the focal point. What do you want to do?"

Mason sighed. "First, I am sorry for hitting you. It was wrong. I have no excuse and I deeply regret my actions and my words."

She put up a hand. "Don't. I'm past it. I mean, I appreciate you saying that but it seems like it happened years ago. This thing we are facing is a life-threatening situation and far more important. Perhaps one day, we can talk about it, but not now."

"Okay. I have to go see someone. I have several fires going at once. My plan for dealing with these creatures has changed. It angers me that they would try to get to me through you and the kids."

"You need help, Mason. You cannot do this alone."

He nodded. "I have help. Clint."

Clinton was talking to Steven. He stopped and looked up. "Yes."

"May I speak to you?" Mason got up from his seat. He glanced at Valerie. "We'll be right back."

Mason headed out of the waiting room and paused long enough for Clint to catch up with him.

"What's up?"

He continued down the corridor. "I am not going to be able to stay here with everyone and successfully handle what we are dealing with."

"I'm still unclear what we are dealing with."

Mason nodded and stopped at the elevator bank, pressing the call button. "I know you are. That's why I wanted to talk to you, privately."

The elevator tone sounded indicating an available car, going up. An elderly couple exited and a young woman with a baby in a stroller got on as they entered. Mason allowed her to select a floor. She chose the fourth floor and Mason hit the button for the fifth floor. Clint watched his father but took his lead and remained quiet as the elevator lifted them up the shaft. They reached the fourth floor. The woman slowly exited, pushing the stroller, and the door closed.

Mason felt the car engage and begin to rise to the next floor. In a swift movement, he turned facing his son and embraced him.

Clint perhaps out of reflex, hugged his father in return, thinking the entire course of events was getting stranger by the moment. He was taken by surprise at his father's strength. The larger man wasn't just giving him a hug, he grabbed hold of the back of his shirt, gripping him like he was about to throw him to the floor. That did not happen. His father picked him off the floor and pushed him back against the wall. Only, there was no wall. There was no elevator. His father set him down and released him. Clint crouched and turned instantly like he was under attack.

"Take it easy, son. Everything is okay."

The first thing that caught his attention was the gigantic fireplace. There was a fire blazing, actually roaring. The massive logs were popping and spitting sparks. The room they were in reminded Clint of an old Roman cathedral with a lot less color. "What is going on? We were in the elevator!"

"I need you to be crystal clear on what is happening, son. Our family needs me, and I need you. I told you I have the ability to move into different realities. The house you are in right now is in one of those realities. I realized that merely telling you was not enough to convince you. Your mother and sisters have witnessed something that has shaken their concept of what is normal and has caused them to consider that what I am telling them may have merit. You and your brother have not had that luxury. I am confident Steven will follow your lead. So, I only need to convince you."

That is when Sid entered the room. "Mason!" He bellowed, a big grin on his face. "Man, I missed you."

Mason laughed. "I know. It's been a long time. How is your Mom?"

Sid waved him off. He watched the young stranger darted behind Mason. "Is this our guest? The one you spoke of?" He put a beefy hand on his face as if trying to speak to Mason secretly. "That's not a 'she'."

"Umm, no, a bit of a change. Please excuse me. Some

things have occurred and I had to move with the punches, so to speak."

Sid nodded. "I am familiar with that one. Well, introduce me."

Mason reached back and grabbed Clinton by the elbow. "Stop that. You are not in danger. Sid, this is my oldest son, Clint. Clinton, meet Sid."

Sid moved closer and bowed. "Very happy to have you in my home."

Clint moved slowly to Mason's side. "He's a giant."

Mason nodded. "He's also my friend. Come with me." Mason led the way to the large front door and pushed it open.

Clint approached with an expression of awe on his face. Outside he witnessed a snowstorm the likes of which he never experienced. Moments earlier he was seated with his brother and sisters in the emergency room of a hospital in the Dallas/Ft. Worth area in the state of Texas. Now he stood here, the cold wind hitting him in the face, next to a giant man that should not exist, looking out at a blizzard that would rival anything the south pole might suffer. It was simply too much. His legs buckled and down he went.

Sid and Mason exchanged a glance. Sid shrugged, reached out and closed the door. "It is kind of nasty out today."

Mason laughed. "That's not it. He has never moved from here to there like I do. He did not believe me when I told him I could do it. I had to show him." Mason knelt next to his son. "My family was attacked, Sid. I need to leave someone in charge that I have some confidence in while I do what I have to do."

"You want me to throw some water on him?"

Mason shook his head. "He'll come around in a few minutes. When he does, I'm taking him back. Is your Mom aware I am coming with a guest?"

Sid nodded. "I just spoke with her. That's where I was when you popped back in. She's adding a few things to your room."

"Thank you."

Mason considered the situation and thought the return trip might work out better with Clint being unconscious. "Sid, can you spare an old blanket?"

"Yes. I can."

A moment later the big man returned with a tattered blanket that would have worked nicely as a leather tarp for an 18-wheeler on Earth. Just what Mason needed. He wrapped Clint in the blanket then wrapped himself. They looked like twin caterpillars in a cocoon. Mason peeked out of the top. "Okay. If things don't get messy, I'll be back with my guest."

Sid waved and this time chose not to cover his eyes.

Mason cleared his mind and called for the Door. He felt the floor fall away and he landed in the elevator. The blanket worked fairly well, absorbing most of the blow as he and Clint slammed against the back wall of the elevator. Mason began to unravel the protective covering when Clint opened his eyes.

"Where are we?" he asked, still dazed. "What's going on?"

"Help me get this blanket off."

The elevator chimed and the doors slid open on the fifth floor. A nurse started to enter the car, saw the two of them unraveling from the blanket and thought better of it. The doors closed and Mason reached out to press the first-floor button. The two men freed themselves of the blanket and Mason pushed it up against the wall. Before the door of the elevator could open on the first floor he opened his own personal Door to other worlds and the blanket was sucked through to return from whence it came.

On their way to the ER waiting room, Clint touched his father on the arm and stopped walking. "What just happened?"

Mason looked at his son. Running from world to world was a way of life for Mason. He wondered how Clint would process what he witnessed. Sidney approached the discovery of alternate realities in a far different manner. He used a different approach with her. He supposed everyone was going to handle this knowledge in their own unique way. It was a difficult thing to be raised in one culture only to move to another; like growing up in Korea, immigrating to Canada. How much harder must it be to experience a new world? He thought perhaps, Clint's mind may decide to tell him it was a dream; one that he may soon forget.

"I am relying on you to keep our family as safe as you can, Clint. Sid and the world of ice and snow is very real. More importantly, there is a world of demons and monsters that are on a mission to capture me. They will stop at nothing to get to me. They will put an end to everything on this planet to accomplish their goal. If they are successful in taking me, I believe the end result for Earth will be the same. Stay at the house with your mother and your brother and sisters. Can you do that for me?"

He nodded. "Okay. I'm supposed to pick up my kids this evening though."

"Can you call their mother and make other arrangements?"

"Yes. I can only do that for a few days. How long do we have?"

"I'm working as fast as I can. I will stay in touch with you. In the event, you need to talk to me and you are not able to reach me, leave a message and make the best decision you can."

Valerie was preparing to go. She looked up as Mason and Clint returned. Mason motioned for her to join him. They moved just a little way from the group. "Clint is coming with you."

"Where are you going, Mason?"

"I will be back as soon as I can. When you guys go to bed, it is best you are all in the same room. One of you should be awake at all times. It is my experience the attacks come when I am sleeping alone. You will be better protected if you are together."

She nodded. "You didn't answer me though. I'm worried about you."

"It's better this way Valerie. When it's over. You and I will have a long conversation."

She looked up at him, warmth and worry in her eyes. She touched his face. "You do look good. I think we need to do more than have a conversation."

Chapter 17

Mason entered the men's room just around the corner from the hospital waiting room. It was a small private restroom with a lock on the handle. He was about to try something new. He always returned to the same point where he exited the Earth; just as he had with Clint in the elevator. He did not think about it. It just happened that way. What would happen if he tried to return to a different spot? If he concentrated, could he return to Earth in the bedroom of his home, or in the motel room? He determined to give this a try.

He closed his eyes and thought about Aiden. He breathed deeply and focused his mind, placing himself in her magnificent bedroom. He imagined her room, looking from left to right, placing each item, giving thought texture and color. He summoned the Door and stepped forward without opening his eyes. One step, then two, there it was, the numbing sensation in his legs. Once his feet lined up on what felt solid he opened his eyes. He found himself in the open area; nothing but light, no floor, no ceiling, no walls. Sensation in his legs slowly returned and he could feel the pulse of the place. Calm filled his thoughts as he breathed purposely, in and out.

The last time he was in this area, between here and there, he thought of the Mercer lab and stepped forward. This time he moved in a circular motion, surveying the room of light. In the distance was a disturbance. He squinted his eyes. There was something there. It was small, perhaps the size of a grain of sand on the beach. Mason reached out and marveled as his hand passed beyond the spot. He pulled it in and the tiny dot enlarged. It was not a grain of sand. As it came closer it took on form and shape. It appeared as a circular window of color and when he looked closely it clarified. It formed a portrait, then two, then it became a mural; hundreds of small pictures within one large picture. Some were joined together, some stood apart, but they were obviously images of places. Four images projected forward, standing out from among the others. Mason studied these four and realized he was looking at a snapshot of his motel room in Dallas, Aiden's bedroom, Mercer laboratory, and the room with the fireplace in Sid's house. Mason straightened. He entered three of these four by passing through the Door. Magdon transported him to and from Aiden's room. How was this option available? He scanned the mural watching as the tiny pictures multiplied. Hundreds grew into thousands, and it continued to expand. The mural extended out to his left and right. Equally, it stretched up and down. Mason could no longer see the end of it.

He wondered how he never experienced this aspect of the Door. His thoughts traveled back when he was a child. For years he was unaware that the tall sliver of light was actually a Door to other realities. How many wonders were yet to be discovered? He lifted his eyes, trying to see the top of the mural and it moved. Or was he moving? He could not tell. He allowed the mural to rush past his vision. He tried to slow it down. He reached out, but his hands found no purchase, they passed through the pictures as though they had no substance. They appeared to be two dimensional without depth. He could not get the mural to come to a complete stop nor was he able to see the edge. He bowed his head and looked back down.

He thought about Aiden's room and the mural changed directions, a blur as it zipped by, bringing him back to that picture. The snapshot of her room extended out from the mural a little and Mason instinctively reached out and touched it with his finger. Instantly, the massive mural folded in on itself, leaving only a two-inch by two-inch picture of Aiden's room floating before him. He took a step back and the picture began to expand. As it filled the space in front of him other features in the room became visible. The items in the picture enlarged and took on depth until they were life size. Within seconds the undefined room of light changed as the picture surrounded him. He looked down and realized he was standing on the hardwood floor of Aiden's room. To his right stood her elegant bed. To his left the bathroom door was closed, light peeking out from the bottom. The knob turned, the door opened and Aiden stepped out, looking radiant. She wore a small black skirt and a matching lace blouse. Mason could see the small bump of her belly.

She stopped, looking up at him in wonder. Slowly she smiled and ran to him, embracing him, the two of them falling back on the bed. She kissed him, then pulled back. "I missed you so much. This is a very nice surprise."

Mason marveled at what occurred. He could feel the

bed under him, and the small woman on top of him. He could hear her voice, smell her perfumed hair, and he began to laugh.

"What's funny?"

He sat up and she joined him. "I don't know how to explain what just happened." He turned to her. "Aiden, I've never traveled to your room through my Door."

She looked at him in confusion. "I thought Magdon brought you here. He didn't?"

He shook his head. "I was in a hospital, on my own world. I came here through the Door! Aiden, I think I can travel anywhere I want through the Door. I can choose my destination."

She smiled. "I am so happy for you, dear. Have you told Doctor Rasmus? I know he would be excited to know."

Mason stood, shaking his head. "No. I haven't spoken to him. Shoot, it's new to me. I need some time to think about it, what just happened and what I saw." He turned back to her. "How are you doing? How is the baby?"

She placed a hand on her stomach and smiled. "We are doing very well. I had some discomfort for a while, some nausea, but the past few weeks have been wonderful. I wish you and I were together." She stood facing him, the two of them inches apart.

He took her shoulders in his hands. "Doctor Rasmus is your pediatrician. You need to be here. I have someone securing a place for you. It will have everything you need."

"You mean a place for us. Mason, you cannot bring me to a foreign land and abandon me with a child to raise."

"No, of course not. I would not do that. We will find

a way through this together. I would never abandon you. Where did you get such an idea?"

"The easy way you just said, 'I have someone securing a place for you'."

"Okay. Point taken. Are you going out?"

She moved past him, deliberately brushing her body against his as she did. "Yes, love. I am going to do some window shopping and may buy something for the baby. When I travel with you, how should I pack?"

"You will only be able to take whatever you can fit in something like a backpack."

She pivoted and looked back at him, mouth open, hands on hips.

He shrugged. "Until I figure out another way, you have to travel light. I could come back and get some things for you. But that is why I'm supplying everything you need on the other side."

"You cannot possibly know everything I might need, or want."

"Well, I can promise to take you shopping for whatever you want."

"What is it like Mason? Your world?"

"You've been there."

"Really. A few minutes in a motel room and I am supposed to know everything about Earth."

"You have been working alongside Doctor Rasmus your whole life. Surely he has told you about Earth."

"I've seen it through the viewer and sure, the Doctor has told me many things. But it's not the real thing."

"I think you will find that it is not so different from Nikon. You have far greater technological aspects of your society. I have a feeling that our political structure is similar. But Earth is a lot less tidy than it is here."

She gave him a questioning look.

"You will be fine. I'll see to that. Come on. I'll spend the day with you and we need to see the Doctor. I have some questions for him before I head back."

They spent the day in the city doing exactly what Aiden mentioned; window shopping, purchasing small items that tickled her fancy and eating at one of Mason's favorite restaurants. She placed a call to Doctor Rasmus' office. He wasn't in so she left a message. When he returned the call, they were in transport. She informed the Doctor of their destination. "We are headed to the public dock on Percival Bay. Okay, great Doctor. We'll see you there."

Percival Bay turned out to be a very large and highly populated park bordered by an ocean of blue-green water. Aiden led the way, weaving in and out, dodging men and women, young and old. Everyone at the park appeared not to have a worry in the world. Several groups of people were busy playing something similar to volleyball, couples and families camped in various spots eating lunch, reading, and socializing. Children ran, playing games and chasing their pets. They reached the dock. Mason was impressed by its size and scope. The wood used to construct the deck was burgundy. It possessed a deep, very rich appearance and it stretched as far as he could see. Benches and tables were constructed of the same wood and placed throughout giving people plenty of space to set up camp or simply relax and enjoy the warmth of the day.

Aiden walked slowly with her arm locked under Mason's. She led with purpose and came to their destination at a small pavilion which seated approximately twenty. Doctor Rasmus was seated under the pavilion. He wore tennis shoes, shorts, a loose-fitting button-up shirt, and a hat that reminded Mason of something Gilligan would have worn from the television show 'Gilligan's Island'. He was reading a book that could have engulfed five volumes of the Encyclopedia Britannica. He looked up, simultaneously setting the big book down, and grinned broadly at his favorite people in the cosmos. "When is the wedding?"

Mason helped Aiden into her seat, though she needed no help, then he sat beside her. He heard a soft buzzing sound like one hundred bumble-bees causing him to look up. A drone floated above their heads. "What can I get for you, Doctor?" the drone asked.

"Ahh. Yes, sir. Bring us some sweet water and a basket of fruit."

"Right away." The drone zipped away.

"Mason." The Doctor continued. "When is your Sidney coming to see me? I have a spike especially for her."

"I'll bring her as soon as time permits. She is currently running errands for me."

"Very good. What new adventures have you to share?"

Mason glanced at Aiden. She wore a silly grin on her face and glossed over, dreamy eyes. "Well, there have been some developments. Perhaps this is not the proper venue."

"I'm a big girl." She purred. "Last time I checked, I'm a bit older than you."

Mason smirked. "That is debatable."

Rasmus interjected, "Developments? Is there some trouble?"

"Doctor, you've seen the world Adramelech comes from?"

"I have. It is extremely dark. I mean literally. It is a bit of a mystery."

"How do you mean?"

"It's like there is no sunlight. For example, with your world and most others, I have to make minor adjustments to the viewer to filter the light out. Not so with Halja. That is what they call it. With Halja, I have to adjust the viewer the opposite way as there is no ambient light. As a result, I know very little about their society."

"Okay. For my purpose here, can you locate this Halja? Do you think you could view Adramelech?"

"I can locate Halja. Finding Adramelech is another matter. If you recall, when we first met, I informed you that you banished Adramelech. When he attacked you in the motel room and you opened the portal, Adramelech was pulled into the portal and I do not know where he landed."

Mason shrugged and watched as the drone brought back the order. It dipped to the table, placing the items gently. It thanked the Doctor and buzzed away.

"I assume he returned to his own reality."

"Yet, when I search, I cannot locate him. I have periodically looked in on his world and I see no activity. Of course, as I said, it is a difficult reality to view. May I ask, to what end? What is your purpose for this inquiry?"

Mason waved the question away. "We can come back to that. I have been thinking about another issue."

"Go on."

"Visiting a reality or world more than once is a new experience for me. Now that I have done it... Well, I am thinking about Sid's world. When I return, it is always two minutes later. No matter how long I stay away, I know I will return in two minutes."

Rasmus nodded, appearing to be deep in thought. "Yes. Continue."

"When I return to my own reality, no time has expired. It is always the same."

"You are wondering why that rule does not apply to Nikon."

Mason pointed a finger at him. "Exactly. I'm gone for a few hours and weeks are flying by over here."

Rasmus cleared his throat. "Honestly, I do not have an exact scientific answer for you."

"But, you have a theory."

"I believe that the same rule applies to this world. You have yet to experience the limit of the time difference. Have you considered that it may be a year, for example?"

"Why would it be so long?"

"Keep in mind that I have no data to back this assumption. Imagine your world as the center of all things. You travel away from that center a little way, Sid's world, and the time difference is two minutes. A bit further, and perhaps it is five minutes."

"I find it very hard to believe that Earth is the center of all things, Doc."

The man shook his head and took a bite of a crisp apple. "Yes, I stand corrected, not Earth. You. The fact that your home reality is Earth, is merely an aspect of the equation."

Mason looked at Aiden who was still smiling at him. "You don't believe that either, do you, Doc?"

"It's the best theory I have been able to come up with so far. I'm working on the math."

"Really?"

"The more I understand what it is you do, Mason. The better equipped I am to assist you."

Mason felt certain the Doctor meant to say, 'The better equipped I am to replicate your methods.'

Aiden turned to the Doctor. "Mason has something else to tell you."

The Doctor glanced at her then back to Mason.

"I opened the Door from my own reality and stepped through into Aiden's home."

The Doctor stopped chewing, his mouth hung open. "You. You. It wasn't just a random drop point?"

Mason shook his head. "No. I think I can exit the portal, anywhere I choose, without having ever having been to where I want to go. I was in a hospital restroom on Earth before I came here. The portal should return me to the same spot at exactly the same time. I am going to try to return to a different location, my own home on Earth."

The Doctor's eyes widened. "This is an amazing development. I can't believe we have been sitting here chatting about nonsense. Why didn't you lead with this information? Mason, Aiden, this is big news!"

Mason sat up. "In a way, I did lead with it. I want you to show me Halja, through your viewer."

Aiden snapped out of her dreamy state of mind. "Mason! No!"

He stiffened. "I'm done running. That bastard brought the fight to my family. I want to mess with his world. I mean his personal world."

The Doctor was shaking his head. "I strongly suggest that you abandon this line of thinking. It is folly. I have seen what Adramelech and his treacherous people can do. You may only succeed in opening a portal they can use to access your world."

"I'm not going to begin the assault on my world. Besides, Doctor, no disrespect, it isn't your business."

"My viewer is my business."

Mason stood. "That's fine. You're are under no obligation Doc. In time, I will find Adramelech on my own. But you may want to consider your position."

Aiden stood as well. She did not look well. She placed her hand on Mason's chest.

Mason brushed her aside but held tight to her left hand. "I can come and go without involving Mercer laboratory, Doc. I don't want to do it that way, but I will. You can assist me, and I'll return the favor. Or we can part ways."

"Now, let's not be so hasty. I'm very concerned with you going to Halja. You are unique in all the cosmos Mason. It is only natural that I would not want to jeopardize you or your abilities." He rubbed his face in distress and mumbled.

Mason thought he was saying 'why, why, why'.

Aiden began to cry.

Mason no longer wanted to be here. He turned and led her from the pavilion. About a hundred feet away, he stopped. "Aiden. Look at me."

She looked up and he wiped her tears. "What? Are you going to try to convince me that everything will be okay? You can go to Halja and destroy a world most likely populated by fallen angels before your world or mine existed?"

"I cannot stand by and do nothing while creatures from

that world infiltrate my world. I have to do something. They have attacked my family. One young man who is close to my daughter is in the hospital. He barely made it out alive. They won't stop, Aiden. They will keep coming, and keep coming until they succeed in killing those close to me. In the end, it is me they want. I realize you are scared but if I am going to face an impossible enemy, I prefer to face him on my feet, and on my terms."

Aiden breathed deep, getting herself together. "I didn't know your family was under attack. You didn't tell me." She paused, then nodded her head slightly. "I understand. It is part of the reason why I love you. You are brave."

"I don't know about being brave, but I do love you too. I don't want to see you come to any harm. If these monsters knew that I had a relationship with you Aiden, they would certainly try to get to you. You should know that I would fight as fiercely for you. My hope is that I can put a stop to this madness before it ever reaches your door."

"You will not face this alone." She grabbed his hands. "I am with you."

"Right now, I need the Doctor, your father, to show me Halja through his viewer. If I can see it, form a picture of it in my mind, I will have a better chance of transporting there, hopefully undetected. I don't want to go in like an attacking army. I want to sneak in, like an assassin. Go talk to him Aiden. Convince him. Tell him I will not attract attention to myself. I will get in and out as quickly as possible. Right now, I am going back to Earth. I will return to you soon."

"How soon?"

"Give me six, perhaps eight weeks." He gathered her into his arms and held her for a moment. They kissed and the Door pierced the day. His eyes stayed on her but his thoughts formed a picture of the living room in his house. The last time he was there he had a nasty fight with Valerie, a lifetime ago.

He stepped back through the Door and Aiden snapped out of view. Perhaps because his destination was his home reality, he did not experience the room of light with the mural. When he planted his second foot he found himself in the place he knew better than any other, his home. The lights were off. The only sound was the air pump in his saltwater fish tank standing in the entry corridor. No one was home which made sense. They were still at the hospital, but they would be home soon. Mason walked over to the tank and fed the fish. He went into the kitchen, opened the refrigerator, and made a turkey and cheese sandwich. His cell buzzed and he pulled it from his pocket.

"What's up, sunshine?" he asked.

"You up, white boy."

Chapter 13

Not wanting Sidney to show up at his house the same time Valerie and the kids pulled up, Mason walked six or seven blocks to the corner store. He didn't have to wait very long. Sidney picked him up and the two of them headed to a house in south Dallas. She was to meet a realtor there. Rob set up the meeting. The realtor was his kid sister, Frankie. She recently received her license and was eager to make a sale.

Homes in the neighborhood were built in the '40s and '50s. The one they were interested in was a three bedroom, two-bath, on a corner lot. It sat on half an acre with a detached garage in the back. There was an additional room above the garage. Mason liked the place. It had some modern amenities added. The bath off the master bedroom was definitely modern. The house came furnished and with all the appliances. He wondered how well Aiden would adjust to a house like this. The wind shower in her bathroom was incredible and there was nothing like it on Earth.

"What do you think?" Frankie asked.

Sidney looked questioningly at Mason.

"It's going to have to do. We don't have much time."

Sidney said, "You can always look for something else

later. Keep this place as a rental. I like it though. You can rent it to me."

Mason nodded and regarded Frankie. She was very young and small. He wondered how Rob could be so big and Frankie so little. Maybe they have different parents. "Good point." he replied, then to Frankie, "You brought the paperwork with you?"

"Yes. Sure. Everything is in my car." She was smiling and looked very perky. "We will need to order an appraisal. My agency has a loan officer unless you wish to use your own."

Mason shook his head. "No. I'm not doing all that. Call the owner and inform them I will buy the place, cash."

Frankie almost laughed. "I haven't even told you the asking price."

"Whatever it is, Frankie, I'm fine with it. Make sure you get a healthy commission. Sidney will transfer the funds. I need you to handle the title transfer and put the place in Sidney's name."

Sidney looked at him in surprise. "What? Really?"

"I don't think it's wise to put it in my name. You're right. This will be temporary. In a few weeks, perhaps a month I'll look for another place. Then this will be yours, free and clear. You can live here; rent it or sell it, whatever you want."

"I don't know what to say."

"You can thank me later." He winked at her. "Right now, I need you to get the other things I mentioned."

"I've got my girlfriends working on that right now."

"Good. You and I are about to embark on our little trip. I'm going to be asking much more of you in the days to come. So, I intend to make it worth your time."

She smiled at that.

244

"Can you have Rob or your friends come to pick you up? I need the truck."

Sidney turned to Frankie. "Could you excuse us for a moment?"

"Oh, sure. I'll go get what I need from my car."

When they were alone Sidney turned back to Mason, slowly moved up close to him. "You can't buy me a house and go running out the door. Where are you off to?"

"I'm on the clock, Sidney. Every hour I spend here is two weeks for Aiden over there." "You can hop around the universe and pop back here without losing a second." She traced the tip of her finger from his Adam's apple to his chest. You think you could make a little time for me?"

Mason snapped his fingers. "Hey, that reminds me. I spoke to Doctor Rasmus. He has the enhancement spike he promised you. We could go get you fixed up."

She smiled. "We return here, and won't have lost a minute."

Mason reached his arms around her and pulled her close. "That's scary. You're catching on."

She reached low and grabbed hold of his crotch. "Just what are you trying to say, wise guy?"

"Do you have any of the cash on you from the storage?"

"No, it's locked in the truck."

The room fell away and they paused in the expanse of light. Mason shifted to his left, never loosening his hold from around her. He stepped back, lifted her off her feet and stepped again. The light faded to darkness and they emerged in the Detection Office of Mercer laboratory. The room was empty. Monitors were tracking the activity in hundreds of locations throughout the laboratory.

"The guard must be on rounds or maybe he's in the john. Come on."

She followed him out the door and down a long corridor. They passed a few workers and got some long curious looks, but no one tried to engage them. They turned down several hallways and stopped outside the door of Mason's choosing. He didn't bother knocking and was pleased to find the Doctor's office unoccupied.

He led her inside and locked the door. Talking was not required. They were out of their clothes in moments. His encounters with Sidney were never like what he experienced with Aiden. It was primal. Sidney took from him what she wanted and he did the same. It was exhilarating and always ended with them in a heap, spent, sweating, working to catch their breath.

They went at it for fifteen minutes. Now they lay on the floor, naked, on their backs, panting. Sidney laughed and rolled over to him. He met her halfway and they shared a long, passionate kiss. She pulled back and said, "I can go another round."

"Okay." He breathed out.

The knob shook. From out in the hall they heard, "I don't recall locking this. Where is my key? Oh, here it is."

Mason gathered her in his arms. "Hold on tight. This may hurt."

The Door deposited them in Mason's motel room. They landed on the hard floor with a thud and rolled several feet.

"Oh, god!" Sidney complained. "That fucking sucks." She got off the floor and began looking for her clothes. She had a visible limp and she was nursing the small of her back.

Mason banged his right knee and elbow. He made a mental note, *try to pad reentry points whenever possible.*

"Where are my clothes?" she asked.

Mason got up and looked around. "I think they may be in the living room of that house. Rob's sister is going to walk back in and find us gone, and our clothing scattered around the living room."

"How did we end up here?"

"When I heard someone coming into that office, I thought, 'where can we go?' and the motel room popped into my head. I think I can direct my destination through the Door with just my thoughts if I've already been to the place I want to go. You know, if I can imagine it, I can travel to that spot. But our clothes started the journey from the living room of that house and since we weren't wearing them, well, here we are. You look awesome by the way."

She laughed. "This isn't cool."

"Relax. I've got clothes here."

"Oh, great. I can rock one of your shirts, but your pants are going to be way too big. You got another truck around here? What about my cell phone?"

"Oh. You're right. Well, I didn't want to return and have Rob's sister walk in on us."

"This is messed up Mason. The keys to the truck are in my pants. If anyone opens the truck, they will find the money. My handbag is in there. What are you smiling about? Are you getting an erection?"

Mason summoned the Door and stepped through, exiting the motel room and entering the living room of the house in south Dallas. He was correct, their clothes were deposited on the floor. Fortunately, they were in a little pile and not scattered about the room. He scooped them up and disappeared before Frankie made it back up the walkway.

Sidney saw him disappear and reappear in the motel room. It was not the same as before. He was gone for about ten seconds.

He tossed her clothes to her and began to pull on his pants. "Get your clothes on quickly. If Frankie reaches the front door before we return she'll wonder where we went. I'll take us back to see the Doctor then we can jump back to the house."

Mason got his shoes on and slipped his arms through his shirt sleeves. He did not bother with the buttons. He picked up Sidney's bra and shirt. She managed to get her panties and pants on. She was putting her feet in her shoes when he grabbed hold of her and picked her up.

"Wait! I'm not done!"

They wasted at least a minute in the motel room. Mason couldn't travel back in time, but he was getting the hang of moving from place to place through his Door. He a handful of locations in the Rolodex of his mind and it was getting easier to navigate those few. Thinking of where he wanted to go was as easy as saying it. The Door adapted well. It reminded him of a computer program learning the habits of its user. He just needed to remember the rules.

The Door deposited them in the office of Doctor Rasmus. The man was seated at his desk and looked up to see Mason holding a half-naked Sidney.

"Sorry to barge in on you like this Doctor. I was in a bit of a situation."

Rasmus cleared his throat. "I see. Miss Sidney. I am pleased to see you again."

She snatched her bra and shirt from Mason, turned her back and finished dressing. "This is embarrassing. I am so sorry Doctor."

"No need to apologize. Mason, we were having a rather serious discussion when you decided to leave us."

Mason nodded and buttoned his shirt. "Yes. That was like an hour ago for me. I remember it well. I've brought Sidney for her spike. You and I can revisit the subject of Adramelech and Halja later."

Rasmus got up and walked around his desk. "As you wish. Sidney, if you will accompany me? Mason, do you wish to join us?"

He shook his head. "You two go ahead. I'll make myself at home here on the sofa."

Sidney turned back around and ran her fingers through her hair. "Are you sure? There isn't anything you could do while we are gone?"

"No." Mason shook his head. "If I leave, even for an hour…"

Sidney held up her hands. "I know, I know. I'd be here for two weeks waiting for you to come back. Might not be a bad idea actually. Aiden and I could get acquainted."

The Doctor raised an eyebrow. "You know Aiden?"

"No, Doc. I'm still waiting for Mason to properly introduce us."

"That's not a problem. I can…"

"Doctor," Mason spoke up. "Tick, tock."

The Doctor dramatically cleared his throat. "Right, right. This way my dear."

Mason sat down and closed his eyes while he waited. The office was quiet. A smile crossed his face as he thought of what he and Sidney did moments earlier right here on the floor. He began to doze off when the office door opened and the Doctor reentered, followed by Sidney. Mason opened his eyes and looked up at them.

The Doctor rounded his desk and took his seat. Sidney stood quietly next to the sofa. She looked very different. Her face and hair was perfection. Her eyes were dazzling green. Her lips a deep ruby red. Her breasts were larger and her curves were curvier.

"*Wow!*" Mason thought as he stood. She exuded feminine sexuality. Her aura changed to something more animalistic. "How do you feel?"

She looked up at him and moved closer. She moved like a cat, slow with purpose. Her voice was a whisper. "I feel fine." She grabbed the front of his shirt and pulled him down. Her face slid past his and she extended her tongue over his ear. "I'm ready to go, Mason. Right now."

Mason glanced at the Doctor. "I need to get her back. Thank you, Doctor Rasmus."

The Doctor nodded. "I designed her spike to enhance her personality. You should know, that I had you in mind as well, Mr. Waters. It is my sincere desire to work with you. I hope you appreciate my efforts."

"Doctor Rasmus, You and I will work together."

Mason summoned the Door and grabbed hold of Sidney. In the next instant, they were on the floor the living room of the house in south Dallas. Mason landed on his left shoulder causing a distinct numbing sensation. *That's going to leave a bruise.* The problem was traveling with Sidney. Normally, he would simply step from one world to the next.

She was dragging him through the portal, causing him to fall whenever returning to her reality.

This time she bounced up and straightened her shirt, getting better at reentry. Mason got up slowly and turned as Frankie came through the front door, carrying a small briefcase.

"Here we are," Frankie said in her perky tone.

Mason put on a fake smile then looked at Sidney. She hadn't noticed Frankie's entrance. Her eyes locked on him. She was in a world of her own and Mason was her sole interest. She closed on him placing one hand on his crotch, rubbing it up and down, the other one his backside. She came up on her toes to lick his neck.

"Um. Frankie, perhaps you could excuse us," Mason said.

The realtor looked confused. She didn't know if she should stay or go. When she saw Sidney pulling her shirt over her head she decided that leaving would be a wise choice.

Mason didn't speak, nor did her protest. Sidney was in charge and he wasn't going to be able to deny her. She removed every article of her clothing. She looked amazing. Whatever the Doctor did, it was perfect. Her breasts were a full cup size larger and though she was already fit, she now sported a firm six-pack. Her thighs were equally muscular, the legs of an Olympic runner. With the exception of the short hair on her head, her entire body was smooth, glistening, brown skin and nothing more. She glowed, and there was something else. Mason could not identify it. She was casting a spell on him.

"I need to talk to the Doc about my spike," he said. "I want abs like yours."

She reached out, unbuttoned his pants and got down on her knees. Gently, she worked on him until he could no longer hold back. When his body finished convulsing she stood up and guided him to the leather recliner positioned next to the small stone fireplace. She pushed him back and straddled him. She bent down and kissed him. He could taste salt on her tongue. As she kissed him she reached down, taking hold of him, positioned him between her legs, eased herself down. His body responded to her as she pressed her nipples into his face. Mason was overwhelmed. She devoured him and he was helpless to resist her.

"Sidney," he said.

She traced her tongue over his lips, biting him gently. "Don't speak." Her body moved slowly up and down; riding him, begging his body for every ounce of fluid he could provide. "I know you like it."

Mason joined her, matching her thrusts. He did his best to keep up with her. He realized his own enhancements gave him the advantage of being able to wear down a much younger woman. That advantage was equalized. The Doctor's voice spoke in his head. "I designed her spike to enhance her personality"

She picked up the pace, bouncing on him like a jackrabbit. Mason wrapped his arms around her and pulled her down as hard as he could.

"That's it, baby. Let it go." She panted, working her hips, sweating.

His body tightened, the muscles in his arms and back flexed. If this were Aiden or Valerie, he would have done serious damage to their bodies. He held her in a death grip, holding her down, crushing her.

She bucked back, moaning, not from pain, from ecstasy.

Mason kept pace with her, this time. Doctor Rasmus programmed her spike for this very outcome. Mason knew it. His own spike continued its miracle work, healing his body, turning back the clock. This was day one for her. What would she be like in a week? A month?

Chapter 19

He told her he needed the truck and that hadn't changed. He pulled his pants up and straightened his clothing. Expecting her to do the same, he turned to find that she'd taken his place in the leather recliner. She didn't seem interested in getting dressed. She was caressing herself, getting ready for round three or four. Mason lost count.

"I've got to go, Sidney."

"Awww!" She pouted. "You're no fun."

"Doctor Rasmus may need to make some adjustments to your spike. I think it's turned up too high. You need to go out there and take care of business with Frankie. I think I see her sitting in her car. She probably doesn't know what to do."

"Man! All work and no play." She jumped out of the seat and crossed the living room, stomping her feet.

Mason found a pen and paper on the kitchen counter, likely left there by Frankie, and began writing. "I need the keys, please."

She snatched up her jeans, removed the keys and tossed them to him.

Mason stared at her. She really looked good. He felt something stirring deep inside. "Once you are done with

255

Frankie, get in touch with your friends. I want everything over here before the end of the day." He crossed the room and held out the paper. "Give this to Rob. I need the stuff on this list, today."

"Yes, sir," she said and saluted like she was in the Army. She took the sheet of paper, read what his scribble and gave him a questioning look.

"Something's been running through my mind; an idea."

"This might be hard to get."

"I'm counting on you Sidney; you and Rob."

"Put your clothes on so you can follow me to the truck. You need the cash. Give Rob what he needs for that. Have Frankie run you to the bank. Heck, ask if she can run you to a car lot and buy yourself a car."

"I want a truck."

"Whatever you like. I'll call you in few hours. Come on. Let's get after it.

***

He drove back to his house, found Valerie's car in the garage and Clint's SUV parked in the drive. With the exception of Rachel, they were all in the kitchen, sitting on stools at the counter or rummaging through the refrigerator.

"What's the word on Conrad?" he asked as he came in.

Valerie got up and met him with a hug. "He's out of surgery. They put him in a room. They haven't said how long they will hold him there. Rachel is with him though."

Mason nodded. "When she needs a break one of you should relieve her and stay with him. No one connected with this thing should be left alone at night. Since I am sure

Conrad will be sleeping while he is in recovery, someone has to stay with him while he sleeps."

Steven spoke up. "I'll go back up there later. Rachel called his folks but they live in California. I don't know how long it will be till they arrive. Anyway, I was at the Rec when Clint picked me up. I need to go back to my place to get a few things if I am going to be staying over here for the next few days."

"Thanks, son."

McKayla said, "Dad, you look exhausted."

Mason sighed and rubbed the thick beard on his face. "I want to shave this off and take a shower. Then I need to rest a bit. I can't remember the last time I slept." He glanced at Valerie. "You mind sitting with me for a few hours?"

She smiled genuinely, her eyes sparkled. "I'd like that very much."

Mason looked at each of them. "I cannot stress to you how important this is. When you sleep, do not sleep alone."

Clint was drinking something, perhaps a soda. He took a long swallow and placed the glass on the counter. "We have discussed everything, Dad. I don't know how you are able to do what you do. I've never heard of anything like it. I can't stop thinking about that giant. I wouldn't mind traveling like that with you again. But, right now I understand we have a job to do. Don't be too worried about us. We will be okay. If you need help though…"

Mason smiled at his son. He was glad to know he was able to assimilate what happened in the elevator at the hospital. "I won't hesitate to call on you or Steve if I need you. Right now, I need you two to help me protect the women in this family. Oh, and Conrad."

He placed an arm over Valerie's shoulder. They walked out of the kitchen. In his own bathroom, Mason removed his shirt, pulled out his electric shaver and a plastic Bic with four clean blades. Valerie took a seat on the edge of the large tub and waited. Once he was cleanly shaven she turned on the shower, made sure it was hot, removed her clothing and stepped inside. There was no need for words. He pulled off the rest of his clothes and joined her. He stood there, letting her lather him up, letting her scrub his entire body. It was not sexual, not even sensual, they were best friends for decades. Recently they grew apart and it led to a brutal argument. However, they were bound by something intangible. At times, they fought hard. They also needed one another. Mason and Valerie could not imagine a life that didn't include one another. Valerie wasn't just tending to her husband, she was applying a healing touch to herself.

Mason let the hot water run over his body and wash away the soap. He turned and stepped into Valerie's arms. The two of them held one another without speaking, the steam in the bathroom engulfing them.

Mason toweled off but didn't bother getting dressed. He climbed into bed and buried himself under the blanket. Valerie followed his lead but propped herself up with a few pillows. She pulled a thick novel out of the nightstand next to her side of the bed and opened it to where she left off. Only a few moments passed until she could hear her husband snoring lightly.

***

In another reality, far, far away, a woman slept. Not counting the baby she carried in her womb, she was alone in the house. Not necessarily an odd thing. Once she entered adulthood she always lived in this house on her own. She furnished the place, decorated it, made it into a home that reflected her personality. She was comfortable here and knew that Magdon or one of the Doctor's other assistants were moments away. The massive mattress covered with linens, blankets, and pillows larger than the occupant swallowed her in comfort. She slept soundly, with an ambient sound of oceanic waves crashing against some distant shore.

In her dream, she was extremely happy. She sat in a rocking chair in the living area of an unknown home. Sunlight beamed through every window creating an atmosphere of bright warmth. Outside, she could hear her husband working; chopping wood, or perhaps gardening. In her hands were knitting needles and she was crafting something. She thought it may be a small cap for the baby. She hummed a tune, a feeling of safety and love filled her. This scene stretched out in time. The longer she knitted the more joy she felt. The baby would be coming soon and she would love the child like no other child was loved.

The dream shifted slightly. The sunlight diminished in jerky increments, shadows stretched across the floor and the house soon became dark. She lay her knitting materials down in her lap and looked up, listening. "Mason?" She called out. "Where are you?"

She listened intently but heard nothing. It was too quiet. There was a little light coming through the windows. Perhaps it was light from the moon. She could not be sure. "Mason?" A sense of dread crept into her. She put the knitting aside and got up from the rocker.

A scratching sound came from her left. It reminded her

of a branch, rubbing against a window. But there were no trees close enough to scratch at the window. She was sure of it. The bad feeling in her body grew. Instinctively, she placed her hand on her belly. The child inside moved and kicked softly. It wouldn't be long now. Scratching at the window again. "What is that? Mason, where are you?" *Why won't he answer?*

She crossed the distance to the source of the sound. The curtain was closed. *That's not right. All the curtains should be open.*

"Scratch!!"

She jumped back and the baby jerked. The fluttering sensation caused by the movement in her womb made her feel nauseous.

"Scratch!!"

She reached out and pushed the curtain aside. There was nothing there. The moonlight cast shadows across the large backyard. She moved closer to the window, trying to locate her husband. A large paw appeared on the glass with long black claws. It bumped into the window and moved from top to bottom. "Scratch!!"

She jumped back, a scream stuck in her throat. The claw retracted and the moonlight took its place. She tried to call her husband, but no sound would come out of her mouth. Her hand reached out to a counter and she balanced herself. Her heart was pounding and she could not get enough air into her lungs.

The back door opened.

This can't be happening. I'm dreaming. Why can't I wake up? She went down on her knees, doubling over, protecting her child from whatever might come through the door.

She could not be sure how long she was huddled on the floor. Nothing came through the door. Instead, she heard a sound, coming from outside, out in her backyard. It was not a sound she was familiar with. The sound was a slow methodical crunch, crunch, crunch; like someone walking through a heavy drift of snow. Crunch, crunch, crunch, then a sound she recognized, a deep growl made by a hungry wolf.

"Aiden." A man's voice called out to her.

"Aiden, help me." She turned her head and strained to hear the man. "Please, help me."

"Mason? Is that you?"

The voice came again, crying. "Please! It's got me. Help me!"

Courage and fear struggled for control within her mind. She did not recognize the voice. Something wrong with it, but she was sure it was not her husband. The door creaked and opened wider. She looked up and saw a man standing at the entrance. He wore a filthy suit jacket with matching slacks. He was unbelievably tall and unrealistically thin. He looked down at her and grinned exposing jagged, rotted teeth. The thin man stepped forward, one step, two steps... "You're coming with me!" The sound of his voice repulsed her. He spoke with wet gravel in his throat.

She was being dragged across the floor. The man snatched her by the arm, pulled her out of the house, out into the yard, where the crunch, crunch, crunch increased. His grip was unbreakable, like a vise on her arm. She was pulled through the doorway, across the back porch, down several wooden steps, onto the ground. She reached up, trying to free herself and she heard the tall man laugh. The sound of his laugh vibrated in her head and she felt she would surely be sick.

She saw what was creating the crunching sound. A creature was digging a great hole in the middle of the yard. The beast was hunched over, its body was half hidden, down inside the hole it was digging. The creature wore no clothing. She could see an arched back with a large spine that protruded from its massive body. The creature was black. Its muscles rippled with every stroke of its forward claws.

The tall man released her at the edge of the hole and the creature stopped digging, turned its large head, and looked at her. Jagged uneven horns jutted from its forehead. It had red eyes with no pupils and when it opened its mouth she could see a full set of wolf-like teeth that dripped with greyish yellow saliva. A high-pitched whine poured from its gaping mouth as it reached out and clutched her by the ankle, pulling her into the hole. It bent down and pulled at her clothing with razor-sharp talons, tearing her garment, exposing her body. Wet mucus drained into her face from the beast's open mouth. A putrid tongue licked her exposed swollen belly, her breasts, and her face. The animal radiated heat and it trembled in anticipation. It was going to ravage her, she was sure of it.

"You may not!" The tall man growled the command and the creature reluctantly pulled back.

Aiden shook uncontrollably with fear for her life and the life of her unborn child. She was racked with terror, helpless to wake herself or to make the dream stop. Her clothes were tattered, her body wet and filthy. She was covered in cool fresh soil. She grabbed her torn nightgown, trying to cover herself and something hit her. Instinctively she closed her eyes and spit as dirt filled her mouth. She threw an arm up to protect herself and another heavy amount of thick damp soil covered her.

The dark beast burying her in her own backyard screamed out a paragraph in reverse; using its massive arms and huge paws, frantically pushing mounds of soil into the hole.

"There are rules." She heard the tall man growl. "It won't last much longer."

The ground beneath her fell away. She fell down an endless black hole. She was no longer in the ground, no longer in her yard, no longer anywhere. She fell into an abyss void of texture, or light.

Chapter 20

Mason opened his eyes. His arm was vibrating. He lifted it in front of his face and could see the spike moving under his skin.

"What is that?" Valerie asked, still seated next to him in the bed.

Doctor Rasmus failed to give him instructions on how to turn the damn thing off. Mason slapped at it, pressed it, shook his hand, it kept vibrating. "It's a beeper. A pager."

"Why is it in your arm?"

Mason sat up. "I don't know how to make it stop."

Valerie threw the blanket back and got out of the bed. She came around and took hold of his arm, inspecting his vibrating skin. "What if we use electricity?"

Mason jerked his arm back. "You would like to do something like that. Next, you are going to suggest a fiery furnace."

It stopped vibrating. Mason thought it might have stopped as a result of him jerking his arm back but he couldn't be sure. He was going to see Doctor Rasmus anyway, this was an item to add to the list.

"Okay. It stopped," Valerie said. "Would you please tell me why it is in your arm in the first place?"

"Its joined with the spike."

"The spike? You're not making sense."

Mason got out of the bed. He felt amazing. He crossed the room and retrieved his cell. "Holy shit. Valerie, I slept for over four hours." He closed his eyes and did the math. Two and a half months. *Damn it!* He still had some things to do but he was going to have to look in on Aiden first.

Valerie draped a thick robe around herself. "Mason. You are going to have to get me up to speed. Nothing you are saying or doing is making sense."

Every minute he delayed, precious time was flying by on Nikon. Mason grabbed his pants and shirt and began to get dressed. He looked at Valerie and grimaced. "I realize I am asking a lot for you to be able to grasp something that for me is a way of life. I've kept it concealed from you because no time passes here while I am away. The reason I look younger, why I have more energy, is because of the device in my arm. It is called a spike. The Doctor that designed it and placed it there also attached a type of pager. He is in an alternate reality. He cannot simply call me on my cell when he needs to reach me."

"So, this Doctor is calling you?"

Mason nodded.

Valerie was shaking her head, confused. "Why is a Doctor on another planet calling you? Oh, my God, I can't believe I just asked that question."

"See. You have been attacked twice by monsters that you cannot explain. Conrad is in the hospital because of the same thing. And you are having trouble believing a trivial thing like someone paging me."

"You're making it sound like I'm nuts."

Mason stopped buttoning his shirt and sighed. "Sorry. I didn't mean to do that. This thing vibrating in my arm... it's the first time the Doctor has called me. Then I just realized I slept way too long."

"You obviously needed the rest. If that thing hadn't started buzzing you would still be asleep. What's the big rush?"

"Well, I have no way of knowing when these creatures are going to attack again. It could be tonight. It seems that each incident is worse than the last. The next attack could result in someone ending up dead. I don't want to look back knowing that it was my complacency that caused it. I need to act quickly and decisively if we are to have a hope of coming out of this thing unscathed."

She was nodding her head. "Okay, okay. But what am I supposed to do while you are out risking your life?"

He shook his head. "You just don't get it. You won't know that I am gone." He approached her and took her shoulders in his hands. "During this conversation, I could have left and been gone for an hour, or a month, you would never know. With the exception of minor changes in my appearance you wouldn't perceive my leaving or coming back."

"Clint said you took him somewhere. In the hospital. Can't you take me with you?"

"Why would I do that? I have set up a situation right here where you and the kids will be safe, or relatively safe. Why would I then expose you to a danger? I needed to convince Clint. If you ask him where I took him he will tell you that it is not a hospitable place. Trust me. You and the kids staying here is the best option. It also gives me a time advantage. Nothing happens here while I am gone. It is important that I stay busy and stay away from this reality."

"This is hurting my head."

He bent and kissed her. "Try not to think too hard about it. Concern yourself with keeping everyone here safe."

She kissed him back then pulled away. "You make sure that you come back to us. What happens to us if you kick the bucket on some distant world? We would all be frozen in time and never know it."

Mason looked at her in astonishment. She may have trouble believing what he told her, but she was paying attention. "I think if I were to die in another reality, this world would carry on without me."

"Can I have the number to that thing in your arm?"

He smiled. "I don't even know how to turn it off, so I certainly don't know how to activate it. If you need me, just call me on my cell phone. I'll be sure to respond."

He took out his phone and pressed a newly programmed tab.

"What's up?"

"How are we doing?"

"I'm actually surprised at how much we have accomplished. I got the keys to the house and the girls are over there right now setting things up. I'm with Rob. We are at a dealership. I'm thinking about a Rav-4, or maybe a Tundra. What do you think?"

"Did Rob get the items I asked for?"

She obviously handed the phone to Rob. The big man said, "It wasn't easy to get the bulbs. I got a portable unit at a hardware store. I picked up ten bulbs at a place where I know the owner. They are packed in bubble wrap and bundled in an old navy blanket."

"What dealership are you at?"

***

Mason met them at the car dealership. Sidney chose a Jeep Renegade. Mason wondered how she got a Jeep from a Toyota dealership. She and Rob were in the waiting room watching television.

"They're prepping my Jeep," she said with a smile and jumped up to greet him. "How are you, big boy? You look refreshed, and clean shaven." She stroked his naked jaw. "That's nice. I like it.

"I'm running short on time."

Rob slowly got up from his seat. "I've got your stuff in the trunk of my car."

They all walked out to Rob's burgundy Cadillac. Rob pressed a button on his keypad and the trunk popped open. He pulled out a wrapped bundle about five feet long and a small device the size of a shoe box. "Here, I put batteries in the portable. He flipped the switch showing Mason that it worked."

Mason accepted the items and examined the portable unit. He hoped Rasmus would be able to work some magic with this stuff. "Thank you, Rob. I trust Sidney has compensated you."

Rob laughed. "Compensated. Ha! You are really Caucasian, man. Anyway, sure. She took care of everything. What about this?" He held up a red and white megaphone.

"Oh. Right, thanks. I need that too."

"What are you going to do with all this stuff?"

"I'll have to explain later. Could you excuse us please?"

The big man nodded, shut the trunk of his car and headed back into the shop.

"This place stays open late," Mason said.

"Sure. They are making a cash sale. They ain't gonna tell us to come back in the morning. So, what are you going to do with that?"

"I'm taking the bundle and the portable light to Rasmus. I have an idea. I didn't want Rob to see me standing here one second with this stuff and then it disappears. Explaining this talent of mine is becoming a full- time job."

"Are we staying the night here? I mean in the motel."

Mason shook his head. "No. I am going to see Rasmus. When I'm done I'll come back here and pick you up. We are going to the Ice World where we will probably be for the next week."

"What about my Jeep?"

"Sidney. Really? I thought you were making progress."

She looked thoughtful for a second then smiled. "No time elapses here."

"Just stand here. We leave, and when we are done on Ice World we come back to this very spot and you can go back inside and pick up your Jeep." He hesitated, then added, "If you still can."

She looked up at him with a big grin. "What? What is that supposed to mean, lover boy?"

"It could mean many things. After spending a week or two with me on another world, you may not be able to return to this one."

Sidney pressed her body into Mason's. "You think you are going to wear me out?"

"That or you might not make it out alive."

She burst into laughter, reached up and kissed him. "Hurry up, old man."

Mason straightened and handed her the bullhorn. "Hold this for me." He closed his eyes, thought of Doctor Rasmus and stepped away from Sidney.

***

In the expanse of light, he opened his eyes and saw the massive mural before him. The pictures changed rapidly. The entire board showed images from what had to be Nikon. Mason saw enough of the city and countryside to recognize the planet. All the images before him were of different places on Nikon. Several protruded above the others. He recognized Aiden's home in one, Mercer Laboratories in another. An image pulsed and he saw what he wanted. In the moving portrait, Doctor Rasmus sat at a table eating something. He was engaged in conversation with someone Mason could not see and busy on a small laptop.

Mason passed his palm over this image and stepped forward into Doctor Rasmus' dining-room. He walked up to the dining table and put the items he carried before the Doctor.

Rasmus looked up, surprised. His mouth hung open. "How? How did you get here?" Rasmus mumbled.

"I learn something new almost every time I use my Door. I appeared in Aiden's room because I pictured her room in my mind. I was able to find you here by simply thinking about you."

"That, Mr. Waters, is amazing." He closed his laptop

and turned his attention to Mason. "What have you brought for me?"

Mason took a seat and placed the items on the table. "I'll get to this in a moment. If you needed to feed say, ten thousand people in one setting, how would you do it?"

"Hold on." Rasmus got up from the table and went into the kitchen. He came back with a silver platter big enough to hold a Thanksgiving turkey and several glass jars. He placed the platter on the table and took a pill from one of the jars. He placed it in the center of the platter. The pill was roughly the size of a large kidney bean. It even looked like a kidney bean. From another jar, he placed smaller pills, about the size of a pea, around the kidney bean.

He picked up a glass of water. "This," pointing at the kidney bean, "is a large bird like a chicken. These smaller pebbles are vegetables." He proceeded to pour an ample amount of water over each pill and the pills reacted immediately.

Mason watched in amazement. It took about twenty seconds for the platter to disappear under a fully roasted chicken, covered and surrounded by potatoes, carrots, tomatoes, and several green vegetables. The whole dish steamed as though it had just come from the oven. Mason took in the aroma and his stomach growled. "That is incredible!"

"This jar holds about five hundred bird pills. I have twenty or so jars on one shelf in my pantry. Other shelves hold various meats, fruits, and vegetables. Every home on the planet is certainly well stocked with food. The manufacturer brings it right to your door. I'll never be able to consume all that I have and they keep delivering it. Once a month there is a shipment at my front door. World hunger was solved centuries ago. I seldom use them. I still like a sandwich made with freshly baked bread. Of course, there are little pills for that sort of thing as well. It's all quite boring. No one cooks food in the traditional way."

"I am going to need some of everything you have; cheese, meat, bread, vegetables, everything. I need it vacuum packed or whatever so I can carry it."

"Sure. When do you need it?"

"Have it ready to go as soon as you can. I'll let you know when I need to transport it. Figure on enough to feed ten thousand, no, twenty, they are very large people. If I have to I will carry it in more than one trip or get Sidney to help me."

"Okay." Mason rubbed his hands together. "That's one problem solved. I'd like to have some of this to eat. It smells great."

The Doctor brought him a plate and some eating utensils.

Mason filled the plate and continued. "You told me and Sidney about the time when Adramelech invaded your world," he said, with a mouth full of chicken.

Rasmus nodded. "Yes."

"You said they were here for many years."

"Yes." He nodded. "It took me over twenty years to repair my machine."

Mason unwrapped the bundle as he spoke. "I assume they went outside during their stay?"

"Rasmus looked at him questioningly. "Well, of course. They can fly. Not much use flying if you are indoors."

"I assume they were outside during the day." He

exposed ten long tubes of glass. "Doctor, do you know what ultraviolet light is?"

The Doctor shook his head.

"I am going to turn on this portable ultraviolet lamp." He flipped the switch on the small box and it produced a tiny dark purple light. He reached out, took the Doctor's hand and grazed his palm with the light cast by the bulb.

Rasmus yanked his hand back and howled. "Oh! That hurts! What have you done?"

Mason flipped the light off. "Sorry, Doc. Put some water on that and you'll be okay."

The Doctor got up and left the room. When he returned his hand was heavily bandaged. Mason thought the man was crying. He sat back down and stared at Mason.

"Are you going to be okay?"

"You show up at my home, uninvited and burn me with something, I don't…"

Mason held up his forearm pointing at the spot where the spike resided. "You called me."

"That was two weeks ago."

"I couldn't come right away. I had to get this stuff first. Why did you call me?"

"You go first. Why did you burn me?"

Mason shook his head. "Okay. Again, I'm sorry but I had to be sure how this light would affect you before I asked you to reverse engineer these bulbs."

"Why would I do that?"

"In my reality, the sun puts out this kind of light." He motioned toward the portable box and Rasmus flinched. "We call it ultraviolet light. Evidently, your sun does not produce this light. The population of Nikon could not exist if it did. I believe Adramelech and the population of Halja suffer from the same negative side effect. They may be supernatural beings, but overexposure to ultraviolet light can destroy them."

Rasmus reached out and lifted one of the long glass tubes. "These radiate the same way as the small light in that box?"

Mason nodded. "Now that you know the danger of this technology, I am sure you will proceed with caution. I need you to figure out how it works, how to produce it and package it in a way that is convenient for me to carry it and use it as a weapon. Remember, it has to be portable and small enough for me to carry through the portal."

"How do you know it will work?"

Mason shrugged. "It's an educated guess. Right now, it's the best option I have. One of the angels from Halja attacked my family on Earth. It was the ultraviolet rays of the sun that killed it."

"This light does not affect you?"

Mason picked up the box and turned the light on again. Rasmus pushed back in his seat. Mason turned the box, shined the light on his own face and smiled at the Doctor.

"How are you withstanding the power of that light?"

Mason chuckled. "I don't know. Maybe it's built into our genetic code. If I stay under a powerful source of UV light long enough it will tan my skin. It can even burn my skin, but I'd have to be out in the sun for a long time to get a burn. Exposure over a long period of time can cause skin cancer. We have some protective products you can pick up at a drug store to protect our skin. You mentioned that when you view Halja it is unusually dark. Maybe their sensitivity to light has something to do with the fact that they live in a very dark environment. I'll bet they have excellent vision. Evidently, Nikon's sun doesn't produce this harmful radiation either, so it didn't have a negative effect on them while they were here."

"You unknowingly took a big risk when you sent Aiden to my motel room. If she appeared on Earth outside on a sunny day, I don't think she could survive."

The Doctor stared at Mason. He spent unknown hours and resources raising Aiden. She was to him a monumental investment. To know that he could have destroyed hundreds of years of effort in the blink of an eye was overwhelming.

"Doctor?" Mason looked at him with concern. "Are you going to be okay? You look very pale."

"You... I..." He lurched and covered his mouth with his hand. He let out a muffled cry and ran back out of the room.

Mason sat there waiting. He couldn't just get up and leave. He needed to stay on top of this.

The Doctor finally reemerged, moving slowly, his hands trembling. "There is so much I do not know. I try and try to work through every scenario and to anticipate what might occur, but..."

"Doctor. Focus. Let's change the subject. Why did you call me?"

He looked up wearily. "Because Aiden has been kidnapped."

Mason stood abruptly knocking his chair over. "She's been kidnapped? Didn't you see the need to lead with that? Where is she?"

"Adramelech has her."

"You told me you haven't been able to locate him."

"Well, that has changed. Somehow, he managed to come here, to Nikon. Or perhaps he sent someone. I don't know the 'how'. What I do know is that she is gone. On a hunch, I located Halja on my viewer and the image of her, in some sort of castle, held in a metal cage, is the first image that came through. I am certain it was intentional to let me see her. I believe it is a trap to bring you to them."

"Show me."

Rasmus looked at him questioningly.

Mason grabbed up the bulbs and the portable unit. "Call a driver, whatever you have to do. Let's get to the lab. I want to see what you saw. I want a team of your technicians on this weapon immediately."

At Mercer Laboratories Doctor Rasmus escorted Mason to a building that resembled an aircraft hangar. The viewer was housed in this building. When Mason saw how impossibly large the machine was he realized it was constructed inside the building. It was far too large to be moved in our out. The building and the machine seemed to be attached to each other. Rasmus led him to a central area where a few chairs and a workstation was located. Rasmus took a seat and pulled himself up to a device no larger than a toaster. It had two lenses and he put his face to the unit. His right hand reached out and took hold of a bowling-ball-shaped device that rolled with ease at his touch. With experienced fingers, he turned the black ball left then right, up a bit, then back down. The entire time his hand moved over the ball he never took his eyes away from the two lenses. After fiddling with the thing for several minutes he got out of the seat.

"Go ahead. I have her centered."

Mason took the chair and put his eyes to the two small glass orbs. Aiden was captive in a man-sized bird cage that appeared to be suspended in the air. Perhaps it was chained to the ceiling. Mason wondered how high she might be from the floor. She wore a tattered nightgown and her left ankle was on a short chain, shackled to the cage. She was filthy and apparently cold as she was huddled down against the side of the cage. There was nothing else in the cage to indicate she had access to food or water.

"You called me two weeks ago."

Rasmus nodded. "Yes. What do you intend to do?"

"I'm going to get her. What else?"

"I want that as much as you do. But you will be walking into an obvious trap. They will have both of you."

Mason sat there silently for a few moments, studying every aspect of what he could make out through the tiny viewpoint. He stood and turned to the Doctor. "They are not expecting me to show up with a weapon. How long do your men need to complete my UV weapon?"

"This is just a guess. Give me two days. I'll try to do it faster. It is new technology, but it shouldn't be too much of challenge."

Mason nodded. "How long is that on my world?"

"Ten minutes."

"Okay, I'll return in two days." He fixed his gaze on the Doctor. "Aiden is counting on us. Her baby is counting on us."

Rasmus nodded.

"Oh, before I go. Show me how to turn off this pager you put in my arm."

***

To Sidney, Mason hadn't moved an inch. One thing changed. The bundle of tanning bulbs and the portable UV box were instantly gone. She looked at the expression on his face and realized something changed. He wasn't the same and she wondered how long he was gone. "What is it? Mason, I can see it in your eyes. What happened?"

Mason chewed on his lower lip. "Adramelech found a way to come after the people that are close to me. Now, he has taken Aiden and is holding her captive."

Sidney had yet to meet Aiden but knew she was important to Mason. She was running around all day preparing a home for this woman. "So, our plans are changing. How can I help?"

Mason shook his head. "No. Our plans remain the same for now. I am going back to Nikon in a few minutes. Once I'm done with what I have to do I'll come back for you. Nothing's changed as far as you are concerned."

"Why don't I believe you? What is it you aren't telling me?"

"It's dangerous. What I am about to do is..." He paused. "I'm pretty sure it's a trap. They will be ready for me. Aiden is chained to a cage. I have to break her free. If I run; if I open the Door to escape without Aiden, then it's pointless. The last time I was in a room with Adramelech he almost killed me."

"Take me with you."

Mason smiled at her. She was a beauty, but deep down he knew she was also a warrior.

"I can't take that risk. I'll be going into…"

"You are planning to take me with you to this Ice World. Isn't that also a risk?"

"It's not the same. At some point, I have to sleep."

She held up her hand. "I don't want to hear that crap. Are you afraid of having me and Aiden in the same room together?"

"No, Sidney. I am afraid of what might happen if I try to move both of you through the Door at the same time. I'm not willing to trade you for Aiden."

"That's comforting. You said you are going back to Nikon."

He nodded. "Doctor Rasmus is crafting a weapon. I'll need it to get Aiden back."

"Take me with you to the laboratory."

"I don't see how that helps anything."

She approached him, put her arms around him and hugged him tightly. "I cannot help you if I'm not with you."

Mason sighed and checked his cell. "Okay. But back up. We still have about four minutes. Honestly, I think this is a bad idea. Let's go set in my truck. At least you will have a softer landing on the return trip. I don't think you want to get dropped in this parking lot."

She smiled, kissed him, and held his hand as he led her to his truck. In the cab of his pickup, he pulled out his cell and checked the time again. "Leave the bullhorn here. I don't need it yet." He placed his cell phone on the dashboard. "In case you make it back and I don't." They exchanged a look and he summoned the Door. "Time to go."

Chapter 21

When they appeared in Doctor Rasmus's office they caught the man with his head down, napping at his desk. Mason shook him gently on the shoulder. Rasmus lifted his head slowly and looked at them with bloodshot eyes.

"Doc, you don't look so good," Mason commented.

Rasmus rubbed his face then ran his fingers through his hair, inadvertently making it stand up. He looked like he just got out of bed and was in need of a hot cup of coffee. "We had some set-backs with your device. Some of my techs were burned. One young man was taken to the hospital. They have to wear full body protection to work on the weapon. Anyway, I haven't slept much since you left."

"How is Aiden?"

"I set round the clock observation on her. About every twelve hours the cage is lowered to the floor and what appears to be a female brings her water and something to eat."

"Isn't she allowed to use the restroom?" Sidney asked.

The Doctor looked at her, noticing her for the first time. "They put a bucket in the cage. I have not seen them empty the bucket. It is horrible. She stays huddled in a ball on the floor of the cage."

Mason reached down and pulled the Doctor to his feet. "Come on, Doc. Let's go see what you've cooked up."

The Doctor wasn't kidding about his technicians needing to wear protective gear. Each person working on the device looked like they were handling the Ebola virus. The Doctor put on his own gear complete with boots, gloves, and a head covering resembling a welder's hat.

Sidney watched with an expression of wonder. She turned to Mason. "Is it that serious?"

Mason nodded. "The UV rays are deadly. I burned the Doctor with that little portable unit. He is creating a weapon that has increased UV radiation. It appears to have them in a very cautious state of mind."

The Doctor picked up a large canvas bag equipped with a small harness. "Follow me."

He led them out of the lab into a relatively empty room. There was a table, a few chairs, and absolutely no windows. He turned to Sidney and handed the contraption to her. "It's fairly self-explanatory. Strap it on his body this way. There are fastening buckles here, here, and here. It goes over his shoulders and rests on his back. Then run the belt around his waist."

Sidney nodded as he explained it to her. Then he turned to Mason. "Once she has it secured you can turn it on using the control handle on the left side. Bring the wand up in your right hand. Test all the controls. It has several applications."

"I don't see a bulb," Mason said.

"I felt the glass was too vulnerable. What if you fall and break it? What if you just bump into a wall? Bad design for a weapon. Once you turn it on you will see the source of light.

I cannot remain in here with you. Even with my protective gear and this visor, that thing will burn my retinas."

The Doctor exited the room and closed the door behind him. Mason picked up the gear and slipped his hands and arms through while Sidney moved in behind him. She hefted the canvas bag so he could fasten the first buckle. She ran the large belt around his waist and fastened it in the front.

Mason's left hand found the proper grip. It reminded him of a joystick. It had a switch on the stem and a button at the top. Sidney wrapped his right arm with the business end of the device. Mason grabbed hold of the handle. It was like holding the butt end of a Samurai sword minus the blade.

He glanced at the switch in his left hand and flipped it up. The device made no noise. A bright reddish/yellow light jumped from the end of the handle in his right hand. It was brilliant and brightened the room like the sun just rose in the east.

Sidney shielded her eyes with her forearm. "Damn! That is bright."

There was enough wiggle room in the handle. Mason could swing the beam of light across the wall. "It's like a giant lightsaber."

"What's the button do?"

He stopped playing with the saber, switched it off, and pressed the button. "Let's see."

Sidney saw movement at the back of the bag. A flap dropped and a metallic sphere, the size of a baseball protruded halfway. Slivers of the metal shifted and the ball glowed pure white. The bar of light emitted from the handle brightened the room dramatically. The sphere blinded them.

They both closed their eyes. Mason felt for the button, pressed it and the ball retracted into the bag.

Sidney opened her eyes and watched a hundred dark circles dance in her vision. The two of them stood there for several minutes, regaining their sight.

Sidney said, "That was fucking intense."

"It was bright. But did you feel anything?"

"Sure. It's warm. Like you're on the beach."

"Yeah. I felt that too. I hope it does the trick."

In the viewing hangar, they waited for the Doctor to focus in on Aiden. Once he had a clear line of sight he stepped back and allowed Mason to see. Mason moved in and lowered his head to the two view plates. He studied the cage and the dark room where Aiden was held.

"Okay. I'm ready," he said.

"Mason." The Doctor spoke up. "The button in your left hand; the one you depress to release the sphere in the back. If you hold it down steady, for five seconds, the sphere becomes an explosive device. It will explode. Nothing within a five-mile radius will be able to withstand the force of the explosion."

Sidney said, "Oh, my god."

Mason nodded slowly. "That's a lot of power Doc. How is the thing powered? It seems too small to be run with batteries."

"The same principle that powers your spike. I use Nano-technology in cooperation with a chemical element similar to uranium. The biggest difference is there is no radioactive component."

Mason nodded. "Okay. I am sure I should be comforted by that explanation, but oddly, I am considerably stressed.

Anyway, thank you, Doctor. You've done a magnificent job but I doubt I will be setting off any bombs."

"You're not going in there alone," Sidney said.

Mason looked at her. "Did you hear what he just said. I'm a walking nuclear bomb. You don't want to be standing next to me if I have to detonate." He turned to the Doctor. "You need to place a medical team at Aiden's home."

Rasmus agreed and made the call.

Mason turned back to Sidney and realized she had walked away. She was returning with something in both of her hands. In her right hand, she held a thirty-six-inch machete. In her left, she held a double-edged blade, long enough that it dragged the floor. "Sidney."

"You are going into battle with a light bulb and a hand grenade. You don't even know if either one of them works. Aiden is chained inside of that cage. How are you going to deal with that?"

"I'll bring the entire cage back with me if I have to."

She held the machete up, admiring it. "I found this in a locker over there. I would prefer a bazooka, but this will have to do."

"You are a dancer. What do you know about swinging a sword? You are not going with me, Sidney."

"God-damn it, Mason! Stop fucking around!" She moved within striking distance and Mason flinched. Doctor Rasmus jumped completely out of the way. "You want to save Aiden. Then let's go."

Mason sighed and half closed his eyes. "I've never attempted this, but then there have been many firsts in the past few days." He looked down at Sidney, standing there with her jaw clenched. She held the weapons so tight her knuckles were losing their color. The tendons in her arms flexed. "I see, you're serious."

"I'm not waiting for something to invade my dreams and attack me or kidnap me."

"You and I are from the reality of Earth. Those weapons and this device on my back belong to Nikon. I am fairly certain I can get us and the equipment to Halja. But you should understand what is going to happen when I open the Door to bring us back. If we are successful and we retrieve Aiden, I won't be able to hold everything."

"If we get out alive and I end up in the cab of your truck, I'm okay with that. At least I'll know we made it. Mason, you have to stay alive. No matter what. If they take you or kill you, then we are all dead anyway and none of it matters. Who's gonna take care of you over there, Aiden?"

Mason stood there and thought about the whole thing for a few moments. "Okay. When we appear in that cage, Aiden may be pulled but since she is chained down. I don't think she's going to go anywhere. We are going to have to break her loose from those shackles. When we get there, I'll pick her up. See if you can break the shackle with one of those blades. Once she is free we all hold on to each other and I'll open the Door. I may not be able to get us all back here together, but the important thing is that we get in quick and get everyone out alive. I can pick up the pieces after."

The Doctor took the long blade and secured it to Sidney's back with some leather straps that he tied around her waist and over her shoulders. He left the handle sticking up behind her head so she could reach up and back to pull the weapon.

Mason put an arm around Sidney and pulled her in

close. With one hand, she held the machete down and away from her body. She placed her other arm around Mason's lower back and locked her fingers inside his belt. The Doctor moved to the viewer and focused on Aiden. She appeared to be asleep in the cage.

Mason summoned the Door and they vanished from the hangar.

***

The bright expanse engulfed them as a massive mural opened at their front. Sidney's eyes darted from side to side trying to take it all in. Mason's grip on her tightened but he did not speak. Nevertheless, she could hear him in her head. She looked up at him. He was not looking at her and he was certainly not speaking. He was studying the thousands of moving pictures that stood before them.

"*Be still.*" His voice told her. "*Don't let go of me. We aren't there yet.*"

She had no intention of letting go. The mural of paintings moved up and then down. It would slow down enough for her to see there was motion inside of each painting; a ship rocked lazily on a turbulent ocean, animals ran in a heard across a grassy plain, people walked along sidewalks in a busy downtown area of some city. Hundreds of the pictures could have been places on Earth, but she wasn't sure. Many of them were like no place she had ever seen. One portrait, in particular, relaxed and hovered in front of them. It was a planet of caverns, all of which were on fire. Everywhere was fire; the ground, the walls. People ran amok, ravenous zombies moving in every direction. Mason discarded the snap-shot and the mural zipped again.

She saw her. The same scene from the viewer was right there in front of them. Aiden lay on the floor of the large cage. The cage dangled from the ceiling of an incredibly large cathedral. The moving portrait before them was of far greater resolution than Doctor Rasmus' viewer. Sidney could see the slight up and down movement of the woman's belly as she breathed. She recognized the small baby bump. She knew at that moment what Mason was doing. He was preparing a home for this woman and her unborn child. She wondered if the child was his and thought the chances of that to be very probable.

She felt Mason pull her in tighter as he reached out to the protruding image of the Mural. He stepped forward and all the light in the world winked out. As soon as their weight registered on the floor of the cage, she heard a metallic clank and the floor gave way. They were all falling; Mason, Sidney, Aiden, and a bucket.

The floor of the cage was set to give way if there was any additional weight. It worked perfectly. Mason and Sidney dropped, a couple of heavy rocks. Aiden's body responded to the gravitational pull of the Door. The chain attached to her ankle did its job. Her limp body jerked and bounced back as the restraints held her in place. The Door blinked out. They were weightless for a few seconds then they slammed into the cold stone floor.

Sidney hit the floor and rolled. She struggled to remain conscious, pushing herself up, reaching out with both hands searching for the machete. "*Got it!*" She scrambled to her feet experiencing a sharp pain in her right knee. "*Oh god. What did I do?*" Above she heard the crying voice of a woman. She crouched and looked up. It was dark in the basilica but her eyes adjusted quickly. *The cage floor gave way.* Aiden was dangling upside-down, being held by the metal clasp around her ankle about thirty feet up.

The floor shook and Sidney knew she had only seconds to think of what to do. She turned to Mason. He was lying in a heap a few feet away, not moving. "Mason!" She screamed. She pushed her body in his direction and fell on him. "Get up!"

Whatever was making the floor shake got closer. It was moving fast, perhaps running and she could hear deep throaty laughter. She shook Mason's limp body. A large spiked hand closed around her waist and pulled her to her feet. It lifted her quickly, off the ground, turning her to see her face.

"We have not met dark child."

The voice of the beast vibrated into her body. Sidney knew who she was looking at. This was Adramelech. She had no doubts. The creature was gigantic. How he stood in Mason's motel room and not put a hole in the ceiling, she could not be certain. He wore body armor from neck to foot or at least she thought it was armor. It was spotless and sparkled in the dim light, made of polished silver and gold. Every joint of the armor; knees, elbows, wrists, fingers, was spiked with what resembled chrome thorns. He did not wear a helmet and that is where she aimed when she brought the machete down.

The beast anticipated her swing and jerked his head to the side. He wasn't quick enough. The blade found purchase and Sidney buried it into the base of his neck where it met the shoulder.

Adramelech blew hot breath into her face and pulled

her in closer. He smiled, revealing a brilliantly white set of teeth, most of which looked razor sharp. The blow from the machete seemed not to have any effect. "I am no mere mortal that you can slice up with your puny knife, whore." His spiked hand did not completely encircle her body but he still held onto her. His grip tightened, pushing the air out of her lungs. With his free hand, he ran the sharp tip of his finger from her neck to her abdomen, slicing her shirt and bra open like warm butter. His smile deepened. "Oh, what my pets are going to do to you."

***

Mason heard that voice; the voice of his motel room attacker, the voice of the animal/man that hunted him in the night. From early childhood, he feared the voice of this beast and all the others that followed. He no longer felt afraid. He remained the target of these creatures, but they changed their tactic, coming for his family. His fear swelled with anger and rage.

Without seeing the action, he was aware that Sidney was in a battle to the death. He turned on his side to face the direction of the fight and felt with his left hand for the switch. He saw Aiden dangling above. She was chained to the cage and he realized immediately how problematic the situation became. He could easily open the Door and escape this attack but the beast held Sidney, and Aiden was chained to the cage. Neither one of them would pass through the portal.

He flipped the switch on the UV weapon and nothing happened. "*Shit! I fell on it. It's broken.*" He got to his knees and shook the wand in his right hand, flipping the switch up and down. "*The button. Try the button.*"

***

Adramelech placed a steel collar around Sidney's neck and clamped it shut. He tore her shirt away and it fell to the floor. The long blade went with it, banging loudly as it skittered across the stone. He reached down and picked up a large coiled chain. The links were the size of a fist. He locked the chain to the collar and dropped her.

Sidney hit the floor on her back, knocking the air from her lungs. Struggling to breathe. She grabbed hold of the chain and pulled. It wasn't long, perhaps six feet, and "*damn-it!*" it was attached to a steel ring in the floor. This place was looking less and less like a cathedral, more and more like a dungeon. Air filled her lungs and she got up on all fours, her right knee burning with pain. She heard an awful sound coming from behind. They were running, three, four, maybe five of them. She was certain she was about to meet Adramelech's pets.

***

Mason could hear the sound of claws skittering across the stone floor. Four-legged animals coming their way. He looked up. He could see them in the gray light. They were long and fast, oversized black wolves. They were snarling and panting, moving quickly for what their master chained to the floor. He saw Sidney about fifty feet away. She was on her hands and knees. She wore only her jeans and shoes.

She looked ready to collapse. Then he was airborne. A spiked hand lifted him off the floor.

Laughter filled the air. "At last! I have pursued you for a long time, Mason." His voice boomed.

Mason looked the beast in the eyes. They were large, dull, and black. "Fuck you." The sphere on his back opened and the world exploded with light. Mason clutched his ears as the great beast screamed in horror and pain. The fist that held him loosened and he fell back to the floor. Behind the mighty cry of Adramelech, he heard other screams and cries. The wolves howled and tumbled as they scurried to stop and run away. There came another cry, a familiar cry that tore at his heart. He pressed the button and the sphere closed. Above him, he heard her sob and he knew he burned her.

He scrambled to his feet and ran to where Sidney managed to get up on her knees. He studied the collar on her neck and felt sure they had very little time before Adramelech or the wolves returned. He could hear strange sounds in the distance but tried to block that out and focus on getting Sidney free. The metal collar was tight and the chain was incredibly thick. The metallic ring on the floor was not as durable.

Sidney saw it too and she pointed to her left. "The blade." She coughed.

Quickly, Mason ran to the long blade, picked it up and returned. Sidney moved as far from the ring in the floor as she could, giving him room to work. It didn't take much. Mason held the blade in both hands and brought it down like a lumberjack. The edge of the blade hit the ring and split it with one blow causing a vibration to run up Mason's hands and arms. He reached down and freed the chain.

"Don't open the Door yet!" She screamed.

"You're hurt."

"We all get out of here together."

"Mason!" Aiden cried out from above. Her words were dripping with pain and terror. "Mason! Save our baby!" She said something else but it was distorted with deep sobs. "He's coming back."

"Take this," Mason said, handing Sidney the long blade. "Get under that cage and wait."

***

He took off running and within seconds Sidney could no longer see him. She dragged her aching body across the floor to a spot just under where Aiden was hanging. She looked up, heard a sharp metal bang, like a lock opening for the first time in a hundred years. The cage was descending. The Doctor said they lowered the cage every twelve hours. Mason found the crank or whatever they used to raise and lower the cage. The air above them came alive with the sound of hundreds of wings. Something else was coming and she feared there would not be enough time.

The two women touched hands. Sidney pulled the crying woman away from the descending cage and lay her gently on the floor. She looked down at her, looked into her wet eyes, noticing her trembling chin, her shaking hands as they fell protectively to her stomach, and her own heart jumped into her throat. She knew there was no way she could leave this delicate flower, this being of pure love, to die in this place. Sidney would give her own life for this one without a thought. Sidney could see that Aiden was cut, bruised and broken. Blood dried and caked at the side of her head forming a sticky mat of blonde hair on her temple. She looked like she suffered a severe sunburn and yet her only motive was to save her child. It was easy to see why Mason loved her, and she knew he did love her. Who couldn't love a woman like this?

"Hold still." Sidney examined the chain that held Aiden to the cage. The clasp around her ankle dug in deep. Fresh blood trickled out and spilled on to the stone floor. Sidney got to her feet. She clutched the weapon in both hands and lifted it into the air. She brought the blade down like she saw Mason do but it only bounced off the chain.

Winged creatures landed and formed a circle around them. There were dozens of them, all naked with what appeared to be a thin covering of hair or fur along their thighs and waists. They looked very powerful. With each slight movement, muscles rippled under their skin. They moved like men and aside from the wings which were now folded at their backs, and feathers that covered their shoulders, they appeared as men. They were white, black, brown, and every shade in between. They stood seven to eight feet tall. They approached Sidney and Aiden slowly, cautiously. Sidney stood transfixed, with the blade above her head ready to strike the chain again. She was distracted and amazed at what she saw. One winged man stepped out from among the rest. He held out his hand in a pleading gesture. As if to say, "We come in peace." She heard it in her head, his gentle angelic voice. "Woman, do not fear."

A short silent moment passed as Sidney stood there frozen, studying them, blade in the air, taking deep breaths, her chest heaving. A sense of calm swept over her; a sense she could trust these men, they were here to help. She considered the one communicating with her. She stared into his eyes; blazing blue sapphires. Those eyes were mesmerizing but they shifted, no longer meeting her gaze. They dropped slightly. She looked down remembering she was topless. This man/eagle was checking her out! He was looking at her breasts. She knew this expression very well; the look of lust in a man's eyes. She followed those eyes as he glanced down at Aiden who, though she was beaten and bruised, was essentially nude. She wore a sheer nightgown so tattered and torn she might as well have been wearing nothing; her small naked baby bump poking up; vulnerable. Sidney looked back at the man, still balancing the long blade at an arc above her head and she saw his penis twitch. The fucking beast was getting an erection and she knew it was all bullshit. *"Do not fear. We come in peace. We are here to help."* Their eyes met again for an instant and Sidney brought the blade down with every ounce of strength she could exert.

"Aiyaaggghh!" She screamed as the blade split the air and crushed the metal link. The chain violently flew apart as though it were made of elastic, one end striking Aiden's leg, the other clanging against the cage. She brought the blade around, pointing it at the birdman. Quickly she moved to a spot between Aiden and the one approaching. The gang of creatures closed in and she screamed, "Mason! Do it now!"

Chapter 22

A bolt of light illuminated the dark structure and Mason witnessed two small forms at the uppermost part of the Door, Aiden and Sidney no doubt, passing into the light and out of this existence. The mighty Door remained open, waiting for him. He looked in the direction from where Sidney screamed and saw outlines of many large men. They opened massive wings, flapped once, twice, rising into the air. He watched as they ascended and he wondered if they had some special ability to pass through walls as they flew up toward the ceiling of the cathedral. He didn't wait to find out.

Mason stepped into the expanse of light alone. The colorful mural jumped out and expanded before him. Each trip through the Door became easier. It took less thought. The mural offered two portraits, Earth and Nikon. He considered these options and felt that Earth could always wait. His reappearance in that reality would be simultaneous to Sidney's. Not so on Nikon. He chose to step through to where he originated from that world.

He stepped out of the expanse of light into Doctor Rasmus' viewing hangar. The Doctor met him with a team of engineers and technicians. "I broke the wand," he said as he unbuckled the apparatus strapped to his back. "But the sphere in the back worked marvelously."

Several of the technicians helped him remove the pack and they scurried away with the device. Mason considered the Doctor. The man looked grim and very tired. "How is she?"

"She is being transported to a hospital that can care for her. I am on my way if you would like to accompany me."

Mason nodded and fell in step with the Doctor.

"The report I received is that she has multiple lacerations, contusions, some broken ribs, all of which will heal. She suffered second-degree and some third-degree burns."

"The baby?"

"Initial indications show the baby to be okay. More thorough testing needs to be done. I regret adding the sphere to that weapon. If not for that…"

"Doc. If not for that sphere it is most likely none of us would have made it out alive. You watched things play out on the viewer?"

He nodded. "Yes, I was able to see some of it. I certainly saw the whole place light up."

"Sidney was seconds from being dog meat. Adramelech didn't care one bit about her. I was the intended target. Once he had me chained down, he would no longer need Aiden. I am certain she and the baby would have been tortured to death. You have first-hand experience with these devils. Do you doubt me?"

"No, I do not. What is your plan concerning Aiden and the child?"

He shrugged. "How do you mean?"

"Do you plan to reside here on Nikon? Given this new

development concerning Ultraviolet radiation, you cannot expect her to reside in your reality."

"She and I discussed this before I realized your extreme sensitivity to UV rays. The plan was for her to remain here until the child is born, under your care of course. As for our living arrangements beyond that, well things have changed. I'll have to talk to her about it. I realized the predicament as soon as I saw the effect of the light on your hand."

"Then you purposely put her in harm's way when you released the power of that weapon on Halja. You knew she would burn!"

"You knew the potential of that weapon as well, Doc. You placed what amounts to a thermonuclear bomb on my back and seemed to be okay with that. There is no way I could have detonated that explosive and gotten out alive. Even if I managed to get the pack off my back, pressed the button and opened the Door, the thing would have snapped back here to your world before exploding. Something like that needs a remote trigger and I would need time to plant it."

The Doctor fell silent. Magdon was waiting for them outside. They entered the man's transport vehicle and headed out at a fast clip. After a few moments, the Doctor turned to him. "You didn't anticipate this?"

"Which part?"

"Aiden being kidnapped or attacked."

"No. I have to tell you at this point, I have to bet Adramelech can reach out and touch any of us. No one is safe and that includes you. When your world was under siege, did you ever see any of them sleep?"

The Doctor thought about this for a moment then shook his head slightly. "I cannot swear to it. I assumed they slept."

"I'm beginning to think they don't. What's more, they've figured out how to enter our reality through our subconscious. I am hoping Aiden can tell us how they came to her; how they managed to take her. I also think they can view other realities just as you do. I mean the apparatus may be different, but how else would they know about my connection with you and Aiden? How could they know I would come for her?"

"Perhaps they did not know. Maybe they are guessing."

"Damn good guess. I'd rather believe they are organized and are using every bit of knowledge at their disposal to get to me. I believe Adramelech sent an emissary to my family on Earth to do to them what was done to Aiden. I am not sure why the first one failed. My wife said she fell back, bumped her head and passed out. Maybe we have to be in a dream state. The second attack failed because in her nightmare she was making mental notes. Perhaps her fight or flight reflex kicked in. The attacker in her dream could not come out into the light. When she woke from the dream that idea was fresh in her mind. She used it to destroy the creature sent to kidnap them."

"She is very resourceful."

Mason nodded. "They all are. Now that they know what they're facing, they are ready to defend themselves. I'll tell you who else is resourceful; Sidney."

The Doctor nodded in agreement.

"I argued with her all the way, trying my best to persuade her to stay behind. If not for her quick thinking and pure determination… Well, I don't want to talk about what might have happened."

Doctor Rasmus had impressive authority at the hospital. They were allowed into Aiden's room without questions. Aiden was asleep. She lay in her bed on her back, propped up slightly. She was heavily bandaged. An IV drip, tubes, and wires ran to and from her body connected at the other end to several pieces of equipment that monitored her vitals.

Mason stood at her side and gently took hold of her hand while Doctor Rasmus scanned a computer monitor, familiarizing himself with her condition. "I don't think it's wise to wake her right now," he said. "There is a cafeteria and a place to get coffee and other refreshments in this facility. It's going to be a while."

Mason looked at the Doctor. "I'd like to stay here, in the room. I don't care how long it takes her to come out of it."

The Doctor nodded. "I'll have someone bring you a comfortable chair."

"Doc. I need you to stay here with her for a few hours."

"You're leaving?"

"Yes," Mason confirmed. "I should only be gone for a moment. If I'm not back in two hours, something has gone wrong."

"I understand. She is an important resource. I see that now. Go get her. I'll remain here until you return."

"Whatever occurs, do not sit here and fall asleep. Make sure there is someone in this room awake at all times." That said, the room split in two by the magnificent light of the Door; a light only Mason could see. He stepped through to the cab of his truck at the exact instant Sidney came down with a thud in the seat next to him.

Mason turned to her with the intention of simply grabbing her and returning to Aiden's hospital room. He realized that choice might be a bit hasty given her appearance. To begin with, she was topless. He looked over the cab of the truck and located her torn shirt and bra on the floor. She was also sporting a large metallic collar accompanied by six feet of thick chain.

Sidney looked at him, her eyes wide. Laughter erupted from her mouth. She fell back in her seat like a giddy school girl celebrating her twelfth birthday. "That was fucking awesome!" She jumped forward and wrapped Mason up in her arms pushing him back on the seat. She stopped laughing as abruptly as she started, pulled back and took Mason's face in her hands. "Oh my god! What happened to her? Is Aiden okay?"

Mason smiled at her and grabbed hold of the chain. "You know, I like this look. It has some fantastic possibilities."

She jerked up and snatched the chain from his hand. "She made it through. You wouldn't be joking if she hadn't."

Mason sat up, reached behind the seat, and pulled out a light jacket. It wasn't much more than a windbreaker, but it was going to have to do. "Here. Put this on."

She grabbed the jacket eagerly and slipped her arms into it. "Where are we going next?"

Mason considered her attitude. She was on an adventure. She had no idea how much danger they were in. He was sure of it. "Is your spike malfunctioning? Why are you so full of glee?"

She pulled the jacket around her, fixed the zipper in place, then zipped it up only a few inches leaving her ample brown breasts almost completely exposed. Mason grabbed hold of the zipper and pulled it up, closing the jacket completely. "Seriously, Sidney. It's not a game. We just faced an incredible adversary. We were lucky to make it out alive and you are acting like we just won twenty thousand on Family Feud."

"I'm excited because we made it out alive. Did you see those wolves? For a second I was terrified. But that feeling was immediately replaced by anger. No, by fury. I wanted more than anything to meet my enemy head-on, and tear his heart out."

Mason chuckled. "Come on. We can talk about it later." He reached up and grabbed his cell off the dash-board. No missed calls, no messages, and why should there be? Only moments passed since he arrived in the parking lot of the Toyota dealership. He placed the cell back on the dash and summoned the Door. Sidney lifted herself up onto his lap, facing him, wrapping her arms and legs around him, pulling him close and holding him tight. Mason could not step forward. He rolled right into the light and onto the cold floor of the hospital room where Aiden rested, and Doctor Rasmus sat half-asleep in a leather recliner.

They got up. Sidney rounded the bed to see about Aiden, while Mason crossed the room to where the Doctor sat and brought him back to full wakefulness. "Doc. You are playing with fire. I told you not to fall asleep. You should have one of your assistants in here with you."

"How is she, Doctor?" Sidney asked.

Rasmus stood. "Sorry, sorry. You are right." He turned to Sidney, caught momentarily by her appearance. "You have a chain hooked to your neck."

"Can you help me with this thing?"

Rasmus picked up the calling device next to Aiden's bed and made his request. He turned back to the slumbering

Aiden. "She is sedated and stable. Her body is regenerating with the help of microscopic technology we are running through her. I presume she will recover consciousness in a day, perhaps two. However, I do not know the extent of the psychological damage she may have suffered. That part of the process will undoubtedly take more time."

Several short males entered the room pushing a cart packed with some electronics and simple old-fashioned tools like a wrench and screwdriver. They pulled Sidney aside and worked on the metal collar. It only took a few moments to release her from the constraint. The collar and chain were carefully packed in a box and placed on the cart.

"I can send that back if you want," Mason said, indicating the chain and collar.

Rasmus shook his head. "They like studying stuff like that. It could hold some secrets that could benefit society; or the government."

Mason shrugged. "Go get some sleep Doc. Ask Magdon to stay with you or anyone for that matter. Do not go home alone. Now that Adramelech knows about the UV weapon, he'll be ready. He will wear full body armor if necessary. If he kidnaps you or anyone else, I don't know if I can rescue you."

"Doctor," Sidney said. "Is there some way I can get a shower and some fresh clothes?"

The Doctor motioned to a door. "Through that door, you will find restroom facilities as well as a blower. I believe that is what you mean when you mention a shower. It serves the same purpose. As for clothes…"

Mason raised his hand. "Does Aiden have some clothes in here?"

Rasmus nodded. "In that wardrobe."

Mason opened the wooden closet and thumbed through the clothes hanging on a small metal pole. "This will do. Have someone bring some more of Aiden's things here."

"Really." The Doctor smiled. "I can purchase Sidney some new things."

Mason turned to face Sidney and Doctor Rasmus. "Where is the long blade, Doctor? And the machete?"

"It is back in the hangar."

"It is difficult to keep items in the wrong reality. It is inevitable, moving things and people to multiple realities, mixing one person's stuff with another's creates unforeseen problems. I'm not always going to be able to keep up with everything. I don't want clothing or anything else for that matter to start popping up unannounced without some system of control. You two following me?"

They both nodded. Rasmus said, "You're right, of course. I am tired. Things are getting past me. Sidney, please help yourself and I will replace her clothing with items I can purchase here."

Sidney looked through the wardrobe and chose an outfit, let the Doctor see what she had taken and excused herself into the restroom.

"You could use some rest as well," the Doctor said, as he opened the door to leave.

"As soon as Sidney is done, I'll let her take first watch."

The Doctor stopped and glanced back over his shoulder, not really looking at Mason, gazing at the floor. "I wasn't sure what to expect upon meeting you. I was aware of your gift and I studied how you used it. It seemed to me that you were squandering something so very precious."

Mason stood there, waiting. He could hear the sound of wind and rain coming from the restroom and knew that Sidney was enjoying a new experience.

"You have many that you care about, and they care for you in return. I have just this one, Aiden. I created her because of you."

"What are you trying to say, Doc?"

"I did not expect that I…" Now he turned slightly so he could see Mason, eye to eye. "Seeing her there, in that condition…" His chin began to tremble.

"You never expected that you would love her so much. We cannot know how much someone really means to us until tragedy strikes, Doc. I know how you feel. You are fortunate because she will recover. Go get some sleep Doctor Rasmus. I'm not going anywhere."

The man dropped his head and walked slowly out the door.

Mason was about to take a seat in the recliner when the restroom door opened. Sidney stood in the opening. She had a towel wrapped around her body; her face, hair, and arms dripping wet. She smiled and motioned silently for him to join her.

In the restroom, she dropped the towel and helped him undress. "This air shower is amazing. Have you been in one?"

"Yes. I think they are fairly common here. We can't stay long Sidney."

She kissed him long and passionately. "Come on. We won't be very long. You'll sleep better."

He followed her into the wind/rain machine. It was not nearly as big as the one in Aiden's house. It did accommodate the two of them for what she intended. Warm air and hot water circled them creating a strong vortex, gently scrubbing, washing and rinsing as they moved upon one another.

She turned her back to him, grabbed his hands and brought them around to her breasts. The wind and hot rain increased. She released his hands and placed her own on the back of his head, running her fingers through his hair. She brought her hands back down and bent forward slightly allowing him access. Their session was intense and ended quickly. They separated, closed their eyes, and allowed the cleansers time to wash over their bodies.

As they toweled off, Mason cracked the door to check on Aiden. She was laying there, undisturbed.

"I want one of these showers in my new house," Sidney said.

"I'm sure the Doc can hook you up. On another note. I suppose I should say, thank you."

"For that? What we just did?"

"No. Thank you for not listening to me, for insisting on coming with me to Halja. You had the foresight to bring the machete and the sword. Without you…"

She moved up close to him, smiling. "You know I love you."

Mason stood there, not knowing what to say.

"It's okay." She continued. "Now that I've met her, I get it. There is something about her. She makes you want to be with her."

"You got that from a few moments on Halja?"

"As soon as she looked into my eyes. Be good to her Mason. I may decide to take her form you."

"I don't think she swings that way."

Sidney chuckled. "You don't know women."

"Let's back up to where you mentioned love," Mason said.

She dressed while they spoke and pulled the small yellow sweater over her head. "Too late. You had your chance." She opened the restroom door and stepped out leaving him standing there in his boxers.

Chapter 23

They camped in Aiden's hospital room for three days. Doctor Rasmus directed assistants bring them food and supplies, whatever then needed. Sidney and Mason slept in shifts making sure that one of them was awake and in the room at all times. They watched her sleep peacefully throughout the day. At night, she tossed and turned. It was concerning. Whatever disturbed her passed after only a few moments. On the third night, she woke.

Sidney busied herself with an electronic tablet connected to Nikon's version of the internet. One of the nurses at the hospital allowed her to use the device. She knew if she lived in this world she would die of boredom. There was no such thing as porn. Social media was virtually non-existent. There was no such thing as Facebook or anything remotely like it. There was no YouTube. She could find no evidence that these people watched movies. *How do they entertain themselves*? She wondered. Everything centered around sciences and arts of varying types. Art might be entertaining, but it was comprised of architecture, statues, and paintings. She wasn't into science. Biology, chemistry, psychology, mechanics, none of it peaked her interest.

The only thing she could find of interest was the massive

amount of information connected to enhancing the human body. This was obviously the fetish of your well to do Nikonian. If one possessed the resources, the alterations, and enhancements were almost limitless. Celebrities from Earth would love to vacation in this world, returning to Earth having lost impressive amounts of weight, develop sculpted and muscular bodies, grow unbelievably large breasts and butts. This would be a popular place to spend one's fortune in an effort to turn back the hands of time. Grandparents would return to Earth looking as young as their adult children. Kids would have a hard time discerning which was the parent and the grandparent. She found one thing a bit odd, however. For all the people who augmented their bodies in one way or a multitude of ways, no one seemed interested in being taller than say five-foot, two inches. Outside of facial make-up and the occasional tattoo, everyone was very Caucasian. Absolutely not one person on the planet was overweight.

As boring as this world appeared to Sidney she found that Nikonians rather enjoyed living long lives. 1000-year lifespans were common. There were those who suffered from accidents and natural disasters who needed medical care. The medical care was incredible. If you were fortunate enough to make it to the hospital in the event of a life or death crisis, chances were favorable that you would walk out alive and most likely in better physical condition than when the accident occurred. Sidney marveled at this. On Earth, if one ended up in a hospice, it was usually considered the end of the line. There seemed to be no such thing as a hospice on Nikon. It wasn't a necessity.

Physical traits and abilities were not the only things that

fascinated clients. Enhanced intelligence was a premium commodity. This was a prize package only those who were stupidly wealthy could afford. The internet had an abundance of sites dedicated to this end. Organizations offering enhancements specializing in Nikonian biology, astronomy, genetics, physiology, and the list went on. The business must be booming because there were so many fields from which to choose. It was easy to see that the upper echelon of Nikon was far superior to that of Earth. Reading the many positive testimonials on these sites she noticed two trends. Those who had the ability to afford the most expensive of mental enhancements listed their occupations as being affiliated with the government in one way or another and they were all male. A renowned scientist in the field of genetics may be making a fortune in that practice but he was also involved in the planet's governing body. This led her to realize another facet of this world. It had one governing body with twelve male leaders of equal power.

After successfully leading the one world society into a new age of enlightenment where crime and poverty were almost non-existent the governing body was disrupted a little over two hundred years ago. One of the twelve, Doctor Brekenmercer Rasmus was given unlimited resources to build a machine that would propel their world beyond the boundary of the known solar system, even the universe as they understood it. Not fully understanding the immense power he would unleash, Rasmus engaged the machine without thorough testing. The device worked for an instant before destroying itself in a magnificent explosion. Their hunger for knowledge and exploration into alternate realities led to an invasion by a species of alien demons, led by the abominable Adramelech. That is how the article described the creature. Sidney gazed at a photo of the demon that clamped a collar on her and fed her to his wolves just days earlier.

She shuddered and clicked the link titled, 'World Leaders Assassinated". 11 of the 12 leaders were publicly murdered in various ways. The entire event was recorded and she watched the episode in horror. It was not a quick beheading. Each leader was executed in a different manner. They were bound and stripped of their clothing. The first was hung upside down with rope wrapped around his lower legs leaving his feet exposed. Adramelech severed both of the man's feet and tossed them to three wolf-like dogs that were obediently hunkered at his side. The man's screaming was cut abruptly as Adramelech sliced his throat leaving his dying body jerking and pouring dark red blood onto the floor. The dogs were all too happy to devour whatever was left.

One of the men was hoisted in a similar fashion, upside-down but his ankles were tied by separate lines so as to stretch his legs apart. Adramelech brought a blade down at his crotch, splitting the man in half to his chest. In a second, clean swift motion, the head was then removed. The man's body jerked for a full minute. It went on like that, body after body, each death more depraved than the last. The video clip was not edited. Sidney looked away when Adramelech severed the jugular of one man, making the other men watch as the dogs lapped fresh blood.

They screamed and cried for mercy. It was obvious, this demon was enjoying his work. He specialized in this art and he had not been able to indulge himself in a very long time. With eleven men gutted, decapitated, body parts scattered about, there was one man remaining. The dogs were rabid. They grew stronger and more ravenous with each kill. Adramelech would not allow them to touch the last man. The video feed focused in on his face and though he looked a bit younger, Sidney could clearly see the frightened hysterical face of Doctor Rasmus.

Adramelech grabbed the rope tied to the Doctor's nude upside-down body and brought him face to face. He growled. "You will rebuild the transportation machine for my use. Your life is spared for this one purpose."

The clip came to an end. There were no subsequent clips. She searched the web for anything else connected to Adramelech. In the alien demon's absence, the newly elected rulers of Nikon left this link up on purpose. They removed anything else about that time period for reasons they deemed necessary.

There was additional information in regard to the Doctor. As scientists were ranked, he led the pack as perhaps the most renowned Nikonians of all time. He was far superior to all others in several fields which included, Nano-technology, Cloning, Synthetic Organic Robotics, Quantum Mechanics, and some fields of study she never heard of. "What is an Interdimensional Physicist?" She whispered.

"It is someone who specializes in the study and application of the ten known dimensions. Doctor Rasmus has devoted his theories specifically to the seventh and eighth dimensions," Aiden responded.

Sidney turned to her, setting the tablet down. "Aiden. You're awake."

Aiden continued in a low tone. "In these dimensions, one has access to alternate realities that start with varying initial conditions; worlds that branch out infinitely. No one world is the same and many are drastically different."

Sidney leaned forward and placed her palm lightly on Aiden's bandaged face. "How do you feel?"

She closed her eyes, smiled, slowly opened them again. "I don't know. I can't really feel my body," she said dreamily. "Is this real? Am I still dreaming?"

"For someone who is dreaming, that was a great definition of an Interdimensional Physicist."

"Okay," she said, still smiling. "Not dreaming. How long have I been asleep?"

"Three days."

"My baby? Is my baby okay?"

"The baby is okay. Don't stress yourself."

"Where are we?"

"We are at the hospital. You are in good hands." Sidney noticed the small woman's eyes begin to moisten. She leaned forward placing her lips close to her ear and began to whisper.

Aiden listened to her words; calm words laced with care and love. "There is no need for stress. Breathe deeply and know that you are safe in the care of those who love you. Allow peaceful thoughts to fill your mind. We will heal one another, you and I. We are friends forever. Feel the love and joy emanating from me. Let it fill you with joy and happiness. You mean so much to us. Your full recovery is our greatest desire. Smile and know that your child is growing, strong and healthy inside of you. Your baby depends on you. Your baby loves you. Mason and I are here with you as you recover." She drifted off with these words fresh in her mind. She thought of Mason. She dreamed of her child.

Sidney could hear deep breaths coming from the woman and sat back up. She noticed Mason watching her from his recliner. He motioned with his hands, *What gives?*

Sidney got up and walked out to the corridor.

Mason got up quietly and followed her. They joined one another in the hall but left the door ajar.

"We may be here for some time." Sidney began.

"It's looking that way. She spoke to you?"

"She woke up but drifted off pretty quick. She's not ready to be taking on anything that is stress related, Mason. I know you want to talk to her, to ask her questions, but I don't think it's such a good idea that she relives what she just went through. It puts the baby at risk."

"Yes. You're right."

"I understand why you want to be here. I also understand that we are not wasting time but in a way, we are."

"I don't know how much damage we did to Adramelech with that pulse of light. Aiden survived it so I have to assume he did as well. He wears some sort of armor. One thing I am certain of, he is more determined than ever."

"How long do you think you can sit here and hope he doesn't launch another attack?"

Mason considered her. "You've got a suggestion?"

"What happens when we get to Ice World?"

"We call together the men of that village and surrounding villages. I want to mobilize them; form a resistance."

"What makes you think that will work?"

Mason shrugged. "First of all, it is a land of giants. They are hunters and warriors. They are eager to help."

"How do you plan on attacking Adramelech?"

"I don't. I want to lure him into attacking me. I have to use myself as bait."

"Did you see what he has at his disposal? At the very least, he has wolves, and half men, half eagle creatures. There is no telling what else he has to throw at us. We won't be able to catch him off guard with the light weapon again. Sitting here, doing nothing, it's getting on my nerves."

"Me too." He agreed.

"Adramelech has us at a disadvantage, several disadvantages. You can put Aiden or anyone for that matter under strict surveillance and he can still get at us because we all have to sleep. You and I should be advancing the plan not sitting here while Adramelech gets the best of us. Let the Doctor handle things here. It's either that or get Rob involved. Or your family. You can't protect everyone, Mason. We are all at risk. We should all be actively working on the solution."

Mason looked up, noticing movement through the open door and pushed the door wider. Aiden was sitting up in the bed.

She looked at the two of them and smiled. "Are you two going to stand out there whispering?"

They came back in, Mason setting down on the side of the bed, Sidney taking up the spot she previously occupied. "Are you supposed to be sitting up like that?" Mason asked.

"I feel okay. Actually, I don't really feel much. I can move my arms and legs, but there isn't much sensation. I'll be okay. What kind of trouble are you two getting into?"

"Sidney is concerned we are losing valuable time."

Aiden glanced at Sidney. "She's correct." Then back to Mason. "He has plans for you."

Mason straightened. "He spoke to you?"

"Not directly. He is very arrogant. He views me as a lower life form. He regards all humans, Nikonians, and most other races as subservient. He tends to ramble. He is obsessed with you, Mason. He finds it offensive that you are blessed with a power that is beyond his ability. He wants to control that power and will stop at nothing to obtain it."

A nurse entered the room. Mason got up and allowed the woman room to work. She seemed pleased with Aiden's progression, checking vitals and recording everything she observed. She advised her to remain in bed and rest. The Doctor assigned to her would be there in a few hours to check on her and they would inform Doctor Rasmus that she regained consciousness.

Once the nurse left Aiden asked Mason about the light that burned her. He explained briefly how the weapon was supposed to work and how it had not worked exactly as planned.

"I had no way of knowing," Mason explained. "But it's true. The light used by the weapon Doctor Rasmus developed is identical to the light produced by the sun on my world. If you are exposed to it, the result will be bad."

"I thought we weren't supposed to increase her stress levels?" Sidney said.

Mason shrugged. "Sorry."

Aiden smiled from behind her bandages in spite of the news. "I have faith in you Mason. I know you are going to find a solution."

"Yeah." He mumbled. "I'm workin' on it."

***

Mason left them and met with Doctor Rasmus at the laboratory. The Doctor called, requesting a meeting. Mason was eager to do something so he jumped at the opportunity. He found the Doctor in a busy room full of equipment and men at various workstations. Once again, the Doctor was in an odd outfit. He would have fit nicely in a Sherlock Holmes novel or perhaps he could pull off young Doctor Frankenstein. The man seemed to love wearing a cape or like today, an absurdly long hospital coat.

"Ah, Mr. Waters. I've been told Aiden is awake. Good news."

"She's regaining her strength and optimistic as always. You called me?"

He hoisted the pack Mason used on Halja. "I repaired this."

Mason noticed he not only repaired the device, it was modified. It was trimmed down to almost half the original size.

"You'll notice the design fits your body much better. Yet, it works as it did before. I reinforced the wand with a stronger alloy. It won't break as easily."

"It looks good Doc."

"Follow me, please."

Mason followed him to an office attached to the large lab. He pulled out a small device about the size of a cell phone. "This is your remote detonator."

"For the bomb in the pack."

Rasmus nodded. "You pointed out a problem in my

design. With this remote, you can secure the pack in a chosen place, travel up to a mile away, and remotely detonate it. It is set to detonate sixty seconds after you give the command."

Mason took the remote and studied it. "If things progress according to plan, I'm not going to want to use this."

"Of course not. No one wants to be in such a situation."

"I don't plan on going back to Halja."

The Doctor did not respond. He looked at Mason and waited.

"The battle will take place on Ice World. I'd prefer not to blow the place up."

"How do you plan to lure Adramelech and his army away from Halja? It seems he prefers to send assassins."

"When I'm ready, I'll make him come get me. As for his army. Well, first things first. If I can manage to take off the head, maybe the body won't be much of an issue."

They walked back into the lab. Mason picked up the newly designed UV pack and strapped it on. "Nice. It fits perfectly."

The two men stood a few feet apart, looking at one another. "I've got to go Doc. Can you have some people attend to Aiden?"

"Leave it to me. She will be okay."

"You cannot leave her unattended."

"Yes, yes. I am aware of the danger. Do not let that be of concern. Oh, I almost forgot." He led Mason to several lockers and opened one. "Here is the food you requested." He handed Mason two large clear packs. The pills inside were tightly packed in a vacuum. Mason could see individual packs inside, each with a different type of pill marked to indicate what each pack contained.

Mason extended his right hand and the Doctor regarded him curiously. He took the hand and they shook firmly. "Thanks for everything. Until I see you again, sir."

The Doctor bowed slightly then released the hand.

Mason held one pack of pills under each arm, summoned the Door and stepped from Mercer laboratories to the hospital.

Sidney managed to squirm in next to Aiden. They were both sitting upright, covered to their waists with a shared blanket, scrolling the web on Sidney's borrowed tablet. Sidney looked up briefly. "Mason, this world is incredible. I am by far the darkest person on the planet and you are without a doubt the tallest. Get this; there are no strip clubs. There aren't even dance clubs. Do you realize how much money we could rake in if we lived here?"

Aiden was laughing. "You are such a bad girl. Why would anyone pay hard earned money to get wasted in a dance club? It is so unsanitary! Aghh!"

"I'm glad to see you two hit it off so well."

Sidney noticed the light weapon strapped to Mason's back, the clear packs under each arm and realized this was no social call. "Oh, man. Are we about go?"

"I leave you for a few hours and you've had a change of heart. Yes. Doctor Rasmus is sending someone to take our place. You and I have work to do. Get your things together. I'd like a moment with Aiden."

Sidney turned to Aiden and hugged her. "Get better, girl."

Aiden hugged her back and kissed her on the cheek. "I'll get better. You take care of our man."

Sidney got out of the bed and tucked Aiden back in. "I will." She glanced at Mason and stepped into the restroom.

Mason rounded the bed, dropped the food packs on the floor and took a seat next to her. He bent down and kissed her gently on the lips. "I am very sorry for…"

Aiden reached up and touched his chin with a bandaged finger. "Don't apologize. My body will heal. If you and Sidney had not come for me, I would not be here at all; me or our baby. I thought I loved you, Mason. What I felt was insignificant compared to how I feel now." She dropped her hand and closed it around his. "Sidney told me about what you are going to do on the Ice World. It is dangerous, Mason. I have faith in you."

Mason sighed. "You mentioned that. I am supposed to be the one doing the talking here."

"I love you so much."

"Yes. Yes, I love you too. I am curious. How did he take you? How did Adramelech kidnap you?"

"Oh, I explained it in detail to Sidney. I suppose he got to me in much the same way he has reached out to you; through a nightmare."

"Yeah, but he has never managed to kidnap me. That scares me. The idea that he can take you or anyone else in your sleep."

"I knew I was dreaming. I became aware of it when it turned into a nightmare. I tried to wake up. It was like I could think but I had no control of my body. They have me on a special drug here. I think it helps me not to dream. It is only a temporary fix. I don't want to take drugs forever and I am concerned about taking anything while I am pregnant."

Mason nodded as Sidney came back out of the restroom. He bent, hugged Aiden for a moment, and kissed her. "We are going to be away for a while." he said softly. When we return you and I can concentrate on our plans for the future."

Aiden kissed him again. "I would like that."

She pushed back slightly and reached out for Sidney. The two women embraced. "I'll miss you. Please, be safe."

Sidney smiled at her. "I will."

Someone knocked lightly on the door and a nurse entered. "Hello, everyone," she said. I've been instructed to sit with you Aiden. Just until someone else arrives. Doctor's orders."

Mason and Sidney stepped back. "Help me with these." He handed Sidney one of the food packs and they exited the room.

They walked briskly down the corridor, into an empty co-ed restroom, and faced one another. Sidney reached out and wrapped herself around him tightly. "I've been wondering about something for a while."

Mason liked how she smelled. He liked being this close to her. She felt good in his arms. But he felt certain she was about to say something about him being married, expecting a child with another woman, and enjoying great sex with a third, the third one being her of course. Perhaps she expected there may be more women in his life. He made a conscious effort to keep the relationships isolated from one another, but she had witnessed him embrace Aiden and kiss her good-by.

"You're wondering how it's possible for a man to be so humble, so loveable, so rich, and so handsome all in one." He looked into her eyes, only inches from his.

"Not even close." She smiled.

Mason opened the Door opened and they vanished.

EPILOGUE

"I thought we were headed to the Ice World," Sidney remarked. She stepped away from Mason but kept one hand fixed on his belt.

They were in the expanse of light. The magnificent mural appeared before them and began offering destinations. Mason looked at the mural but his mind was on what she might ask.

Sidney had at times gotten angry at him. He had a way of pissing women off once they got to know him. This was a flaw in his character he sometimes wondered about but never really cared to address. He could be charming. He had an expression he practiced in the mirror when he was much younger. He smiled slightly and looked at his reflection with half-open eyes. Yeah, that's the look. Like, you really don't care if the girl notices you or not cause you have better things to do anyway. Sidney had been pissed a few times, but they never fought. That aspect of his life was reserved for Valerie. He never wanted to fight with Sidney. He purposed to remain calm. No matter what she had to say. He would not add fuel to the fire if she got angry. He loved her and determined to keep that thought at the forefront of his mind.

Without taking his eyes off the mural floating in a sea of bright light he asked, "What's on your mind?"

"It's okay to let go of you in here?"

Mason realized this was a question. He shrugged. "I think so. Give it a try."

Sidney released her grip and took a tentative step away from him. She turned her attention to the mural and stood there in apparent awe.

"It's something, isn't it?" Mason asked quietly.

Sidney nodded. "All those places. So, many worlds. There aren't enough days in a lifetime to visit them all."

"No. We don't even visit all the places on Earth in a lifetime. We get stuck in a routine. Live our lives with myopic vision, not willing or maybe even afraid to look up and consider the possibilities."

He stopped talking and they stood there for a moment in silence looking at the changing mural. "This isn't what you have been wondering about though. I chose to stop here, before moving on to the next chapter in our journey. Perhaps there are a few things we should discuss."

She turned to him. "Because there may not be time later? That's what you are leaving out. You're saying it, but not out loud."

Mason pursed his lips but remained silent.

Sidney crossed her arms under her breasts and shifted her weight to one side. "When we first met, you took the time to outline your situation. Even though I expected everything you said to be bullshit and at any minute the predator in you would reveal himself. The same crap I see in all men. But, that didn't happen. Not like I expected anyway."

"Rob is a good friend. But he tried to get in my panties once. I had to set him straight because we worked together."

"Not a paying customer."

She gave him a glance, her eyes narrowed, her jaw clenched. "I'll let that slide. My customers paid for a dance. I was a dancer. What you are referring to is called prostitution."

Mason opened his mouth but she put up a finger.

"It's best you don't say anything else until I'm through."

He closed his mouth, nodded, and she continued, noticing the mural had almost stopped moving. Portraits crept by. She wondered if the mural was a living organism no longer interested in offering destinations, turning its attention to the conversation of these two humans.

"Men are mostly the same, deep down. I have a problem with how they sometimes treat women. But I keep that shit to myself, look for an angle, and try to work the situation to my benefit with my dignity still intact. In the club, that first night. You could have chosen any of those girls. They would have followed you eagerly. You could have picked a different club. You came in my club and asked for me, specifically. Why?"

Mason waited a beat. "Is that your question? That's what you've been thinking about?"

"So, he answers my question with two of his own." She said turning slightly toward the mural. She looked up at him tapping a finger on her forearm. "No. It's not. I'm working my way up to the thing that's been itching at the back of my mind. But, let's start there. Why me?"

"I've learned a few hard facts about myself, growing up," Mason replied. "I like getting my way."

"Who doesn't?"

"It's a character flaw, Sidney. I will push and push. I will manipulate to get what I want no matter if it is good for me or not. Weak women don't work for me. I will run right over you if you have no backbone."

"You didn't know me when we first met. Unless you were stalking me, how did you know I was the right girl? You sent another dancer to get my attention."

"Well, this isn't going to sound good. It's my experience that African-American women are strong. They don't put up with nonsense. Valerie is that kind of woman. It is all but impossible for me to run over or manipulate her. I guess you would have a similar character. I just walked into that club randomly. You were the only black girl I saw. You were and are pleasant to my eyes, Sidney. I didn't know for sure. You'll recall I didn't want you to dance for me. I needed to get to know you. You could have walked away at any time. I am very thankful you didn't. I am glad you are with me now."

Her posture visibly eased. She didn't uncross her arms but the tension drained from her face. She nodded her head slightly. "That night and the following morning we discussed quite a bit. You told me a fairly detailed account of what had occurred in your motel room. Having encountered Adramelech face to face, I can imagine what you went through, alone in that room. No one even knew you were there." She paused long enough for Mason to look at her. She held his gaze and asked her question. "Why were you in the motel room in the first place? You have a home, a wife, adult children with multiple options of where you could have spent the night. You chose to be in a motel. You even rented the place for a week. Why?"

Mason blinked. She wasn't asking him anything he expected her to ask. He was certain she was going to come at him about his multiple relationships with women. 'How can you love me and Valerie, and Aiden all at the same time? Who do you care for more? Are you planning to divorce your wife? I saw you with Aiden. I can see you love her. How could you do this to me?' She came at him with nothing like that.

She didn't tense up but she was tapping her finger again. "Mason? Why were you in a motel room?"

"We had a fight." He started. "Valerie and I had a fight. I hit her. I put her on the floor." He was ashamed of every word coming out of his mouth. His chin trembled and his eyes watered. He could no longer look at Sidney. "I wish I could go back to that moment and do it differently. I ran like a coward. I got that motel room and got wasted. I drank so much I passed out."

The mural was no longer moving. There was no motion in the images on the mural. Nothing moved in the expanse of light. A casual passer-by might view the scene and swear it looked like a display in a wax museum. The humans in this display didn't even seem to breathe. Time ceased in that instant, but if the passer-by looked closely he or she would see a tiny sign of life, there on the man's cheek, a tear escaped his eye and rolled down his face, leaving a thin wet trail.

Sidney saw Mason as a boy in a man's body. At this moment, he was broken. He was reliving the argument with Valerie, perhaps seeing what he could have done differently. She was glad he could not go back to that moment to change things. They would never have met. She made a decision

327

there in the room of light, the massive mural to her left, perhaps somehow recording this event. She moved slowly and put her arms around Mason, her head against his chest. She could hear his heartbeat. "I may never have all of you, Mason. But, I'll take what I can get."

He put his arms around her and said quietly, "I don't want to lose you. I don't have all the answers, but I know I don't want to lose you, Sidney."

She held him tighter. "I'm not going anywhere."

They didn't speak for a while. But in this place time had no meaning. There was no real sense of up or down, or of a passage of time. At some point, Mason heard her say, "Let's go."

Mason wiped his face.

"You are going to have to make things right with your wife. She may have forgiven you, but you have to do better Mason. She gave you four healthy children. She's been there for you no matter what. No woman like that deserves to have her husband strike her."

"You're right," he said quietly.

"But not right now." She watched as the mural moved, picking up speed, offering destinations. "You see where we are going?"

Mason straightened. "I don't need the mural to go somewhere I've been before. Sid is waiting for us. We're going to his home."

The mural, anticipating this choice placed an image of Sid the giant working a fire in a large fireplace with a long metal rod.

Mason nodded. "Yeah. Sure. That's the place."

Sidney clutched him tightly and Mason reached

out toward the mural. The expanse rippled, the mural disappeared, and they were standing together in a large medieval home of wood and stone. Sidney eased her hold on him but Mason held her tight. "Thank you," he said.

She looked up and kissed his eyes, his cheek, and his mouth. "Mason. There's a giant man standing there staring at us."

THE END

Printed in the United States
By Bookmasters